ONCE UPON THE END

Also by James Riley

Half Upon a Time

Twice Upon a Time

ONCE UPON THE END

Book Three in the Half Upon a Time series

JAMES RILEY

Aladdin

New York London Toronto Sydney New Delhi

ALADDIN

An imprint of Simon & Schuster Children's Publishing Division
1230 Avenue of the Americas, New York, NY 10020
First Aladdin hardcover edition May 2013
Copyright © 2013 by James Riley
All rights reserved, including the right of reproduction
in whole or in part in any form.
ALADDIN is a trademark of Simon & Schuster, Inc., and related logo
is a registered trademark of Simon & Schuster, Inc.
For information about special discounts for bulk purchases, please contact
Simon & Schuster Special Sales at 1-866-506-1949 or business@simonandschuster.com.
The Simon & Schuster Speakers Bureau can bring authors to your live event. For more information
or to book an event contact the Simon & Schuster Speakers Bureau at 1-866-248-3049
or visit our website at www.simonspeakers.com.
Designed by Jessica Handelman
The text of this book was set in Goudy Old Style.
Manufactured in the United States of America 0413 FFG
2 4 6 8 10 9 7 5 3 1
Full CIP data is available from the Library of Congress.
ISBN 978-1-4424-7422-2
ISBN 978-1-4424-7423-9 (eBook)

Dedicated to anyone who wishes they knew
how their story ends. Just look ahead to the
last page; it's so much easier that way!

Special thanks to my editor, Liesa Abrams,
who believes in me like I believe in the invisible
gnomes who actually write all my stories.
Thank you, Liesa, for making my life and
the gnomes' books so much better.

ONCE UPON THE END

CHAPTER 1

Once upon a time, a dragon held a princess captive, and a hero did everything in his power to save her.

This was not that time.

"Don't you get it?" the princess shouted, her anger growing. "If you don't defeat the dragon's riddles, it's going to eat me!"

"I understand," said a boy in black armor and a midnight blue cloak, the uniform of the Wicked Queen's Eyes. "But I don't do that kind of thing. Not anymore."

"You're going to just let me die?!"

"Looks like it."

"But if you defeat the dragon, all its riches can be yours! And your fame will spread across the world, with children singing your name and old men telling your story by the light of dying fires!"

The Eye shrugged, then turned to walk away.

"You can't be serious!" the princess shouted after him.

"Good luck," the Eye told her, and kept walking.

The dragon roared, a clawed hand launching out to grab the Eye by his cloak. "You will not leave without facing me, Initiate! The Queen demands it!"

The Eye stopped and slowly turned around to look the dragon in the eye.

"Your task is to outwit me, Initiate," the dragon said. "You will not leave here alive if you cannot. Answer my riddles, and win both your freedom and the princess's. Fail, and I eat you both."

The Eye nodded. "Deal.

The dragon smiled, revealing thousands of teeth. "The first riddle is this: What walks on four legs in the morning—"

"A human being," the Eye said. "Are we done?"

The dragon's mouth dropped. "But . . . that is the correct answer! A human being walks on four legs when it crawls as a baby in the morning of its life, two legs as an adult at midday, and three legs at the twilight of its life, when it needs a cane to walk. You are right, Initiate!"

The Eye just waited.

"However, there are *three* riddles in total!" the dragon

declared, and the princess sighed loudly, as did the Eye. "What can run but never walk—"

"A river."

"Stop it!" the dragon roared. "I don't know how you knew these answers, but this last one will *stump* you—"

"Of course the tree falling makes a sound. It's a tree, falling. Who cares if anyone hears it?"

The dragon shrieked in rage and unleashed a wave of fire that enveloped the entire room.

When the fire went out, the Eye was nowhere to be found.

"He did pass, you know," the princess told the dragon. "That wasn't exactly fair."

The dragon opened its mouth to respond, only to collapse to the ground. The Eye stepped off the unconscious monster's head and resumed his walk out the exit, sheathing the sword he'd used to knock the dragon out as he went.

"My hero!" the princess shouted, running after him. "You freed me from the—"

"Nah," the Eye said, and didn't turn around.

She stopped in her tracks. "But what about your fame and riches?!"

"All yours."

And with that, the Eye kept walking, while the princess turned to the dragon and snorted. "YOU need some harder riddles next time!" she told it, smacking the unconscious beast on the head.

The Eye continued on, only to find his path coming to a dead end at a mirror on a wall. As he approached the mirror, his reflection grew closer as well, and waved to him.

"Hello, Initiate," his reflection said.

"Hello, me," the Eye said, if just to be polite.

The reflection saluted the Eye with his sword, smiling a friendly smile. "Guess what I am?"

"My second challenge?"

"Nice one, Initiate!" the reflection of him said. "You've got a quick head on those shoulders! Let's see if you can keep it there, shall we?" The reflection aimed his sword at Jack. "The Queen grants great power to her Eyes. But power that's granted can easily be taken away if one misuses it. Only a wise user of the magic of an Eye can pass this test, for only a wise user would know better than to use that magic against the Queen."

"And what exactly do I need to use it on?"

"Me!" the reflection said. "You'll have to use your magic to defeat me before I kill you."

The Eye pulled his sword off his back and faced his reflection. He struck out at the mirror, and the reflection blocked his attack exactly, just from the opposite side, as a reflection will do. Only, unlike other reflections, this one's sword came right out of the mirror.

"I wouldn't recommend that," the reflection said. "Everything you do, I do. Hurt me, and you get the same."

The Eye nodded and put his sword back in its scabbard. One of the first things he'd learned in training was the magic of tricking light into ignoring you, into not even seeing you, into going right through you.

The Eye closed his eyes and concentrated, convincing the light that he wasn't there anymore, that it really should just go on about its business, that there wasn't anything to see here.

Then he opened his eyes.

The mirror was empty. Or, more accurately, it was reflecting his invisible self.

With that, the Eye pushed his way into the mirror and kept going.

A short distance later, a rosy glow filled the corridor, and the Eye found a man sitting before a fire, his back to the entrance. The Eye walked over to the man and saw that he held a glass of something red and cheery-looking, while the fire danced over his face.

"You made it!" the man said with a smile, and gestured for the Eye to sit down.

The Eye took a seat and found a glass of something thick and black on the table between them, a table that hadn't been there a second ago.

"Congratulations on making it this far," the man told him, fire glinting in his eye. "Most don't."

"Which challenge do they fail?" the Eye asked.

"Oh, most know enough at this point to defeat the dragon, though not a small amount miss a riddle or two," the man said absently. "But quite a few never make it past their own selves in the second challenge." He frowned. "There's probably a metaphor there. Still, even when they do make it through, most seldom arrive here so quickly. Or so healthy! Do you even have a scratch?"

The Eye shrugged. "Looks like I finally found something I'm good at."

"Being an Eye?"

The Eye smiled. "If that's what you want to call it. So, what now?"

"Oh, that's easy," the man said, placing his glass of red something on the table, next to the glass of thick black liquid. "You'll drink from one glass, and I'll drink from the other. That's it."

"I hate to say it, but the red one looks a bit more appetizing."

The man laughed. "I'd hope so! The other is Death."

The Eye nodded. "And the red one?"

The man watched the Eye carefully. "That one grants the Queen your service, body and soul. If you betray her, if you consider betraying her, if the thought even crosses your mind . . . your blood will light on fire, and you will burn from the inside out."

The Eye raised an eyebrow. "Sounds bad."

The man shrugged. "One Eye betrayed the Queen, and now the rest have to suffer, I suppose. The Charmed One never had to drink this, or the Queen wouldn't have had to kill him with his own sword." The man looked over the Eye's shoulder. "*That* very sword, in fact."

"That's what I'm told."

"So, my Initiate friend," the man said, gesturing toward the drinks. "The choice is yours."

The Eye reached out and took the red drink. "But if I drink this, and you drink Death . . ."

"Then I'll die," the man said. "It won't be the first time. I betrayed the Queen long ago, my friend, back when she was just a princess. And this has been her punishment for me until the end of time."

"Well, if you're okay with it," the Eye said. "So, I'll drink from this glass, and you drink from that one."

The man nodded and reached for the glass. "You have made your choice, then!"

"I sure have," the Eye said, then dumped his red glass into the other one.

The man's hand froze midway to the glass. "What have you done?!"

The Eye brought his empty glass to his lips and drank deeply of nothing, then placed it back on the table. "Just drinking from my glass."

The man stared at him for a moment, then sighed. "Why is it your family always has to take the hard path?"

The corners of the Eye's mouth twitched. "You can't always control what you're thinking, and the last thing I want to happen is a stray thought making me burn from the inside out."

The man just shook his head. "You'll still burn, my friend. She can hear your thoughts. She knows all. But have it your way."

And then he took the full glass of loyalty and Death, brought it to his lips, and drained the entire thing.

"By the way," the man said, starting to shake. "As a reward for passing the test, I thought I might do you a favor and show you something."

The Eye raised an eyebrow, and the man held a now-trembling hand up, then gestured. His hand dropped back to his lap while a bright circle of fire showed two boys, one in black armor, one in royal clothes.

"Your future," the man said, then coughed over and over.

The Eye looked closer and watched himself fighting the royal boy in the Wicked Queen's throne room. He seemed to be toying with the boy, then finally knocked the royal's sword away and sent the prince to the ground. His self in the fire circle held his sword over the prince's head, then the sword dropped, and the image disappeared.

"One will betray her, and one will die," the Eye said quietly. "I'll have to keep that in mind."

The man didn't answer, and the Eye didn't disturb him. Dying over and over every time some new initiate came by couldn't be easy, and the last thing the Eye wanted to do was disturb what little rest the man got.

He stood up to leave, only to find himself waking up to a room lit only by candles, his sword glowing softly by his side. The room was empty except for a tiny seat on a table just to the Eye's left, upon which sat a man no taller than six inches.

"You passed!" Thomas roared, slapping the Eye on the shoulder. "Congratulations! I was sure you'd die at least once!"

"Can you die *more* than once, sir?" the Eye asked. Even in the haze and confusion, he knew better than to be impolite to the captain of the Queen's Eyes.

The tiny man winked. "If anyone could, it'd be you, boy! You realize that might be a record-setting pass of the test? Faster than your sister, even!"

"Permission to tell her that over and over, sir?" the Eye said, rubbing his temples. He might have passed, but it'd left a test-size pounding in his head.

"You know, the test is different for every initiate," Captain Thomas said. "What challenges did you face?"

The Eye shrugged. "Lots of little monsters, each one only about half a foot high. Creepy, huh?"

The captain stared long and hard at the Eye, who just matched his gaze innocently. Finally, Captain Thomas looked away. "You'll have to fill me in more later. We can't keep the

Queen waiting. She asked for you specifically as soon as you passed. Seemed to know you would. I told her you'd die, I really did. But she was so sure!" He chuckled. "Should have known better than to question Her Majesty! Still, if she were wrong about anyone, it'd have to be you."

The Eye quickly stood up, straightened his midnight blue cloak, his black armor with a white eye in the center, and saluted. Tom saluted back, then climbed up to the Eye's shoulder and gestured with his sword. "Onward!" he shouted. And with that, the Eye left, his captain riding on his shoulder.

If there was one thing Jack had learned as an initiate, after all, it was that one never left the Wicked Queen waiting.

CHAPTER 2

The sun wasn't even up when the birds began singing. Every. Morning. Birds would flock to the window, pushing against each other to all tweet as loudly as they could, all in harmony, practically fighting over each other to get space on the windowsill.

It was like something out of a horror movie.

The worst part, though, was that May couldn't ever get their song out of her head.

Tweet tweet . . . tweettweettweet . . . tweet tweet tweet.

"I'm *not* going to Cinderella for you!" she shouted, holding her pillow over her head.

The birds could hear her, of course. Whenever she started yelling at them, they'd stop singing for a moment and begin tapping at the thin window glass, practically cracking it with every tap. She tried shutting the curtains, but the birds just flew around to the other window or sang down the chimney, following her wherever she went.

Only one thing ever scared them off.

The pirate monkey leapt at the window, shrieking his little monster head off. The birds exploded in every direction, now tweeting in terror instead of song, which always made May feel a little bad . . . until she remembered the horror they brought to her every morning.

Tweet tweet . . . tweettweettweet . . . tweet tweet tweet.

Every morning for three months.

When the birds had all flown, the monkey landed on May's pillow and smacked it, letting her know it was time to get up. Or more likely that he was hungry. Or wanted to annoy her. There were plenty of options.

May shoved the monkey off her and sat up with a sigh. The sun had just risen outside, but as usual, clouds covered the Wicked Queen's kingdoms, where her parents had lived before they'd both passed away. May yawned widely as she meandered over to the window, trying to get a look at what was happening before the birds came back.

Outside, people walked quickly through the town of Charm, hoods covering their faces, all careful not to look at each other. Between them roamed bands of goblin guards, pestering random people whenever they felt like it, shoving a piece of paper in their faces.

She shuddered a bit, knowing what was on that paper.

Just up the hill, a castle sat in quiet watch over the little town that May was meant to grow up in, over the once nice but now falling apart house that her father had bought for his new wife after May's mother had died. And in that castle—

Someone screamed May's name downstairs, her father's now not-so-new bride. "We're *waiting!*" her stepmother shouted.

The monkey shrieked in a very similar tone, and May gave him a dirty look, then started to close the shutters, only to stop abruptly. Off in the distance, in one of the castle's windows . . . had something moved?

Everyone thought that the royal family had long since escaped the Wicked Queen's rule, run off to wherever someone would take them in. Her stepsister Esmerelda, the younger of two, claimed the castle was haunted now, swearing she'd seen odd lights and a ghostly shape dancing on the roof beneath a full moon. Esmerelda's sister, Constance, had then called

Esmerelda a fool for believing in such things, followed by Esmerelda claiming Constance's feet looked like they belonged to an unkempt giant.

Things had gone downhill after that.

May pulled on a dirt-and-stain covered frock that was longer than she was, sadly missing her jeans that were tucked in one of her dresser drawers. A ripped-off sleeve of a ratty dress worked as a belt and held up enough of the frock to let her walk, at least.

Cinderella's working clothes. A costume she'd put on every morning to act like the dutiful stepdaughter, all to keep her safe. To keep everyone safe.

Sometimes she thought about going down in her jeans and T-shirt, letting her entire family know what she thought of them, and running out the door with a laugh. But that wasn't happening any more than the birds were going to stop singing.

"May!" her stepmother screamed from downstairs. "Don't make me come up there!"

"I'm hungry!" shouted Constance. "Make me breakfast already!"

"If you're not down here this minute, I'm locking you in the attic for a week!" threatened Esmerelda.

"This is why they're the villains in this story," May told the monkey, who just shrieked back at her hungrily. Honestly, he was a close second.

Living a fairy tale sounded good, until you realized you were only getting the bad parts, and all the fairy godmothers and happily ever afters weren't coming.

As May tromped down the spiral staircase outside her attic bedroom, the monkey running in front of her and almost tripping her several times, she ran one hand down the brick walls of the house, wondering not for the first time if she could feel the magic that the fairy queens had placed there. Phillip hadn't wanted her to stay, not without some protection, so his family had begged Merriweather for one last favor: As long as May remained in her stepmother's house, only a fairy queen could find her.

Even Phillip had forgotten the house's location as soon as May had forced him to leave. And she'd forced him to pretty fast. After Ja—after *someone's* betrayal and the Wicked Queen's promise that between . . . *someone* . . . and Phillip, one would betray her and one would die, well, May wasn't taking chances. She'd made Phillip promise to never come anywhere near her ever again, as long as she was safe.

And with the fairy queen's magic, he didn't have a choice.

That meant all she had to do was stay hidden, stay in her family's home with her, uh, loving family, and Phillip wouldn't be hurt. And neither would . . . anyone else.

The prince had fought it, of course. May secretly suspected he was more nervous about leaving with Penelope than he was about May's safety, but that was his problem.

Hers was making sure that no one else suffered because of the Wicked Queen.

As she continued down the long spiral staircase, her hands ran over first one picture frame, then another, then a third. All hidden on the stairs leading up to the attic were portraits of her father, her grandfather, and her great-grandfather. Her father's eyes seemed kind, though haunted, while her grandfather and great-grandfather stared disapprovingly at the painter, not the most pleasant reminder of anything. Both looked gaunt with black hair, something her father had somehow avoided with the same blond hair she had. Recessive genes or something.

The hall had become something of a memorial, given that all three men had passed on without leaving much behind. Her father, attacked on the road, out trying to sell his goods to keep up with his demanding new wife and two new stepchildren at home; her grandfather, killed by an Eye, if the stories were true.

And her great-grandfather . . . well, there were dragons involved, according to her stepsisters, but while her sisters had continued in horrible detail, May had tuned them out.

There was no picture of her mother. Her stepmother had removed all traces. At least she had passed away relatively peacefully from sickness shortly after May was born.

Cinderella's life. All the bad parts, and none of the fairy godmother coming to save her. Not after May had traded that away for being saved from a genie six months ago.

"Morning, ladies!" May said as brightly as she could, giving the monkey a push with her foot out into the room, maybe a bit too hard. The monkey shrieked, and all three women screamed, despite this same thing happening every day for three months.

"Kill it!" Esmerelda said, and May noticed that both sisters had already dressed up like they were going to some sort of fancy-dress ball. Sadly, without any money coming in, their fancy dresses were falling apart, and no one could afford to repair them. May had been given the job shortly after arriving. Having never sewn anything in her life, she'd quickly had the job taken away from her as well. That was the first time her sisters locked her in the attic.

Fortunately, the monkey had his ways in and out, and had

snuck them both food. Or, more accurately, had snuck himself food, and May had fought him for it.

Constance swatted at the monkey with a broom but was far too slow, and the little monster escaped back upstairs with an armful of fruit that had been sitting on the side table.

May flashed a smile at the three glaring women. "So, what'll it be this morning?"

"Something edible this time?" her stepmother said, her tone icy.

"I wouldn't get your hopes up, mother," said Esmerelda, her tone even colder than icy. Like an absolute zero sort of colder.

"Just try not to poison us this time," Constance said, not even bothering to make her tone cold, she cared so little.

"I will," May said, starting to leave.

"Wait, you will try, or you will *poison* us?" Esmerelda asked.

"No, of course I will!" May said, flashing an entirely much too innocent look.

Her stepsisters glared at her, while her stepmother didn't even look up. "By the by," the woman said. "Some gentleman came by earlier looking for you." She held up a familiar-looking piece of paper.

The paper, ripped and frayed at the edges, had WANTED written in large black letters, with a drawing of May on it. BY ORDER OF THE QUEEN, it went on, FOR INCITING REBELLIOUS ACTIVITIES.

"Let me know if I should run to find him," her stepmother said, giving her a sideways look. While she stayed in the house, the fairy queen's magic protected anyone but her family from seeing her. But May knew that if she took one step outside, her stepmother would be first in line for any reward.

May took the paper from her, hopefully keeping any of her stepmother's ideas in check, and went into the kitchen to give breakfast a try. She honestly had poisoned the women a few times when trying to make the meals at the beginning of her stay here. But now she'd gotten cooking down to the point that at least it didn't make anyone sick. And some things even tasted almost not bad.

As she cooked, she glanced at the paper every so often, each time getting a chill down to her toes. The goblins could knock all they wanted. They could even search the house. But the fairy queen's magic would ensure they'd never find her here.

But one step outside . . .

A scream outside caught May's attention, and she looked out the window. Across the street, four goblins were dragging a girl about May's age out of her house.

"It's not her!" a man shouted at them. "She doesn't even look anything *like* her!"

He was right. Whoever the girl was, she didn't look anything like May. That wasn't stopping the goblins, though.

One of the goblins held up the paper to the girl's head. "It's not that close, sir," he said to a goblin sitting on a horse.

"I, for one, am not going back to Her Majesty empty-handed again," the goblin on the horse said. "This one is close enough. Take her."

"Hey!" May shouted, throwing open the window. "It's the girl! The one the goblins are looking for! She's making a run for it!"

The goblin on the horse bolted upright, looking all around him, but couldn't find the source of the voice, as May was still inside her house and therefore invisible to him, despite being just a few feet away. "After her!" he shouted at the others, and the four goblins went running off in four directions, releasing the girl.

The man grabbed his daughter and pulled her back inside, while the goblin on the horse just laughed. "Better hope we find her, or we'll be back," he told the man before riding off.

May slammed the window, not able to look at her neighbor

anymore. Hopefully, he'd take his daughter and run. But where? The Queen controlled these lands for hundreds of miles in every direction. Where could he go?

He was as stuck as she was.

Breakfast and some more insults done, May went to work on the laundry, hearing the girl's terrified shouts in her head. Would the goblins come back? Would they find some other girl May's age and just take her?

Washing the windows, she thought she saw the man and his daughter ride off, but it could have been anyone, really. And when making lunch, May heard the monsters come back. From the sounds of it, they found an empty house, but May couldn't bear to look.

"I miss the dances," Esmerelda said at teatime, which May hadn't even known existed but now was a separate meal every day.

"Me too," Constance said. "Mother, if we give May up to the goblins, do you think the Queen will grant us our own kingdom?"

May froze. "You couldn't," she said. "They wouldn't see me, even if you brought them here. The magic makes sure of it."

Her stepmother nodded. "The girl has it right. Otherwise, I'd have given her up right after she arrived." She held up the cup of tea. "All this trouble for a weak cup of tea? It's just about unbearable!"

"Can't we just *carry* her outside or something?" Esmerelda asked. "Wouldn't that break the magic?"

Her stepmother gave May a steady look. "I enquired about that when the fairy queen cast her spell. She claimed that May can only leave under her own power. Maybe that is something to test out, though. Perhaps another day." She stirred her tea, then sipped at it again, making a face. "Or perhaps sooner."

Cleaning their rooms came next, followed by dusting and dinner. Finally, the sun went down, and May was allowed free time to sit in her bedroom, as long as she didn't come out.

It was the best part of each day.

As the monkey picked at the bread she'd brought him, May sat with her arms crossed on her windowsill, the shudders open again, the night air playing through her hair. The castle on the hill was dark, just like every other night, but every so often, whether she imagined it or not, May thought she saw a light in it.

A light meaning someone lived there. Her "prince." Some guy who looked like Phillip and couldn't use contractions.

She uncrumpled the paper beside her, looking at the picture of herself. BY ORDER OF THE QUEEN.

They wouldn't stop. They'd never stop looking for her, not while she hid away.

BY ORDER OF THE QUEEN.

The words terrified her.

But not as much as living out this story terrified her. Not as much as staying here, hidden away, causing other people harm terrified her. Those in the city around her. Phillip . . . other people.

A minute later, May was dressed in her jeans and T-shirt, the only objects she had from her old life all tucked into her pockets: a cell phone that hadn't worked for six months, a piece of paper from a Story Book, and a set of pipes that had once belonged to the Piper.

At the bottom of the drawer was a glass slipper, something she'd been left by Merriweather. For a moment, she considered taking it, too, but then stuffed it back into her drawer, under her working clothes. The slipper belonged to Cinderella, and Cinderella sat around waiting for life to get better. She was done with waiting and done with this whole story.

Everything set, she sat down on her bed and played the pipes, a song she'd practiced many times but had never had the guts to actually play on the pipes themselves.

A song calling out for her fairy godmother.

Only, not Merriweather. Merriweather wouldn't come, not after May had traded Cinderella's life for protection against a genie six months ago.

But May had someone else in mind anyway.

Music floated in through the window, a harmony to the song she played, and May watched as a beautiful woman appeared out of nowhere, her eyes containing no pupils, her dress black as a starless sky.

"Now, *this* is interesting," Malevolent said to her, a wide smile on her face.

The monkey shrieked and leapt at May, but to defend her or to hide, May had no idea. Just as his hand touched her hair, the monkey, room, and house all disappeared, and May found herself back in a throne room she hadn't seen in six months.

"Now," Malevolent said. "There are so many ways to kill you. However will we decide?"

CHAPTER 3

Until now, Jack had never been allowed close to the Queen's castle. Signs posted on every corner warned ALL HUMANS TO STAY INDOORS FROM SUNSET TO SUNRISE! and DANGER—NO HUMANS OUT AFTER DARK! but who those signs were for was a mystery, since Jack didn't see any humans on the street, beyond a few that had been turned to stone at one point or another, mostly with terrified expressions on their faces.

Now, goblins roamed the streets—goblins, and worse. Trolls weren't allowed in the city, but you could hear them howling outside the gates throughout the day and night. And Jack wasn't sure where the dragons or ogres were kept, but there was certainly no room for them in the city.

What there was room for, in every dark corner, were the . . .

well, something. All he knew was that the shadows moved when no one was around, even in bright sunlight. Not that the sun ever shone inside the city. Much like everyone else, the Sun Giant was far too afraid to ever come out of hiding, not this close to the seat of the Wicked Queen's power.

Along with the howls of trolls, Jack could hear voices raised in fear from every side. By order of the Queen, thousands of humans throughout the city were making wishes, wishing to the fairy queens, insuring that the fairy queens could not turn their gaze on the human world without being overwhelmed with terrified voices. A horrible yet effective way of keeping them distracted from whatever the Queen might be doing.

"Don't you just love the BIG city, Jack?" said Captain Thomas from his spot on Jack's shoulder. Captain Thomas laughed at his own joke, but Jack couldn't bring himself to join in. The city was far too bleak.

His apprenticeship had taken place entirely outside the city, so while he'd been training, he hadn't seen much of anything beyond his instructors, the one other recruit who hadn't lasted more than a week, and a few moving shadows. Jill had dropped him three months ago, and he hadn't seen her or his fairy since . . . not to mention the father Jill had promised back in the Fairy Homelands.

"The Queen's been anxious to see you again, my boy," Captain Thomas said, his tiny, glowing sword pressed almost casually against Jack's neck, as if it could be an accident and wasn't entirely on purpose as Jack knew it was. One step out of line, and that'd be it.

"I'm pretty anxious to meet her myself," Jack said. "There were some nights I thought I'd never get this far."

"Oh, your family's always had talent for such things," Captain Thomas told him.

His family? Did that just mean his sister, Jill, or—

"Stop here," Captain Thomas told him, and a tiny pinprick in his neck instantly froze Jack's forward momentum. They were at the gate out of the capital city toward the long, treacherous rock pathway that led to the Queen's castle. The pathway's sides were sheer cliffs, rising hundreds of feet above the water to a castle of dark, almost black stone, jutting turrets and piercing towers. Lights flickered madly from window to window, far faster than any human could move, and with a random insanity that made Jack nervous just watching it.

"Oh, don't be scared!" Captain Thomas said, slapping him with his tiny palm. "What's the worst that could happen? The Queen burns you to ashes? I stab you in the neck and drop you from that pathway? Creatures of darkest magic invade your soul and curse you to an eternal torment?" He laughed again. "It's not like you'd be the first! Buck up, lad!"

"You're a huge comfort," Jack told the little man.

Captain Thomas's eyes narrowed. "Is that a height joke?!"

The gate creaked open, saving Jack from a potential death by tiny man. Captain Thomas slapped his neck, and Jack made his way up the treacherous path, promising himself not to look over the sides at any point, and breaking that promise exactly thirty-four times in the first minute.

The height made him a bit woozy, but the jagged rocks at the bottom of the cliffs clarified everything a bit too much, honestly. Fortunately, the man on his shoulder distracted Jack with tales of other Eye initiates who'd died right here, or on that stone over there, who'd fallen there, NO, THERE! all the way up, so that helped. Hugely.

And yes, that one *was* a size joke.

The gate to the Wicked Queen's palace wasn't guarded any more than the gate leading from the city had been. And just like that former gate, this one opened on its own as well, then closed just behind Jack, leaving a faint odor of iron and selfishness in the air, with maybe an earthy hint of fried potato, of all things.

"Excuse the smell," Captain Thomas said, patting his chest. "Lunch isn't sitting particularly well."

Well. That explained the smell of selfishness. The miniscule Eye hadn't offered anything.

Inside, flickering torches lit what little of the palace Jack could see. Corridors ran off in every direction, as if anywhere he looked, there was another hallway hiding potential creepiness. Each step Jack took, a tingling in the back of his head made him jump, like something was JUST. RIGHT. BEHIND. HIM.

Of course, there *was* something there. The shadow creatures, whatever they were, seemed to be everywhere.

Captain Thomas led Jack down hallway after hallway, meeting no one, backtracking at times but never lost. If the captain was trying to confuse Jack, it was working. Honestly, even if he *wasn't* trying, it was still working. Overall, though, they seemed to climb more stairs than they walked down, and finally they came across a set of tarnished silver doors easily four times as tall as Jack, a beautiful stag carved into each one, facing each other and rearing back, as if ready to attack.

"The Queen's throne room," Captain Thomas said in a whisper. "Here's where I offer you the only advice I have in this type of situation."

"Yes?"

"Try not to die too much."

"Perfect."

Jack started for the doors, which, as always, opened by themselves. A slight pressure lifted on his shoulder, and Jack turned to find Captain Thomas leaning against the far wall as if he'd been standing there for hours. "You're not coming in with me, sir?"

"Oh, she wants to speak to you alone. Don't worry, you're no danger to her. She could handle the entire Order of the Eyes all on her own, let alone you."

Jack smiled at that, purposefully not thinking too hard about it. When a certain Queen could read any of your thoughts, after all, you learned to keep your mind away from anything that could get you killed. He'd spent the last three months training himself not to think about dangerous things, like schemes, plots, or certain blond girls with blue streaks in their hair.

Some of those thoughts were easier to block out than others.

With a final deep breath and a salute to Captain Thomas, Jack walked in.

Enormous golden vases exploding with fire lit the throne room every ten feet or so, sitting between marble columns long since marked with some kind of obscure alphabet. Jack walked slowly, not able to make out who or what was waiting for him at the end of the room, the fires were so bright.

Fortunately, not everyone had that same problem.

"I was beginning to think the Mirror must have been wrong," said a voice warm with ice. "But of course, it never was, so this must be exactly when you were meant to arrive."

"I bow before your wisdom," Jack said, wondering if he should actually bow but choosing to instead keep walking toward the voice. If he squinted, he could just barely make out a human shape sitting on what looked to be a throne sculpted from dragon bone.

The voice laughed, and Jack suddenly remembered helping this same woman up stairs made of snow in the Palace of the Snow Queen barely six months ago. He stepped closer and found himself staring up at a woman as beautiful as a barren field of stone, her hair black as night except for a streak of white here or there. Those imperfections just served to make her more striking, as did the deep purple gown she wore, covered by a robe that almost sparkled in the pure blackness. A blackened bone crown rose from her hair, pronouncing this woman every inch a queen.

"Your Majesty," Jack said, and this time he did bow.

As he looked back up, his eyes locked on a coffin carved from ice to the left of the throne. Snow White, at the right hand of the Queen, almost like a trophy.

"My newest Eye," the Wicked Queen said with a smile. "Do you come to betray me, then?"

Jack paused. "No."

She looked at him carefully. "You speak the truth. But why should I believe your words? Isn't it far more likely that you're here to attack me when I'm defenseless and vulnerable?"

Time to go all in. "You're thinking of my *sister*, Your Majesty. She is the one planning on betraying you."

One of the Queen's eyebrows raised slightly. "Indeed?"

Jack shrugged. "So she told me when she was trying to convince me to join the Eyes and help her with her plan."

The Queen smiled. "And you would betray her so quickly to me? Even if it means her death?"

"You won't kill her, Your Majesty," Jack said. "You'll keep her close and not tell her you know so that you can use her as an Eye. And then when the time comes, you'll be ready for any attack and watch as she fails. THEN you'll tell her you know. At least, that's the smart thing, so I imagine that's your plan."

"So much like your father," the Queen said, still sounding a bit surprised.

"I really hope not."

"So you aren't here as some misguided attempt to help my granddaughter, then?"

Jack gritted his teeth, purposefully not picturing anyone, certainly not at the very mention of her. It'd been three months, and the last thing he needed was some blond princess's face popping into his mind to knock him off track.

"I want just *one* thing from you, Your Majesty," he said. "And to get it, I will follow any order you give."

"And what might that be?"

Jack pulled out his grandfather's Story Book and opened it to the marked page, then held it up for the Queen to see. "I want to leave," he said, showing her a picture of the Huntsman carrying the Queen through a blue fire portal. "I want to leave this world and live in one without magic or royalty."

The Queen's eyes widened just a bit, and then she stared at Jack with a curious expression.

"That is quite a request," she said. "After all, I would not gain much from you leaving. Still, there are possibilities. How far would you be willing to go, though?"

"Whatever you ask."

"You would tell me where May is, then?" The Queen sat back on her throne and smiled.

Jack ground his jaw closed so hard it gave him a headache. "If I knew, yes. However, I have no idea where she is."

"Again, you tell the truth," the Queen said thoughtfully. "I would not have thought you'd let her out of your sight."

"She has her story to live out, I have mine."

"Quite the story hers is, too," the Queen said. "A handsome prince, true love . . . things we all wish we could find, no?"

Jack took a deep breath, then two, then three. She was baiting him, that's all this was. If he couldn't get through this, he certainly wouldn't have any chance of reaching the other world. "Everyone . . . wants different things, Your Majesty. I'm not particularly interested in a handsome prince myself."

The Queen laughed. "You're a remarkable boy, Jack. And no matter, if you truly don't know where she is. I have my best hunter out after her, so it should only be a matter of time."

"Let's hope she hasn't found a red hood, then, Your Majesty."

"Indeed," the Queen said, her eyes locked on his. "But let us return to your request. I could grant your wish. And if you give me your oath to follow my every order, I will do exactly that."

"Then you have it," Jack said, bowing his head.

The Queen stood up and gestured, and Jack's sword jumped into her hand. She pointed the sword at Jack, and he kneeled down in front of her.

"Then I declare you one of my Eyes in all things and every land," she said. "And if you disobey me even once, I will kill you."

"I know the price of betraying you, Your Majesty," Jack told her, his mind on the image he'd seen of his sword hanging over Phillip.

CHAPTER 4

Y ou're not going to want to kill me," May told Malevolent, backing away from the fairy queen in the creature's own throne room. "Here's the thing. We can help each other. I think, at least. I didn't have a ton of time to plan this out." She paused. "Honestly, I don't really even know your full story—"

"You won't live to hear it," Malevolent said with a smile.

"But that's not the point," May said, continuing quickly. "Don't you think there's a reason I called *you*? I've got something you need, and you've got . . . well, all this." She gestured to the whole castle, magic, everything. "Which would be very useful to me right now."

"And how would a child like you help me?" Malevolent said, smiling like a cat would smile at a mouse if cats smiled.

"Now, let's not either of us get angry at what either of us says, okay?" May said, holding up her hands and backing away. "I mean, I know you weren't thrilled with us when we left last time, but that's what I can help with. You remember that prince who was with me—"

Flames flickered out of Malevolent's eyes, and she growled, her mouth opening a bit too wide and dragony for May's taste. "You wish to hasten your death, I see."

"No, see, that's where you're not getting it!" May said, backing away faster. "I can help you with that! He's my friend—he'll listen to me, the prince!"

"You *both* will die by my hand!" Malevolent shouted.

"Okay, this isn't exactly going how I hoped it would," May said, her back slamming into the wall behind her. Well, this had been fun. Well done all around. "I thought you'd be more interested in surviving, but I can see that's not high on your list."

"Your little . . . *prince* . . . can do *nothing* to me!" Malevolent growled, her voice getting deeper as her skin began to glow.

"He might not be able to alone," May said quietly, "but he found his princess."

Malevolent's eyes went wide, and suddenly she looked like a human again. "What? It . . . cannot be . . ."

"Oh, it can be," May said, pushing forward. "It can be all *over* you if you don't listen to me for a second. Sleeping Beauty. He woke her up. Probably looking for you right now, if I know Phillip. He likes going out and finding his giants, you know? Not really a guy to just relax at home."

"The Mirror, it foresaw this," Malevolent said, glancing all around. "Together, they will destroy me! I cannot . . . she promised!"

May started to say something, then paused. "Wait, who promised?"

Malevolent grabbed her by her shirt and held her in midair, the fairy queen's pupilless eyes filled with terror. "You must save me! You must protect me!"

"That's what I've been . . . I WILL protect you, you just need to do something for me first!"

Malevolent sneered, despite her fear. "You WILL protect me, or I will burn you here and now!"

"Do it," May told her, then closed her eyes. "Fire me up, if you think that's a smart plan. 'Cause Phillip and Penelope will just *love* seeing their friend turned to ash. That'll calm them down and make sure they won't attack, especially after you tortured him last time he was here."

The fairy queen shrieked in rage, then dropped May to the floor. "What is it you want, you foul little beast?"

May stood back up and glared at Malevolent. "I want your help to make the Wicked Queen . . . go away."

This, of all things, made Malevolent laugh. Not for long, and not very hard, but it was definitely a laugh. "I would sooner take my chances against the prince and his princess."

"Fair enough," May said, and turned to leave. "Good luck. I'd try it as a dragon, it'll look better when they make the cartoon."

Malevolent growled again, and grabbed May's shoulder. "NO. I will help you. What is it you need?"

May turned back. "I need a way to fight her. A way to beat her, since I don't have all that magic and stuff that you both seem to have been born with."

"*She* is not a fairy kin," Malevolent sneered. "Any magic she knows offends this world."

"Help *me* offend the world too, then," May said. "Whatever I need! I can't let this go on any longer!"

"You could not learn enough magic to make a difference, not in a hundred years," Malevolent told her. "Not such as you. But there might be . . . another way."

"Another way—perfect!" May said. "What's the other way?"

"A weapon against the Queen," Malevolent said, turning around and swirling her hand as she hummed silently. A tiny glass ball appeared in the air and danced around.

"Perfect!" May said again, and grabbed for the ball, only to have her hand pass right through it.

"This is but an image," Malevolent said, grinning annoyingly at May's mistake. "I call it the Fairest, and it was hidden away many years ago."

"The Fairest, huh?" May said, staring at the glass ball. "Well, it fits the Wicked Queen theme, I guess. So what does it do?"

"It is a weapon of sorts," Malevolent said with a grin that May instantly didn't trust. "Without it, you will surely perish."

"That's optimistic," May said. "So where is it, and how do I use it when I find it?"

"Throw it at the Queen, and the glass ball will do the rest," the fairy queen said, still smiling mockingly. Honestly, it was so irritating. "As to where it is . . . I can send you there."

"Great," May said, spreading her arms. "Let's go!"

Malevolent's eyes flamed up again, and May took a step back involuntarily. "I . . . cannot go to this place. My kind are barred from it, for we never sleep."

"That's . . . an odd end to that thought," May said. "Wait, where is this place exactly?"

"You've been there," Malevolent snapped. "Every night. All humans go there, but without physical form."

"What, dreams?!" May said. "Those are just memories or images from . . . oh, forget it. I'm so tired of correcting you people. This weapon of yours is in . . . dreams?"

"If that's what you call it."

"What would *you* call it?"

"The breakdown of all reality, a land subject to no rules save those of its lord, an all-powerful creature who rules your night-lands."

"Let's stick with dreams, just because it's shorter. Okay, so *I* go find this Fairest thing in dreamland and bring it back? What kind of dream is it stuck within?"

Malevolent gritted her teeth once more. "If I knew that, I would know it because I traveled to these . . . dreams . . . and found the Fairest myself!"

"Well, so what do I do, just fall asleep?"

"You must enter the realm entirely, not just within your head, if you are to have any power of your own," Malevolent said, then began to hum.

"Wait, you're sending me there with my whole body?!" May said. "You know, dreams can be dangerous!"

Malevolent just smiled that truly irritating smile as everything began to swirl around, and the world disappeared.

CHAPTER 5

R ise, my Eye," the Wicked Queen said, and handed Jack the hilt of his sword. "I have need of something, and quickly. It's but a tiny thing. One similar to a task I once set your father to."

His father? Lian had claimed the man was here within the Wicked Queen's lands, but this was the first he'd heard of him since. His father had worked for the Wicked Queen?!

Well, was that really so surprising, given that his sister was currently?

"What's the task?" Jack said.

The Queen raised an eyebrow. "You aren't going to ask what your father was doing, serving me?"

"I'll find that out when I catch up to him. Just part of a lengthy chat we need to have."

"There is a giant living in the clouds," the Queen told him, watching him closely. "Your father tried to steal a few items from him but left something very important behind. I want that item."

The giant. A lifetime of mockery, of pitying looks, of everyone associating Jack with his thieving father, came flooding back, and Jack had to grit his teeth to stay on topic.

"What kind of item are we talking about? It's hard to steal something when you don't know what it is."

"A harp," the Queen said. "A harp sculpted from gold, in the shape of a woman. Do not speak to her, as she speaks only in song, and her music might destroy you."

"Destroy me?" Jack raised an eyebrow. "That's . . . unusual for a harp, or am I wrong?"

"She was created by the fairy queens," the Queen said, tapping a finger on her throne. She apparently wasn't full of patience. "Her power rivals the Mirror's, in her own way. Fortunately, that's exactly the way in which I have need of her."

"How big is this harp exactly?"

"No bigger than you are tall."

"Oh. Should be pretty easy to carry while I'm running from giants, then."

The Queen glared at him. "As soon as you've found her, play

these chords." She closed her eyes, and three loud tones sounded throughout the throne room. "Play those, and the harp's magic shall bring you back here immediately."

"And the giant?"

The Queen finally smiled. "For that, you'll need to see an . . . ally of mine. Follow my light." She held out a hand, palm up, and a little bolt of blue exploded over and over just above it. The bolt of blue floated out of her hand and back out the hall the way Jack had come.

Jack started to follow the bolt of blue, then turned to look at the Queen one more time. "This harp . . . and you help me get away from all of this. Right?"

"Do what I say, and you shall have all that you desire," the Queen said, her smile widening.

"Well, that sounded purposefully vague," Jack muttered, then followed the bolt of blue out the door.

The bolt led him up stairs and down hallways, twisting and turning until Jack wasn't sure he could find his way out, though that wasn't any different from how he'd come into the castle. Far too late he wondered if he should try a trick a boy from Giant's Hand had once taught him: leaving bread crumbs behind you in order to find your way home if you got lost.

There were only two problems with that plan. Problem number one: Animals tended to eat the bread crumbs, so it didn't work so well in woods. Fortunately, that wasn't so much a problem here. Unfortunately, that led to problem number two: Jack had no bread crumbs.

It was a sad day when you couldn't even pull off a plan doomed to fail.

The bolt led him on, twisting and turning farther than the Queen's castle could possibly have extended. At times, he was sure he was hundreds of feet above ground, maybe even in the highest towers of the castle. At other times, it felt like he had ended up deep underground.

He briefly wondered if the Queen would come looking for him if he never came out.

Then he even more briefly wondered if the bolt of blue was purposely trying to get him lost.

Fortunately, before he could wonder if the bolt was mocking him with its bolting, it exploded onto a wooden door, which unlocked at the explosion. Jack opened the door to find another, this one made of iron, also unlocking at his touch. A third made of steel, a fourth made of brick (very heavy), and a fifth made of bone all unlocked as he reached out for them.

Finally, behind the fifth door, a large room opened before him, one shaft of light shining on the dead center of the room. Jack glanced up at the light source and found none. There was no hole in the roof or anything.

A bit odd.

The sourceless light shone on more steel and iron, this time in bar form. Or maybe more accurately, in cage form, steel and iron intertwining playfully in gradually smaller and smaller cages, one inside the other.

Jack slowly approached the cages, expecting them to unlock just as the door had, but no lock tumblers tumbled. In fact, all he could hear was someone slowly breathing, watching as he came closer. Okay, he didn't *hear* the person watching, but that was hardly an important detail at this point.

Someone was breathing, and that same person was watching him.

"Hello?" Jack said.

"Hello, boy," said a tired, gravelly voice. "You're late."

That's when Jack saw him, a man hunched over in the very middle of the cages, iron cuffs on his wrists and ankles, barely able to move, by the looks of things.

"Father?" Jack said, his voice barely above a whisper.

"Are you asking? Because any boy of mine shouldn't have to."

Jack nodded. "Just making sure."

And with that, he took his sword off his back and threw it straight at the tiny spot that led all the way through the bars of the cage, straight at his father's chest.

The sword hit something glowing and translucent, and a hand grabbed it before it could hit the ground.

"Don't you just love family reunions?" Jill said, a sword in each hand.

CHAPTER 6

Phillip stood with his arms folded behind his back, covered by his royal vestments, staring out the window. Beyond the glass, adventure waited. Beyond the glass lay creatures of all-encompassing evil, and warmth that would make a shadow smile. Beyond the glass was his destiny.

His destiny to sacrifice himself for May, fighting against the Wicked Queen.

"Your Princeness," said a boy not much younger than Phillip and holding a pig. "Did you hear me? I said my pig can see the future, and he warns of terrible things!"

The pig oinked in agreement, and Phillip sighed.

"What does it see?" said a dazed voice from behind him. "What *kinds* of terrible things?"

A girl with hair of bronze, wearing a dress woven from golden thread by hand, no spinning wheels, leaned forward to put her ear next to the pig's dirt-covered snout and listened intensely, nodding every few seconds. "Phillip," she whispered, still nodding. "You really should hear this!"

Just beyond the glass. Would it be so wrong to leave once more? To forsake his duties, to leave his kingdom and . . . everything that came with it? To once more find his destiny under a full moon and a hungry sun, his sword gleaming like a star?!

"Seriously, I think you might want to listen to this," Penelope said with a frown. "HOW big?"

The pig oinked, and the boy nodded. "See what I mean, Your Princessness? Dark tidings are on the wind, and you'd be wise to heed the warnings of my pig here!"

"Thank you, Pig Keeper," Phillip said, and placed a few gold coins in the boy's hand.

The boy's eyes went wide as he felt the weight of the gold, even as he absently corrected his prince. "Uh, Assistant Pig Keeper, actually. But, my Princeness, what did I do to deserve—"

"Use it to give your divining friend a grand meal and have one yourself," Phillip said, patting the boy on his shoulder as he led him toward the door. "Mother, who's next?"

"That's it for today, darling," said a woman seated on an intricate opal throne, dressed in a dress very similar to Penelope's, only with elaborate stitching in silver. This woman feared neither spinning wheel nor evil fairy queen but still managed to love her son as warmly as her now-deceased husband. "Well, for your subjects. But there's still the matter of the wedding."

She may love him warmly, but she also could stop Phillip's heart with one word.

"I believe I am late for . . ." Phillip began, then froze at any possible lie. Why could he not tell even the simplest untruth, even to his own mother?!

"For what?" his mother said, her gaze filled with as much steel as her dress was with silver. It was not a lightweight piece of clothing, yet nothing would so much as stoop this woman.

"I'm sorry, Your Majesty," Penelope said, grabbing Phillip's hand and pulling him toward the door. "He meant to say he's late to take me into town, like he's been promising since we got here. Today's finally the day! You're welcome to come, we're just going to see . . . well, the entire thing."

"That sounds . . . lovely, dear," Phillip's mother said. "I will leave you two to it, however, as I have seen the town before, once or twice."

"Thank you, Your Majesty," Penelope said, and a minute later they were alone in the courtyard.

Phillip smiled at Penelope in thanks, and gently removed his hand from hers. "Did I really promise that?"

Penelope looked up with a shocked expression. "Of COURSE! Are you accusing me of lying to your mother?!"

Phillip instantly blushed red. "Of course not, I am deeply sorry that I even—"

And then Penelope laughed. "I like that color you turn. It makes you look like a tomato. A very dignified tomato. A tomato above all other tomatoes, one that rules his garden with a squishy iron fist."

Phillip blinked at that, unsure what to say and even more unsure how they had ended up outside the castle gates with two guards smiling evilly at him as Penelope somehow had his hand again, dragging him farther into the city. How did the girl *do* that—turn off his mind so easily?

"Where first?" she asked, her head bobbing around to look at everything.

"I, uh, had not really planned on an outing tonight," Phillip said, then shrugged. It was preferable to speaking to his mother about the wedding. "How about the marketplace? It is quite something to see, and it might give me the opportunity to drop my sword off at the blacksmith to be sharpened."

"In case we meet a dragon or something," Penelope said, looking up at him with her eyes barely open. The girl seemed perpetually either on the brink of falling asleep or as if she had just woken up. Phillip was never quite sure if he had her full attention, and if he did not, what that might look like.

The citizens of the town of Tailorsville nodded respectfully to their prince, as well as the mysterious princess who had arrived with Phillip three months earlier, claiming to be the long-lost princess of a neighboring kingdom, destroyed during the war. Penelope had no family left and had never known them . . . in fact, she had grown up without knowing many humans at all, living in the Fairy Homelands, surrounded by some of the most magical and oddly incomprehensible creatures Phillip had ever met.

He was beginning to see where Penelope might have picked up some of her habits.

The marketplace rumbled with activity, with calls of breads for sale, customers haggling with shopkeepers, farmers showing off their wares, and children running everywhere.

A few children screamed in delight from the opposite side

of the market as Phillip strode purposefully toward the black-smith, Penelope at times behind him and at other times in front. He wasn't sure how the girl moved, as he never seemed to see her. It was as if she just . . . appeared wherever he was not looking. Strange.

"You don't like this idea of a wedding, do you?" she said while feeling a magical cloak of rain deflection. "Hmm, smooth! But why would someone not want to be rained on?"

Phillip started to answer the first question, then the second, then decided the first was more pertinent and a question that needed to be answered. "Penelope," he said, taking the princess by the shoulders and gently turning her around to face him. "You are correct. I do *not* like the idea of this wedding. Our parents betrothed us at a very early age—"

"Well, to be fair, I'm apparently your true love," Penelope said, making a half-disgusted face at him. "Otherwise you wouldn't have been able to kiss me awake back when that Eye girl hit me with a spindle, putting me and everyone close by asleep. And somehow making vines grow. Huge vines. I didn't get that part. So I must be your true love, which is good to know, in case someone sets the sleeping curse off again. Oh, I see we're back to dignified tomato?"

"Yes, well," Phillip said, and pulled her into the shadow of the blacksmith's booth. The children's delighted screams echoed closer, as if they were moving in this direction. "I do not know that there is anything to that, beyond the silly belief of some old-fashioned fairy queens—"

"Don't say such things about my sisters," Penelope said, staring a bit more intently at him, though still with her half-closed eyes. "Even if I am your true love, it doesn't mean that *you* are *mine*. And I never *asked* you to fall in love with me."

"I did NOT do any such thing!" Phillip shouted. The children seemed to be screaming in his head now, as if they were everywhere. What was causing all this commotion?!

"Well, then this must all be a dream, and I never woke up," Penelope said with a shrug. "Listen, I'm sorry I don't feel the same way about you—"

"YOU do not feel the same about—that is not the point!"

A girl of about four years of age shrieked in his ear, and for a moment, the prince lost his dignity, if just a bit. "If you are quite through?!" he said, turning to the girl.

And that's when he saw a monkey dressed like a pirate, robbing the poor blacksmith while a small group of children waved and shouted encouragement. The blacksmith looked from Phillip to the monkey and back, almost pleading with his eyes.

"YOU?!" Phillip said to the monkey.

The monkey shrieked in joy and threw himself at Phillip, hugging his most likely vermin-infested body against Phillip's chest. Finally, it looked at Phillip and held out a lock of bright blue hair.

"Malevolent," the monkey shrieked.

The pirate monkey. Phillip's bit of magic that he had arranged, just in case May ever found herself in danger. The monkey had been put under a spell by his court magician to appear to Phillip instantly if May's life was ever threatened.

Apparently the town was as far as the magic had taken it.

Phillip was halfway across the market before either the monkey or Penelope caught up. Finally. This was the moment the Wicked Queen must have seen. This was the moment Phillip had been born for.

And it would be the most noble of deaths.

CHAPTER 7

May smacked the blaring alarm to her right and shut her eyes again. Ugh. School. Too early.

Then she sat bolt-upright. "Wait, I don't have to go to school!" she shouted to no one. "There's no school in fairy tales!" Maybe not 100 percent good news, but still, the school part had been a nice relief. She swatted her old alarm clock off her old night-stand. "Nice try on that, by the way. But we're not going to do the whole *Was this all a dream?* thing."

"You're not supposed to be here, not like this," said a voice from somewhere behind her, which shouldn't be possible, since all that was behind her was her bedroom wall. May whirled around and found herself no longer in bed, now fully dressed, only . . . wrongly. Her black PUNK PRINCESS shirt was pink, and her blue hair was on the wrong side, like she'd come out the other side of a mirror.

Well, Alice had dreamed the whole Wonderland thing, hadn't she?

Oddly, the changes felt completely normal, just like weird-ness always did in a dream. Maybe that's also why she wasn't surprised to find a man made entirely from glass, like a translucent statue, with sand flowing through him like in an hourglass, standing right in front of her.

"You're dreaming, but you're also here," the man made of sand said. "I don't see many of you physically in my world like this."

"I don't see many of *you* anywhere like anything," May told him. "Who are you exactly?"

"You know me," the man said. "I build your dream stories. Whatever I imagine comes true for you here every night."

"You could stand to brush up a bit on plot and character, then," May said with a grimace. Maybe the Sandman didn't enjoy criticism, but seriously, every dream she'd ever had was all *over* the place. "Or at least just tell one story, you know? I feel like I'm living four or five different ones in dreams. Sometimes all at once."

The man stared at her strangely, his glass eyes darkening a bit. "The fairy queen sent you, didn't she? The one who sent all those goblins."

May paused. "Goblins? She didn't say much about that—"

The glass eyes darkened further. "I imprisoned them all forever in their nightmares."

May backed away, only to find herself in a room no bigger than a closet, bumping up against the wall. "Nope, I've never heard of any fairy queen. Just made it here myself! I'm not here to cause any trouble, just, you know, find some glass ball called the Fairest, take it back to the real world, use it on a bad lady, that kind of thing."

The glass man gestured and spilled sand out before him. "You will do no such thing," he said as May watched the sand fall, almost mesmerized. She blinked and found herself in class, her teacher Mrs. Murray standing in front of her, hand out, as every other student in the class stared at her.

"Well, May?" Mrs. Murray said, stamping one foot. "Where's your thousand-page book report on a book you've never heard of, let alone read?!"

May's stomach dropped, and she struggled to speak but couldn't. . . . Her mouth was too dry. "Glargh," she said, which just seemed to anger Mrs. Murray more.

"No book report?!" Mrs. Murray shouted. "You know what we do to children who don't do their homework, May!" With that, all the other students began shouting insults at May as they swarmed her, picking her up and carrying her out of the classroom and into what looked like a zoo.

Into the Spider-Snake-More-Spider Hut of Fun.

"NOOOOOOOOOOOOOOO!" May shouted, struggling to get away, but the other kids just tightened their grip and carried her toward the Hut door. This was all like a bad dream!

Uh, of *course* it was. Why exactly had she fallen for that? "Alright, sand guy!" she shouted over the kids' insults. "I'm not buying this anymore! It's just a dream!"

That made her feel better. Only, the Hut kept getting closer.

"Seriously, just a dream," May said, struggling against the kids, beginning to panic even more. "JUST A DREAM!"

Mrs. Murray opened the door to the Hut of Fun. An enormous snake uncurled itself from around a spider bigger than May was, and both licked their lips. Even though neither one actually had lips.

"DREAM!" May shouted, frantically pinching herself.

"You can't wake yourself if you're here physically," the man of glass told her, his face expressionless. "Instead, you're stuck here until something pulls you back out."

Well *that* wasn't good news. Would Malevolent know to pull

her out? Would she even care if May was being eaten by giant spiders and snakes in her dream?

Wait, this *was* her dream. She'd had this nightmare before . . . or parts of it. Sort of. But that meant it was happening within her head, somehow, even if she was here, somehow, which just gave her a headache, somehow. But if it really was within her own head—

May squeezed her eyes closed just as the kids tossed her into the Hut, concentrating on someone, anyone, who could help her. Concentrating on help as hard as she could, even as she fell toward the worst things in the world.

She landed on something hard, and for a moment, May didn't want to open her eyes in case it was something that was not only hard but spider- or snakelike. Finally, a pleasant breeze on her cheek convinced her that she wasn't being attacked, so decided it was okay to check things out.

A man dressed in a midnight blue cloak with black armor beneath it stared down at her, a large oak tree behind him swaying in the wind. His armor had a large white eye right in the center of the chest.

"You must be May," the Eye said, offering her a hand. "Jack has told me so much about you."

CHAPTER 8

You know what's fun?" Penelope said to the goblin holding a knife to her throat. "Rescuing princesses. I don't know why only boys get to do it. I think they keep it a secret just so we won't rescue the princesses before them."

The goblin snorted. "And what a good job you're doing. Who's going to rescue *you*, then?" He pointed up at Malevolent's dragon castle, rising into the air above them. "More guards?"

Phillip stepped out from behind the goblin and held his sword to the monster's neck. "I believe that would be me."

A deep voice behind Phillip growled, and the prince felt something annoyingly sharp and metallic pressed into his back. "Would it?"

"This is getting too complicated," Penelope said with a sigh.

"Ambushes on top of ambushes? Enough twists—it's too hard to keep up!" With that, she fell forward, kicking backward. The goblin behind her slammed into Phillip, who in turn hit the goblin behind *him*, and all three went down in a heap. Both goblins yelped out in surprise, then began to snore, and Phillip noticed two tiny wooden needles sticking out of their arms just inches from his own.

"From the spindle that Lian girl used on me," Penelope told him, looking a bit embarrassed. "It absorbed some of the curse, so I broke it into a bunch of different pieces. Looks like it works! They should be out for a couple of hours, unless, well, someone kisses them."

Phillip pushed the first goblin off himself, then carefully got to his feet, deliberately avoiding close contact with any wooden needles. "You . . . might have told me about those," he said, keeping a few feet between himself and the princess. "How many more do you have?"

Penelope felt around in a pocket of her light green traveling cloak, covering a darker green dress that his mother had insisted she wear, despite Phillip actively encouraging a more travel-friendly outfit. And to be fair, that was only after he had encouraged her not to come at all, then tried to leave in secret without her. Unfortunately, he had been caught by the princess quite quickly. "As many as I could throw in my pockets," she said. "More back at the castle."

With that, she turned and led the way up the beach, toward the stump of a beanstalk rising out of the sand. Above them, the dragon castle's mouth lay open, operating as a drawbridge for the goblins patrolling the surroundings, though there were now two fewer awake guards doing so.

"Next time, I will handle the goblins," Phillip told her, leading the way into the woods surrounding the castle.

"Were you meaning to handle them this time?" Penelope asked, and Phillip had no idea if she was mocking him or serious. "Maybe you were just waiting for your moment."

"I do not need your help here," he told her, pushing on through the woods.

"At least you're here already, to not need my help. If I'd left you to it, your horse would get here in about three days."

She had a point there, not that Phillip was very interested in hearing it. He *had* intended to ride here, not considering that there might be a faster way. All Penelope did was sing a little melody, and a stout, black-haired fairy queen had appeared to take them. "She owes me a favor," Penelope had whispered to him. "I once helped her rescue a wooden puppet from a whale."

For May's sake, Phillip had let the fairy queen transport them right to the beach. Unfortunately, the fairy queen had not been willing to drop them in the castle, fearing Malevolent's reprisal.

It was just as well. No one else needed to be hurt here. Now all Phillip had to do was figure out a way to leave Penelope safely behind, and he would go on alone to face his fate.

"I suggest a frontal assault," Phillip whispered to Penelope, taking out his sword. "Last time I was here, a fairy queen tormented and tortured me, claiming I would one day kill her." He glanced up at the princess. "I intend to prove her correct, if it is all the same to you. But there is no reason that you should not stay here, where you will not be hurt."

Penelope held up a shard of the spindle. "Or I put you to sleep right here and go do the hard work without you. Your choice."

Ah. With that, Phillip nodded, then strode up the thin stone bridge, the sleepless princess falling in behind him, both with weapons ready. Before them rose a dragon castle containing a small army of goblins, an evil fairy queen, and who knew what other evils.

It would be a grand final adventure. And all he had to do was call out a challenge, then attack. On the other side, only two goblins guarded the gate, but Phillip knew ten times that many, at least, lay just beyond.

And then, for just a moment, Phillip thought about Jack. Jack, whom he had once thought of as a friend, before things had changed. But once, if Jack had stood where Phillip did now, his friend would have said something funny, as likely as not, and Phillip would have laughed inside, even as he kept a serious expression on his face for May's sake. Then Jack would have done something clever, potentially outwitting their foe, potentially failing miserably. Odds might have favored the latter, but Phillip always admired the attempt.

All he had to do was call out a challenge to the goblins.

Instead, he reached over and politely took two of Penelope's spindle splinters from her hand. When she gave him a questioning look, he just shrugged. "This one is for an old friend," he said, then quickly and quietly climbed one of the drawbridge's chains.

The chain creaked a bit, but no more than it did whenever a wind came up, and the goblins never noticed until both collapsed into one pile, snoring away.

Goblins would be a fine last adventure, but there could be better. And better awaited him just inside the castle, in the form of a very large black dragon.

CHAPTER 9

Jack stared at his father, chained and caged on the ground in front of him.

"Really, just *everyone* hates you, huh?" he said.

"Everyone is a lot of people," his father said, staring straight ahead. "I'd bet that just by numbers, that isn't true. But who am I to say?"

"Very clever," Jack told him, taking his sword back from Jill.

"You're not the first person to tell me that."

"Are you two going to be done any time soon?" Jill asked.

Jack paused a moment, taking everything in, then began the speech he'd been waiting for years to give. "Father. If I can even call you that. After all, does a *real* father leave behind his—"

"We don't have time for that," Jill said, covering his mouth with her hand to keep him from speaking. "Your issues can wait. There's too much you need to know. Some things have changed since I last saw you."

Jack looked at her and nodded, and she removed her hand. Then he turned back to his father and continued his speech. "Does a *real* father leave his only son to, and I'm being kind when I say this, go off and be a filthy, horrible thief? Are those the actions of a man who loves his children?"

Jill rolled her eyes, but his father turned his gaze up at Jack. "Sounds like you've got a great grasp of history, don't you, kid?"

"A *thief*," Jack repeated. "And what did your criminal activities result in? A giant rampaging through the land, killing and eating and destroying wherever it went. All for what, Father? Money? Treasure?"

"Well, what can I say?" his father said, gesturing around his empty cage. "I just couldn't resist all that gold I brought back here. Isn't it pretty?"

"Why did you do it?" Jack asked, gritting his teeth.

"Didn't we just cover that?" his father said, glaring at him.

Jack hit the cage with his sword, making both ring loudly. "Answer the question!" he shouted.

"And get in the way of all your indignation?!" his father shouted back. "I wouldn't dream of it!"

"HE DID IT FOR OUR MOTHER, YOU IDIOT!" Jill shouted, pushing Jack back away from the cage.

Of all the answers Jack expected, that wasn't at the top. Or on the list. Or even a distant possibility. "Our . . . what?" he said. "But our mother died during the war."

"She sure did," his father said, back to staring straight ahead again. "Do you have any idea why they lock me up like this, boy?"

"Stop it," Jill said to him. "This is getting us nowhere, and we have no time. Jack, what did the Queen say she needed?"

"Why do they lock you up like that?" Jack said quietly.

"Because this is the only cell they've ever found that can hold him," Jill said quickly. "He's escaped from every other one."

"And what do you think I do when I escape?" the man said.

"He attacks the Wicked Queen, and she almost kills him," Jill said. "I get that this is all some sort of macho father/son thing, but does it really have to be *now*? There'll be so much time later, if we can just—"

"Why doesn't she?" Jack asked just as softly. "Why doesn't she just kill you?"

Jill sighed. "Because she *needs* him, Jack. Just like she needs me, and like she *thinks* she needs you! She's always needed our family—we do something she *can't*, now that she doesn't have her Mirror anymore!"

"And what is that?" Jack said, his voice sounding like it was coming from a distance, certainly not from within his own body.

His father laughed suddenly. "Of course you wouldn't know, boy. You show no sign of using your mind, why would you know what it could do?"

"Cleverness," Jill said, glaring at Jack. "This stinky, chained-up man here is one of if not *the* sneakiest, cleverest, shrewdest person to ever live. There's nothing he can't figure his way out of, no one he can't outwit. NO ONE. Which makes him a very powerful enemy . . . or a huge advantage, if you could somehow force him to make your plans for you."

"And why . . . why would he ever plan anything for the Queen?" Jack asked, already knowing the answer.

His father's gaze dropped to the floor. "Your mother . . . I never should have fallen in love with her, boy. I knew I shouldn't. I don't know if it was destiny or coincidence or just horrible luck, to fall in love with an Eye—"

"An EYE—"

"Stop it," Jill said, slamming Jack's dropped jaw closed

again. "Yes, she was an Eye. Don't interrupt, or we'll never get through this."

"She and her brother both grew up under the Queen's reign," his father said. "I, of course, figured stealing something from one of the Queen's Eyes would be a fun challenge and maybe hurt the Queen in the process. I wasn't involved in the war, I was so young . . . but I got caught. By her. Your mother."

"You don't remember her, do you?" Jill said, moving across the room to stand against the wall.

"No," Jack said. For some reason, he found it a bit difficult to speak, like he hadn't had a drink of water in weeks.

"She was so smart," Jill said without looking at him. "She could outthink Dad in a minute."

"And did, all the time," Jack's father said, almost smiling. "She certainly did when I first met her. Had me thrown in chains a lot like these before I even knew what was going on. Of course, she cheated with that sword of hers. She always cheated."

"Always?" Jack said.

"Well, I was gone as soon as she turned her back," his father said, still just a hairsbreadth away from a smile. "But no matter how far I traveled, no matter how many adventures I had, I always kept coming back. I told myself it was for the challenge.

Your mother knew from the start, she told me later. Said she just waited for me to catch up because she knew I wasn't as smart as she was."

"She could talk him in circles," Jill said, still looking at the floor. "You should have seen her."

"Gray eyes," his father said. "I couldn't get them out of my head. I'd close my eyes and see hers. She was all I could think about. By then, her brother, your uncle . . . he was having a little trouble with the Queen, and ran away." He sneered. "He deserved what he got. But your uncle put your mother in just as much danger and left her behind. So I . . . I ended up rescuing her right out from under the Queen's nose." Now he broke into a smile. "And we had the happiest years of my life after that."

"He's saying we were born," Jill supplied helpfully, smiling herself now. "And then, um, someone got hurt. You know, by accident."

"You pushed me down a hill!" Jack said indignantly.

"You were always a fragile boy," his father said, looking at him now. "That head of yours, especially. I'm surprised you haven't broken it again."

"So at what point did you decide to steal from a giant and ruin all our lives?" Jack said, refusing to get pulled in. He'd hated this man his whole life! Just because maybe some of what he'd done hadn't been so bad, didn't mean—

"The Queen found Mother," Jill said softly. "After your accident. You were living with Grandpa by then, to heal your big stupid head, which I still think was your own fault, by the way. You should have aimed at something other than a rock when you fell down the hill. But I went to bed one night with Mom tucking me in and woke up the next morning with her gone. Dad hadn't heard a thing. The only thing left was a blackbird cawing on the windowsill. It dropped a note for Dad and flew off."

"The Queen's raven," his father said, and Jack threw a look at Jill, who almost imperceptibly shook her head for him not to say anything. He turned back to his father as the man continued. "The note said that the Queen had your mother, and the only way we'd see her again is if I had something to trade. And along with the note—"

"Beans," Jack said. "So up you went."

"And came down with a goose that could lay golden eggs," his father growled. "All the gold the Queen could ever need to pay for her armies and her war, and I delivered it to her. Though at least I did see your mother again."

Jill curled her hands into fists.

"Her body, at least," his father continued, his voice dead of any emotion. "The Queen had killed her, you see. To punish your uncle."

"You keep mentioning an uncle—" Jack said, but Jill interrupted him.

"NO. We're definitely not going down that road. Get back on topic!"

"Fine," Jack said to his father. "So here you are, still making the Queen's plans for her. She killed our mother, and you still do what she wants?!"

"I've escaped more times than I can count, but every time she brings me back she steals something from me, something precious," his father said. "Memories. Memories of your mother." He grabbed his head with both hands, growling in frustration. "They're all I have left, and she pulls them right out of my head, then burns them in dragonfire. It's as if our time together never happened. And if I don't do as she says, she'll take the rest, boy. She'll take EVERYTHING from me." He shook as he finished and stared at Jack, hatred swimming in his eyes. "So I plan for her. I scheme. I outwit her enemies, including myself. Including *you*."

"Me?" Jack said. "But you didn't even know I was coming here—"

"Who do you think sent Jill? Who do you think had her help you, under the sea, in the Fairy Homelands? Even while I came up with the Queen's plan to destroy the fairy queens, I made sure Jill could save them, through you. And the Queen *knows*, Jack! It's all a game to her! She tortures me here, making me plan her horrible tasks, then watches as I desperately try to stop them from happening! And she must know why you're here as well, because she had me outwit you from the start!"

Jack started to say something, then stopped. His father might be right . . . or he might be wrong. There were things that Jack knew that no one else did, and right now, it seemed smart to keep those things secret. "So you're fighting against the Wicked Queen, while also her chief strategist. You're coming up with plans, then plans to stop your plans, then plans to stop those? Is that even close?"

"Close, but not the end of it," Jill said. "You and me, brother. WE have to be the end of it. You've met our father, and you know what's happening now, why no one's been able to defeat the Queen, either in battle or by tricking her. We're going up against the most clever person to ever live. And now, you and I have to outwit him."

"Except I'm supposed to be stealing something else from the giant in the clouds," Jack said.

"Ah, the harp?" his father said. "Wondered when she'd try for that. You'll need my help to accomplish that task. You're nowhere close to smart enough. Jill is, of course. But that's probably why the Queen is sending you."

"Well . . . that's just insulting, first of all," Jack said.

"The truth insults you a lot, doesn't it?" Jill said, not unkindly.

"Yes, but now's not the time," Jack told her. "So, what do I need to know?"

"Three things," his father told him. "First, don't underestimate this giant. The giants on land might be stupid, but this one . . . he's their king or lord or something. I was never quite clear on that. Either way, that giant brain of his isn't just for decoration."

"So he's smart. Next?"

"It was nice knowing you," Jill told him, shaking her head.

"Second," Jack's father said, shaking his head too, "you're going to be the size of a mouse to him, so take advantage of that. You'll be faster and quieter than you might ordinarily expect and have a lot more places to hide. Use it. If he never knows you've been there, you might have a chance."

"These really are helpful," Jack said. "Hide, huh? Try not to let him know I'm there? Brilliant."

"And third," his father said, "when he catches you, as I've

already figured out he will, you must under no circumstances, never ever *EVER* let him follow you when you leave. The only reason he didn't destroy everything in his path is because I had to trick him back up."

"YOU tricked him?" Jack said. "I thought Phillip's father died trying to kill him!"

"There's quite a bit more to that story than you know," his father told him. "But there's no time for that."

"We'll finish that, and more than a few other things, when I get back," Jack told him.

"You mean *if* you get back," Jill supplied helpfully.

"Stop it," he told her. "Did you get what I asked you for, by the way?"

She nodded, and tossed him something in a bag. "Not sure why you'll need it or anything. Won't exactly help much if the giant eats you, but whatever. You wanted a strong healing potion, I got you one. The Draught of Irrational Bodily Repair, if you want to get specific."

"And this is the same sort of thing that was used on that knife I told you about?" Jack asked her.

"That or something close," she told him.

Jack gritted his teeth but let it go. He couldn't ask anything more without explaining himself, and right now, he couldn't tell anyone anything.

"I'm going to ignore all this," his father said. "But that's not all Jill has for you, I'm guessing."

Jill sighed. "You really are way too smart," she told the man, then reached back into her hood. A golden fairy yawned, stretched, then stepped into her hand. "Sleepy time is over?" Gwentell the fairy asked. "Fine. It's about time you finished all your testing, stupid man-child. Can we go steal from a giant already?"

CHAPTER 10

They would be too late at this rate. Whatever the evil fairy queen intended to do to Princess May, she would have done it by the time they reached her.

Phillip sidestepped a goblin sword, then swung down and backhanded the creature with his own sword. Not killing the monsters added a level of difficulty to the task, but for all he knew, the goblins had no choice in the matter, controlled as they most likely were by Malevolent. And if nothing else, he could sympathize with having no control in matters of one's own life.

Behind him, Penelope seemed incapable of being hit, continually moving as the goblins attacked, almost swimming gracefully upstream against a goblin river. Phillip tried to keep an eye on her whenever he could, but keeping an eye on the girl was harder than he would have thought: She was never in the same place twice. Yet she did not move as quickly as an Eye . . . she just seemed to anticipate where the goblins meant to strike, as if she were aware of everything they meant to do.

Aware, and yet half-asleep. An odd combination, but it seemed to work extremely well.

"DIE!" the goblin in front of Phillip yelled, yanking the prince's attention back to the front.

"Not just yet," the prince told him, driving the hilt of his sword into the creature's forehead. The goblin's eyes crossed, and it dropped to the floor, on top of two already-unconscious goblins.

"Can I suggest something?" Penelope asked, ducking under a sword that otherwise would have taken her head off, then continuing the motion to sweep a leg around and knock her attacker off its feet. "Maybe we could find a different way to go that might have less goblins?"

"I would be happy to hear of one," Phillip grunted, his sword deflecting a goblin's axe into the wall. "I fortunately did not spend enough time here to become familiar with any shortcuts, the last chance I had to visit."

"That's not what I meant," Penelope said, then grabbed Phillip's hand and pulled him right out the closest window.

In his life, Phillip had seen quite a few sights that would make grown men weep, all with a bravery that Jack might have called foolish. But bravery was not about feeling no fear, as Phillip had quickly discovered. Instead, bravery meant conquering your fears, and that, anyone could do, foolishly or no.

Still, the thousand feet of nothingness outside the window presented quite a large fear for him to overcome.

Penelope, meanwhile, had begun to climb up the side of the dragon castle, moving more quickly than Phillip had seen her move on solid ground. "We're going up to the top," she shouted down. "Less goblins there, I'd think."

Phillip swallowed deeply, then followed her up a bit more slowly, carefully picking his hand- and footholds. Truthfully, he had been this high on the beanstalk last time he had been here, but then he had something solid beneath him. This time, his fingers dug into less than an inch of stone here, his toes flexing on top of the same below him.

"Where did you learn to climb so well?" he asked, knowing that fears had much less of a hold on you when you could turn your focus elsewhere.

"You get used to it when everyone around you can fly," Penelope told him, smiling her half smile back down at him.

"Maybe you should spend a few years in the fairy homelands. It's a pretty nice vacation spot."

"I will keep that in mind for later," Phillip said, purposely not adding that he did not believe there would be a later for him.

Beneath him, he heard the first goblins exit the window, pushing each other to climb up after them. Their large feet and hands would make things more difficult but not impossible. He would have to hurry.

Fortunately, the higher they went, the more the wall angled inward, flattening out into the dragon's back. Indeed, Penelope had reached a spot flat enough to be jogging up the side instead of climbing. "I'm going to try something, okay?" she said, quickly running out of sight.

"Perhaps you should wait for me before—" Phillip gave up, knowing she could not hear him. Instead, he put his efforts into climbing faster, hoping that whatever she did, he would not be too late to protect her.

And then he heard it. Singing. Beautiful singing, a song he could neither get out of his mind nor remember for the life of him.

Fairy queen music. Fairy queen *magic*.

Spurred on by the idea that Penelope was in danger, the

prince quickly reached a portion of the wall flat enough to scamper up, then turned that scamper into an all-out sprint. There was Penelope, standing right in the middle of the dragon castle's back, singing quietly. As low as her voice might be, though, Phillip could hear every note clearly, as he imagined anyone in the castle could. Such was the power of the fairy queens, and yet here was a human girl who somehow had been able to match it.

Who *was* this girl?!

Phillip quickly reached her and grabbed her shoulders, shaking her gently to stop her. She opened her eyes halfway and smiled a bit. "Let's see if that helps anything."

"What did you do?! What spell did you cast?"

Penelope shrugged. "It wasn't magic, not really. It was more . . . an invitation."

The ground beneath them began to rumble, first only a little bit, then more and more until it became difficult to stand.

And then an entire section of the roof exploded upward, rock flying all around them. Phillip grabbed Penelope and shielded her, yet most of the rock flew out and over, landing on the beach and in the ocean, and all Phillip felt was a heavy wind, followed by nothing, then the wind again, over and over.

Almost like wings beating.

The prince turned back toward the hole, then looked up into the green eyes of a furious black dragon.

"YOU!" Malevolent shrieked.

"An invitation?" Phillip asked quietly.

"Maybe more of an insult?" Penelope said, shrugging again. "I didn't know what most of the words meant, but I figured they'd get her attention. I might have said some mean things about her mother, actually."

"It seems to have worked," Phillip said, right as the dragon spewed fire at the both of them.

CHAPTER 11

And you are . . . ?" May said to the man wearing the armor of an Eye, wishing she had some sort of weapon. And then, just as she wished it, there they were in her hands, two ray-guns that looked like they were straight out of some cheesy science-fiction movie.

Perfect.

The man opened his cloak to point at the white eye on his armor. "I'm assuming you've seen this before?"

"Oh, I sure *have*," May said, then shot both guns right at the white eye, and the man exploded into a million pieces.

And then the million pieces unexploded, reforming into the Eye right behind her. She whirled around and shot again, but this time the shots zigzagged around him, and he shook his head.

"This isn't only *your* dream anymore, child. You asked for help, and I offered. But to get you where you need to go, you needed to leave the comfort of your own head behind."

"Deep and vague," May said, lowering her guns. "You must be the Charmed One. Jack's mentioned you a few times too."

"All good things?"

"Mostly about how you were trying to train him to become evil. Unfortunately, you won. He ran off to become an Eye. Nice job." She quickly raised the guns and shot, hoping to surprise him. The rays hit him again, and again he exploded, but for a second time, he just reappeared behind her.

Well. That was irritating.

"The lord of this world is on his way," the Charmed One told her. "You have time to debate my actions, or you have time to ask for my help in finding what you seek, but not both. Which shall it be?"

"Debate!" May shouted, and shot, only to have the ray whiz off in the opposite direction from where she aimed it, missing by a mile. "YOU made Jack do this, didn't you?"

The guns disappeared out of May's hand, so she concentrated, and the ground shook out of nowhere, again and again, like enormous footsteps.

"Giant?" the Charmed One asked her, not turning around to look.

"Dinosaur," May said as a humongous Tyrannosaurus Rex bent down to swallow the Charmed One whole.

At first, it seemed that she might have actually gotten to him, as he didn't reappear anywhere. And then the dinosaur turned to look at May and spoke in the Charmed One's voice. "You cannot hurt me here, May. You cannot hurt me *anywhere*. All I am is an idea, and ideas can't be harmed. Only passed along or ignored."

"Why did you take him?" May asked, gritting her teeth to keep from calling in the air force. "Why did you *take* him from me?!"

Abruptly, the scene shifted all around her, and May gasped.

Jack was staring right at her. And he was dressed exactly like an Eye.

"Jack?" she said, her voice barely a whisper.

He looked right at her, then bent down on one knee, his hands held out for hers.

May reached out for his hand, only to look down and see that she held an apple in hers. And her clothes were different . . . she was dressed in black robes with golden trim, far richer than anything she'd ever worn before. Her hair was no longer blond but black, and her hands had hints of wrinkles.

"I accept your poisoned apple," Jack said to her, and took it from her hands. "And in return, I pledge my loyalty."

"Stop talking like Phillip!" May yelled, but that's not what came out. Instead, a voice that sounded like both May's and . . . someone else's said, "I accept your oath. You are now under my control."

She was the Wicked Queen. And as the May inside her new royal clothes screamed, the Jack in front of her brought the apple to his lips and took a bite.

"NO!" she screamed, and suddenly she wasn't the Wicked Queen, she was May, and she was pulling on Jack to yank him away from the Queen with all her might, but he wouldn't move, he just sort of slumped to the ground, he wasn't breathing, what was happening–

"May," said a voice, and she felt a hand on her shoulder. "This is the glass man's doing. Let me help."

The Charmed One pulled a sword from off his back, a sword that looked exactly like Jack's, and handed it to May, then nodded back at the apple now lying on the ground. May screamed in anger and stabbed at the apple, which exploded into the man of sand's shape. Something tinkled like broken glass, and the sand man screamed as sand went flying.

"Catch what sand you can!" the Charmed One yelled, and May caught as much as she could as the Charmed One grabbed her hand and yanked her forward, just as the scene shifted, then shifted again, over and over.

Shift: An upside-down cliff, where to fall was to be safe.

Shift: A dark castle, the one from up the hill from May's house, only the lights go on abruptly, blinding May, and someone's in there with her, someone glowing. . . .

Shift: A future where nothing exists, only roaming elephants carrying cities on their back, cities the size of small dogs, inhabited by butterflies.

Shift: May pushes off from the ground in the middle of her old neighborhood, gently floating into the air. She'd always known she was adopted, since she was the only one to survive her planet exploding, but to have superpowers? Who knew!

Shift: War breaks out between the colors blue and red, though green seems jealous that it wasn't involved. Yellow, meanwhile, hides in the corner.

Shift: The Wicked Queen gently reads May fairy tales as she tries to fall asleep, purposely skipping over the story of Snow White.

Shift: An oak tree in the middle of a quiet field of grass—

And there, the Charmed One stopped. "We have lost the glass man within your dreams," he told her. "But he will continue to hunt you down, not resting until you are imprisoned here forever. For he is the guardian of this land, and what he does, he does for the sake of every dreamer. If a person could appear in the dreams of others without their knowledge, that person would gain untold power over them."

"I'm not here to gain told *or* untold power," May said, breathing hard from the run through crazy. "I'm only here to find . . . a weapon. The Fairest."

"A weapon?" the Charmed One said. "That's an interesting way of viewing it."

"I really hate this whole vague thing, by the way," May said.

The Charmed One shrugged. "That means we must travel to his castle and most likely defeat him to find what you seek."

"So we just stab him until he breaks again?"

The Charmed One shook his head this time. "First, we cannot harm the guardian beyond repair, for that would leave these realms in danger. But fortunately for that, there is very, very little you can do to actually harm the glass man. His sand makes up this realm, and to kill him, you would have to destroy everything here."

"Destroying dreams?" May said. "You know, if that's all it takes—"

The Charmed One frowned. "It appears that you have other worries as well." And with that, a window appeared between them, showing a black dragon diving toward Phillip and Penelope.

"WHAT?!" May shouted. "No, he can't hurt her, I need her help! And *also* to get me out of here!"

"You worry about *her* instead of them?" the Charmed One asked.

She grimaced. "I've heard how this goes. Not to mention I've read the story. And seen the movie. What I haven't read is something about some glass man made of sand . . ." She trailed off, realizing what she just said, then shook her head. "Ugh, I have. The Sandman. I hate this place. Not everything is literal, people! Sometimes things are just metaphors!"

"Are they?" the Charmed One asked her, raising an eyebrow.

"Don't you even *dare* start," she said, pointing at him threateningly. "Where is the Sandman's castle? I don't have time for vague."

"There are no locations here," the Charmed One said, his voice fading out with the scene, as everything shifted to a castle made entirely of translucent bricks of glass, sand falling slowly within.

"Well," May said, "that certainly speeds things up." She glanced around and sighed. "Annnnnnnd he's gone. Yet I'm still talking." She closed her mouth deliberately, staring up at the castle, then realized she was holding a handful of sand. She pushed as much as she could into her pockets, then dusted her hands off. Where the sand fell, tiny little flashes of light exploded, then faded out. Odd.

Okay. She was here at the castle, yes. But she didn't have a weapon. She couldn't hurt the Sandman. And the Charmed One hadn't said one word about how she was supposed to use the sand he'd told her to bring. So really, nothing really new for her.

She did know one thing, though. There was no way that she was ever, *ever* going to call this place a sandcastle. Nope. Not gonna happen.

With that, she set out into the sandcastle (ugh, there it was already) in her dreams to find the fairest one of all.

CHAPTER 12

The sandcast— the *castle* of *sand* was empty. May probably could have seen that from the outside, given that it was made of glass. But all the swirling sand gave her a headache. Where was the Sandman, anyway? Out writing nightmares?

She made her way through the glass castle, searching for a dungeon or a cloudy room or something where the Fairest might be held. Where would one hide something in a glass castle? One wouldn't, probably, just like one hopefully wouldn't throw stones (she laughed to herself at that, then rolled her eyes), but that answer didn't get her anywhere, besides to maybe a more logical world to live in. But to be honest, *that* wasn't happening any time soon.

The castle looked bigger on the outside than the inside . . .

either that, or she was just a lot quicker than she thought, because she managed to walk through the entire thing within seconds. Seconds? Wait, it couldn't be *that* small.

But this *was* a dream, and dreams went by much faster, didn't they?

If only she could fast-forward to the point where she found the Fairest.

"She belongs to me," said a glassy voice behind her, and she whirled around to find the Sandman, with what looked like a newly sculpted glass plug keeping his sand inside his glass body.

"Why do you always appear right behind me, anyway?" May said, pushing her hands into her sand-full pockets.

"Sleep always catches one unawares," the Sandman said, tilting his head a bit.

"Oh, aren't we proud of that little line," May said. "You think you're so smart? Maybe you should . . . take a FALL!" And with that, she tossed a pile of sand into his face.

Had her comment made sense? She'd better clarify. "As in, FALL ASLEEP!" There.

The Sandman brushed the sand from his face and looked at her curiously. "I'm not entirely sure what you hoped to accomplish.

But I do not have time to play your games. Shall we take a look through your nightmares again?"

And the castle disappeared, only for May to smooth a long, blue gown over herself. "But I couldn't possibly!" she said to Merriweather, who stared down at May with a loving smile. "This gown is far too nice for someone like me!"

"You need to look pretty if you wish to impress the prince," Merriweather said. "And I'm here to help with that, to help you get away from this life!"

May felt the fabric between her fingers dreamily, then abruptly screamed, long and loud. "Are you KIDDING me?!" she shouted, throwing the dress at Merriweather. "THIS?! You're not making me live this, NO ONE is making me live this! I'm NOT Cinderella, I don't care about a stupid dress or some prince, and this is not who I *am*!"

"Isn't it?" the man of sand said, and May stood at the top of an elaborate set of marble steps leading down into the most beautiful ballroom she'd ever seen. She, like the dancers below her, wore a mask to hide her identity. These masquerade balls were such fun, and she'd wished for so long that she might attend one. To be here, to perhaps be near the prince . . . !

But would that ever happen? From her vantage point atop

the stairs, she could see her prince, swirling around in a dance with a girl in a large pink dress, one that looked like it'd taken a bit of magic to make itself. She looked down at her own blue dress and marveled at its magnificence once more. Only a fairy queen could create something so beautiful.

NO. SERIOUSLY, DRESSES?! She growled and kicked both glass slippers off her feet, which hit the dance floor below, shattering into a thousand pieces. "I DARE YOU TO MAKE ME TRY THOSE ON LATER!" she screamed as loudly as she could. "I *DARE* YOU!"

The crowd parted all the way to the prince, who broke off his dance with the girl in pink. His mask, a large double-diamond-shaped covering, hid his entire face behind it as well as most of his hair. He held out his hand to her and, in a familiar voice, said, "You should embrace who you are. Your dreams show you the real you."

May picked up one of the bigger shards of her slipper and threw it like a baseball at the prince. "I am who I SAY I am!" She picked up more of the rounder shards and threw each of them as she yelled. "I! AM! NOT! CINDERELLA!"

The prince caught each shard, then pushed them together in his hands. A moment later, he bent down on one knee, opening his hands to reveal a glass slipper. "If the shoe fits, May."

And that's when May recognized the voice.

It was Phillip's.

No. NO! The dream was in her head, and she didn't know who the prince was, so she was just giving him Phillip's voice. It couldn't be, he was from "Sleeping Beauty," and she was from "Cinderella." It didn't make sense; he couldn't be the prince, he was in the completely wrong story . . . wasn't he?

This was the worst nightmare yet!

She furiously dug her hands into her pockets, her dress morphing back into her regular jeans and T-shirt as she did, and pulled out a handful of sand. "I will make my *own* story, Sandman!" she yelled. "And no one else gets to write it for me!" Then she threw the sand in an arc in front of her, spraying it throughout the ballroom.

The dance disappeared, and May looked up from a movie camera, surveying the scene. "No, no," she said, gesturing for the boy wearing the name tag SANDMAN to move left. "You're too close. Back it up a little, I want to pull out a bit."

The boy moved to the left. "Here?" he asked.

May looked back into the video camera. "Yeah, that works." She looked back out. "You." She pointed at the girl wearing the name tag FAIREST. "Get away from him. Actually, come over here." She waved for Fairest to come back behind the camera. "Now, Sandman. I want to see you angry. You've just lost your prisoner to the amazing and wonderful heroine." May pointed at the girl with a blue streak in her blond hair, wearing a name tag that said HEROINE.

"And can we get her some more weapons? I wouldn't mind if she had, like, two swords, one for each hand."

A man with a white circle on his chest popped out and handed Heroine two swords. Heroine took one in each hand, then aimed them both at Sandman. "Everyone ready?" May asked, looking back behind the camera. "Heroine, this is the scene where you defeat Sandman. And . . . ACTION!"

"You cannot win that way," the glass man told her, and the actors disappeared as the Sandman advanced on her. "I will not allow you to use my world against me anymore."

May threw sand again, and bottle after bottle of caffeine-filled soda rained down on them, threatening to keep the Sand-man (and sleep) away forever, only to disappear immediately as the glass man waved a hand. "I will lock you in nightmares that you'll *never* wake from," he told her, taking another step closer.

More sand, and this time a thousand armed marines appeared between them and disappeared just as quickly. "I will hold you prisoner until your body withers away," the glass man said, his voice rising in anger. "Your mind will be trapped here until the end of time. I will—"

"Hold up," May said, noticing something for the first time. She hadn't been close enough to see before, or hadn't looked, but there it was. The man had sand everywhere in his body . . . everywhere except his eyes.

May's mouth dropped. "Oh, *gross.*"

"What—" the man of glass said, but May concentrated, throwing the last of her sand, and suddenly the scene shifted so that she was behind him. She concentrated, and Heroine's swords appeared in her hands.

Then she drove one of the sword's hilt into the back of the Sandman's head on the right side and heard a strange popping noise. She quickly dove forward, catching the Sandman's right glass eye, then rolled out of his way as he began to scream.

"The Fairest is in the eye of the beholder?!" May shouted at him, showing him his own eye. "Are you *kidding* me?" That phrase didn't sound exactly right, but she figured it was close enough. She held the eye up to hers, where she could clearly see . . . something inside. Maybe even something moving.

Again, *gross.*

"You will give that back or—"

"Nah," May said, a swirling feeling pulling her away from here. She smiled at the glass man. "Looks like my ride's here. I'm going to go wake up, but you have yourself some sweet dreams!"

And with that, the scene changed one last time.

Only, May didn't find herself back in Malevolent's castle.

Instead, she found herself back beneath an oak tree, in a field of grass with a warm wind blowing.

This time, there was no Charmed One.

There was, however, a Jack sitting beneath the tree.

CHAPTER 13

Penelope tipped forward, dragging Phillip to the ground as the flames burned through the air just above them. Stones from the demolished roof offered a bit of cover, but not enough.

"Staying down would probably be a good idea for a second," the princess told him, but Phillip shook his head, even as Malevolent flapped her wings, coming around to get a more direct angle at them.

This was it. He had known it was coming ever since the Wicked Queen had promised that one would betray May, and one would die. And since he would never betray May, die it was.

But that was not the only prophecy at play here.

"Malevolent!" Phillip shouted, standing in the midst of blackened stone, his sword aimed at the dragon. "It is time!"

The dragon shrieked in rage and dove directly at him. Penelope tried to yank Phillip back down, but he pulled himself from her grasp, his sword ready for the dragon. He would die, of course. But he would take this demon with him.

Malevolent's jaws opened wide, but Phillip swung out with his sword, cutting the dragon inside her mouth. The dragon screamed in pain and lost control, one of her wings slamming Phillip full in the chest, sending him flying across the castle's roof. Malevolent hit the castle hard as well, coming to a halt only a few yards from the prince, who was having trouble seeing straight.

Phillip tried to stand, but the roof swayed dizzily, and he ended up on one knee. The dragon, meanwhile, had no such trouble and was quickly back up on her feet, her snakelike neck weaving in a way that the prince had trouble following.

"You are *nothing*," Malevolent spat, then snapped at one of Phillip's shoulders too fast for him to follow. Pain filled his arm, and he almost dropped his sword but managed to swing it, far too late to do any good, as the dragon's head had snaked away.

"You think to fight *me*?! One of the thirteen?" Malevolent laughed, low and without any humor. Her head snapped out again, and pain filled his other shoulder. Both arms went numb, and the prince dropped to his knees, barely managing to keep ahold of the sword's hilt as the blade hit the roof hard.

"I think . . . exactly that," Phillip said, pushing himself to his feet, gritting his teeth and struggling to hold his sword up. A wing lashed out, sending him flying across the roof again, and this time he lost the sword completely. It fell away, but it was all Phillip could do to stay conscious.

"I need no magic to end you," Malevolent said, almost slithering across the roof after him. "To think I feared you all this time! You, some simple human, some powerless boy! The Mirror could not have been more wrong!"

"You may . . . kill me," Phillip said, breath coming a lot harder to him than it should have. "But the Mirror . . . did not lie. I will take you . . . *with* me." How exactly he would do that, he was not certain, though. Standing at this moment did not seem possible, let alone holding a sword. Wherever it was.

Talons as sharp as his missing sword dug into him, and suddenly he was flying high above the castle. He struggled against the dragon's claws, but he was far too weak, and the dragon was much too strong.

"Shall I drop you, little Prince?" Malevolent said, flying higher and higher. "Shall you plummet to your doom?" She let him go, and plummet he did, the wind whipping by so fast he could not breathe.

He glanced down and saw Penelope staring at him, something in her hand. Was it his sword? No . . . it was smaller, and the wrong color. She was screaming something, but the wind was too loud—he could not hear. Not that it would matter in a moment when he hit the castle.

But the moment passed, and again he felt the dragon's claws digging into his sides. His fall slowed but did not stop as the dragon tossed him to the roof, which he hit hard, knocking what wind remained right out of his lungs. He rolled as he hit, struggling not to black out as the edge grew closer and closer, only to stop just inches from his face.

"Shall I rip you to shreds with my teeth?" the dragon said, and he felt hot breath on the back of his neck. Something impossibly sharp touched his skin, and he tried to roll to the side, away from her jaws, but he was far too slow. Malevolent toyed with him, snapping just inches from his face, then his heart, then his face again.

"These deaths seem much too quick, little Prince," she said, her eyes blacker than her shining skin. "No, I believe you and your princess should burn instead, knowing that this finally makes us even for what your fathers did."

Phillip watched the dragon rise into the air, higher and higher, knowing he wouldn't be able to move, and if he did, he would probably just end up falling off the side of the castle. Malevolent circled higher and higher, getting enough elevation to follow him and Penelope wherever they might hide, wherever they might run.

"What are you *doing?*!" the princess said, skidding to a stop at his side. "Why aren't you letting me handle this?!"

". . . I am sorry?" Phillip said, sincerely confused. What was she talking about? "Please, help me up. I will perish doing so, but I am destined to destroy her, so I must fight."

Penelope just stared at him for a second, touching his face, with a tiny smile.

Then she slapped him.

"Not everything's about you," she told him, standing up. She pulled out the object Phillip had mistaken for his sword while falling a few moments ago and smiled at him again. "She's mine, Your Highness. She's *always* been mine. After what she's done to me? Are you kidding?"

Above them both, Malevolent circled once more, rising as far as she meant to go, then turned and began her dive, flames spilling out of her mouth like water.

"You curse me?" Penelope shouted at the descending dragon, holding a wooden spindle to her hand. "Because you feel left out, you hurt people I love? You take my family away? You take my *life*?!"

She stabbed the spindle right into her palm. "Let me return the favor," Penelope whispered, then collapsed to the roof, instantly asleep.

She'd voluntarily cursed herself again! Phillip was immune, given that the fairy queens who had protected the girl from the original curse had needed him to wake her up. So he stayed wide awake.

Malevolent and everyone else within the curse's range were not so lucky.

The dragon shook, looking confused for a moment before the spell took over completely, sending the now-sleeping Malevolent into a dive. Phillip pushed himself to his feet, then picked Penelope up in his arms and dove out of the way of the plummeting dragon.

Malevolent hit the roof like a cannonball, taking Phillip, Penelope, and half the castle's roof with her. The prince hit the floor below hard, cradling Penelope in his arms as the dragon continued on, crashing through floor after floor, rubble collapsing in after her as she went, finally coming to a stop at the very bottom of the castle, from the sound of it.

Phillip held Penelope close until the rumbling stopped, then looked up to find his sword embedded in some rubble just inches from his head.

Apparently he wasn't meant to die just yet.

Though had it ever been *close*.

CHAPTER 14

May took a seat next to Jack as he absently pulled petal after petal out of a flower. A gentle, warm breeze flowed over both of them. May pulled her knees up, wrapped her arms around them, and just looked at the grass, at the field, at the tree, and at Jack.

Neither of them spoke for the longest time.

"I hate that you're here," Jack said finally, still pulling petals off one by one. "I thought I stopped this."

"By leaving?" May said, laying her head on her knees.

"I thought I had some sort of control here," he said, shaking his head. "It took months, but I thought I finally had stopped dreaming about you."

"You've . . . dreamt about me?"

"You'd know, wouldn't you?" he said, not looking at her.

May just looked at him. "Why did you leave?"

He finally looked at her and shook his head. "You're a dream. That means you're me, and already know why I had to go."

May bit her lip, then just went for it. "Yup, I'm a dream. So you can tell me anything, and it's basically just telling yourself. So why did you leave?"

"How could I stay?!" Jack shouted. "Where is the Charmed One, anyway? I don't have time for this; I'm supposed to be stealing from a giant. Turning into my father. Becoming everything I hate." He stared at May. "You're definitely a dream. The real May would be insulting me a lot more."

"Sometimes she does that," May said softly. "But sometimes she . . . just doesn't know what to say."

"Yeah, well, I'm sure you'll have plenty to say to your prince," Jack said, turning his back to her. "Could you please leave? Like I said, I've got a busy day."

"Prince? You mean Phillip, or . . ." She stopped. He didn't mean Phillip. He meant Cinderella's prince.

Unless her nightmares weren't true, and those two princes were one and the same.

"Don't say Phillip's name—he might appear too," Jack said.

"Charmed One? Seriously, I could use some vague advice or something! Anything but more of this!"

May stood up too, then reached out and took Jack's hand to turn him toward her. He pulled away and glared at her. "Just . . . go," he said.

"Why did you leave?"

Jack laughed. "Are you serious? You've never stayed this long before. I went because I made a mistake, May. I made a lot of mistakes. And I couldn't just stay, not like things were."

"Mistakes?"

"Your grandmother?" Jack said, gritting his teeth. "The woman you wouldn't talk about for the past six months? The woman who *I* told you was Snow White? The woman who *I* let out? The woman who's currently about to start a second Great War? Her. For one. And she's just one of *many* mistakes."

May flinched, looking down at the ground. "That wasn't . . . your fault. You don't need to run away."

His eyes widened, and he pointed out toward the field of grass. "GO."

May groaned in frustration. "You can't join her, Jack. You can't! I don't know what you think you're doing—"

"I'm doing what needs to be done!" he shouted. "I'm not

Phillip, I'm not you. I wasn't born into a royal family, May. I was born with a mind, and that's about it, and that's what I'm going to use now. Whatever I need to do, I'll do!"

"You need my help," May said, her voice softening again. "You have to know that, Jack. Whatever's going on, you can't do it alone. You need your friends. You *have* to know that!"

"You've got the wrong guy," Jack said, bitterness swimming behind his eyes. "I thought the same way once, but I was wrong. I know what I'm meant to do now. One of them will betray you, and one will die, right? I know what I have to do."

May's entire body went cold. "What do you mean, you know what you have to do? What are you planning?" She grabbed his arm, but he tore it away.

"LEAVE," he said, his eyes closed tight, and May could feel a tug on herself, like a river current pulling her away.

"NO!" she screamed. "You can't do this, whatever you're planning! She's not worth it! NONE of this is worth it!"

"LEAVE," he said again, and this time the current almost swept her away.

"Jack, I'm not a *dream*!" she screamed. "The Charmed One can tell you! I'm here in the dream world! I'm stuck here, but I'll find a way *out*. Don't do anything . . . don't do anything crazy!" She was practically begging him now. "PLEASE. *Wait* for me. I'll come find you, I promise. Just don't do anything! WAIT FOR ME!"

Jack started to say something, then stopped, just staring at her. Finally, he sighed. "I'm sorry," he whispered, and it was like a whirlpool appeared directly beneath May. The force of it yanked her off her feet and into nothingness, but as she was pulled back into the waking world, expelled from the dream world by Jack, she could hear the Charmed One's voice.

"Another dream about the girl?"

"The last one I'll have, I promise."

The Charmed One's head appeared, staring down the whirlpool at May. "Yes, I would imagine so," the knight said. "But don't worry. Just a dream."

"She almost seemed . . . real."

"Dreams always do."

And with that, May slammed into the floor of Malevolent's castle, almost crushing the glass eyeball clutched tightly in her hand. She gritted her teeth at the pain, then looked to her right to find a dragon tail sticking out of a heap of rubble, and Penelope helping Phillip climb down the stones.

"You *are* here!" the prince shouted. He and Penelope rushed to her side. "But how? Did you return when we killed Malevolent?"

May stared at him, wondering how much to say. "Not exactly." She reached out a hand, and Phillip gently helped her to her feet. The prince noticed the glass ball in her hand, and she shook her head. "Long story."

"You'll have plenty of time to tell him in the Queen's dungeons," growled someone from the throne room door.

All three looked up to find an enormous man wearing a bulky black fur cloak, with more goblins than May could count lined up behind him.

"Any more cursed wood pieces?" Phillip said to Penelope.

"Not enough," she said.

A man no bigger than May's hand appeared out of nowhere on Penelope's shoulder, then dropped off, striding away with several splinters of a spindle. "They're safe to take, Wolf," the little man said, and after getting over the oddness of him, she noticed the white eye on his chest.

Another one. Apparently, they came in all sizes.

As the Eye and the goblins led the other two away, May pushed the Fairest glass ball down deep into her pocket, then held out her arms for a goblin to chain together and lead her away with the others, prisoners of the Wicked Queen.

CHAPTER 15

Is she gone?" Jack asked, his back to the Charmed One.

"She is," the knight said. "I did not realize you were still having this problem."

"I didn't think I was." Jack turned around, letting out a breath he hadn't realized he'd been holding when he found the Charmed One alone. "I'm sorry about that. I'd thought I'd figured out how not to dream about her anymore."

"There are always setbacks in such things," the knight told him. "I often dream of Snow, though I welcome the sight of her."

"Yeah, we're different people," Jack told him. "But that's not why I'm here. I finished my training, and the Queen has one last test for me. I'm supposed to steal something from the same giant that my father robbed."

The knight raised an eyebrow but didn't say anything.

Jack waited, then shook his head. "Forget it, there's no time to go into all that. But I'm afraid this is going to push things back."

"You didn't mention anything about what you plan to Jill—"

"Nope. Not her or my father. I couldn't be sure who was listening."

"You *can* be sure who was."

"Anyway, Gwentell is back," Jack said. "I haven't asked her about the raven yet, but unless I'm wrong about everything, the plan goes forward. Though I'd still argue that it's a bird, and there have to be more reliable sources of information than something that runs into windows by accident."

"If only," the Charmed One said, turning to look away from Jack. "But you're not wrong. I have seen the object you're looking for. I was shown it by someone with much the same goals as you have. If Gwentell confirms everything, you should move forward as quickly as possible."

"I will," Jack told him. "By the way, that suggestion to use Gwentell was smart. Thank you."

"The sword of an Eye grants you knowledge beyond that of

the natural world," the knight said. "Communicating with magical creatures is something few Eyes realize they can do and even fewer know how to take advantage of."

"I would have been okay taking less advantage of that, actually. She's not so thrilled with me usually."

"You don't know her as well as you might think you do," the Charmed One said. "She has watched over for you since the beginning and so far has managed to keep you alive."

"Keep *me* alive?!" Jack said, giving the knight his most incredulous look. It wasn't enough, but he tried. "By insulting me every time she opens her mouth? Was I dying of not being called stupid enough times a day?"

"Humility can be a virtue," the knight said, the corners of his mouth rising just a little. Jack noticed—and noted—it. He'd get the Charmed One back for that, even if the man didn't necessarily exist anymore. "But yes. Under my request, she has watched over you and served you where she could."

"Big help she was in the Fairy Homelands," Jack said. "She slept through the whole thing!"

"And gave you warning of the curse, if you remember."

Jack coughed, covering his blush. She *had* given him about two seconds of warning before Jack had hit the curse himself.

Whoops. "Yeah, well, good for her. Anyway, back to this giant thing." He sighed.

"The Queen does this to you on purpose," the knight said. "She knows how you feel about your father and his actions. She wishes to see how far you'll go for what you want, if you'll become the man you have always hated."

"She could have just asked."

"This way, she gets something out of it." The Charmed One paused. "She must be preparing for something. What was it that she needs?"

"Some singing harp . . . I know."

The Charmed One gasped, which didn't help Jack's feelings on anything. "The harp?! We have even less time than I thought. She will put her plans into motion the moment she has that, Jack. There's no more time. You must be ready the moment you return."

"Good, it wouldn't be right if there weren't some world-ending pressure." Jack shrugged. "Aren't I just making things worse, though, if I give her this thing?"

"She won't go through with your request to leave this world if you don't," the knight told him. "You have no choice. But be wary. She will use the harp for horrible purposes."

Jack sighed again. "I really hope I'm not wrong about all this."

"The Story Book is your proof," the knight reminded him.

"Right," Jack said. "A magic book that may or may not be reliable anyway. How could it go wrong?"

The Charmed One chuckled. "You have to have faith at some point, Jack." He started to reach out a hand, then dropped it quickly. "Now, before you leave, what is your plan for the giant?"

"Don't worry about that," Jack said. "I got advice from an expert." And with that, he pushed himself out of the dream just as he had pushed out the fake dream-May. He really didn't want her showing up out of nowhere again . . . it was humiliating for her to just appear when the Charmed One was walking him through a training exercise.

His eyes opened to two beady little golden eyes staring at him.

"Finally," Gwentell said. "Could you be any lazier, stupid man-child?"

Jack blew out as hard as she could, sending the fairy flying off his face. Then he spit and spit again. "Were you stepping in my *mouth*?!"

"You should see what I stepped in *before* that," the fairy said, sticking out her tongue.

"You are *evil!*"

"You are *stupid!*"

Jack frantically scraped at his tongue, trying desperately to get the taste of something horrible out of his mouth. "Did you find the bird?" he asked, or tried to, around his fingers.

"Didn't I say I would?" the fairy asked. "Yes, I found it. How could I not, when you gave such explicit instructions? 'Find me a black bird. How many can there be?'"

"I was a bit more detailed than that," Jack said a bit defensively.

"You failed to mention that it's the same bird that has been following us since we first met," the fairy said, shaking her head.

"Wait, what?"

"How did you not see it?!" the fairy said, stamping her foot angrily. "I kept pointing it out when I first decided to protect you!"

"When you first decided—I couldn't understand you then!"

"Your stupidity is always your excuse, isn't it, man-child?"

"You *knew* the Wicked Queen was watching us, even back then, and you didn't say anything?!"

"I believe I just told you that I said *many* things—"

"Forget it!" Jack shouted. "So, what did the bird have to say?"

The fairy gave him a look. "Birds do not speak, man-child. I feel as if you should have known that."

"What did it caw, then?"

The fairy paused, then handed him a tiny folded-up piece of paper. "It confirmed your . . . idea. Congratulations. Now what does that mean?"

Jack took the paper and gave her a sweet smile. "Sorry, can't tell you. You're far too talkative, and we can't risk anyone hearing. Did you make sure the bird's tied up or something? Can't have it getting back to the Queen."

The fairy nodded, giving him a dark look, then said something low and hostile that Jack couldn't hear.

"Right back at you," he told her. "Now, I have to go become everything I hate by stealing something from a giant, potentially dooming the world and everyone I know. Do you want to come or not?"

"The possibility of a giant squishing you?" the fairy said. "I would not miss it!"

A knock at the door forced Jack to throw open the window and toss her out, causing some horrible shrieking and shouting of words that Jack would rather not have understood. He opened the door, only to find no one there.

At least, no one at eye level.

"Final test, eh?" Captain Thomas said, striding into the

room. "And a fine adventure it is. You won't make it back, but that can happen."

"Well," Jack said, "I really have enjoyed our time together, even if it's getting cut short."

And then he quickly excused himself, the tiny man's glare burning into him, probably somewhere around his ankles.

CHAPTER 16

This is why I told you to leave me alone, Phillip," May
whispered through clenched teeth.

The prince and Penelope sat next to her, all chained together
and seated around a fire on the beach beneath Malevolent's
castle, armed goblins in a circle around them. The wolf, meanwhile, hadn't come near them yet. Apparently he was off check-
ing on their ride home, back to the Wicked Queen.

"You were in danger, Princess," Phillip said. "I had to rescue you."

She wanted to yell at him, tell him he'd made things worse,
but he just looked so concerned, she couldn't. She couldn't do
that to him. It'd be like taking away his entire reason for being.

Phillip turned to Penelope and offered her some of the

dirt-covered bread the goblins had tossed their way. Penelope looked at the bread, then at him. "Okay, Phillip, we need to talk."

Phillip looked at her blankly, still holding the bread between them. She looked at him, then at the bread, then took it out of his hand and put it back on the ground. May tried to stop her, then gave up; it's not like the bread could get any dirtier.

"I get that this is what you do," Penelope said, gesturing around at herself and May, absently dragging Phillip's chained hand along with her. "You rescue princesses. I get that. And on some level, it's sweet. But on a lot of other levels, it's ridiculous."

"Sorry?" Phillip said.

"Don't apologize yet, I'm not done," Penelope said. "May, feel free to jump in here."

"I'm . . . okay with you handling this for now," May told her, having no idea where she was going.

"Up on the roof," Penelope told Phillip, gesturing up to the top of the castle above them, "you tried to protect me. But you were the one who needed protecting. I had a plan, Phillip. I had magic. You . . . you've got a sword."

Phillip sat up straight, his eyes flashing angrily. "I have killed more giants than—"

"Shh," Penelope said, and touched his mouth with her finger. "I don't care. What I care about is that you almost got yourself killed because I thought you had to. Because the Wicked Queen *told* you that you were going to die. Does she seem like someone any of us should be listening to?"

"But the Mirror—" Phillip said.

"I'm not sure what mirrors have to do with this," Penelope told him, "but last I remember, they're for seeing if you have anything in your teeth after eating. Try to stay on topic here, Phillip. I don't want to have to worry about you next time."

"Worry about *me?!*" Phillip said, and one of the goblins chuckled.

"See?" Penelope said, pointing at the goblin. "He's with me."

"He is a monster!"

"HEY!" the goblin shouted. "*You're* the ugly one, human!"

Penelope bobbed her head from side to side. "Okay, that's an interesting point about culture, but that's not really our focus right now. You need to understand that we can handle ourselves, both of us. Yes, May needed help—"

"Yeah, you were a huge help, getting me caught by the wolf!" May yelled.

"But that doesn't mean that you need to go running in,

swording everything in sight, only to get smacked around by a dragon."

"Or getting us caught by the wolf!" May added again.

Phillip just gave her a look of confused horror.

Penelope patted his leg. "I get it. You mean well. And you did save me, back in the Fairy Homelands. But let's be honest . . . you were born for that. I'm your true love, and that's all that was important for that spell. So yes, you heroed just fine there. But that's not who you're meant to be."

"And who . . . exactly . . . am I meant to be?" Phillip said carefully.

"I hope it's someone who uses contractions," May said quietly.

"You're meant to be king someday!" Penelope said, getting the closest to annoyed that May had ever seen her. "You have a responsibility to your people, Phillip. Take care of *them*. Be a great leader, a noble one . . . that's what they need. They don't need you getting eaten by any old dragon that happens along just because some window says so!"

"Mirror," May pointed out.

"It's all glass," Penelope said with a shrug.

Phillip opened his mouth to say something, then shook his head and went silent.

Penelope patted his shoulder, then turned to May. "So what were you doing there, anyway, May?"

"Turns out, a whole lot of nothing," May told her. "I . . . well, I asked Malevolent for help in defeating the Queen."

"You WHAT?!" Philip shouted, and the goblins all began to laugh.

"And then you had to go and dragon-slay her before I got the rest of her plan!" May shouted back.

"You asked Malevolent for HELP?!" Phillip said.

"She just said that," Penelope told him. "Weren't you listening?"

Phillip turned to Penelope. "YOU hated her more than I did! Why are you not upset by that?"

Penelope shrugged. "I did what I needed to. She got what she deserved, but that's over now. Why hold on to it? Besides, if she was helping May, maybe she was trying to make up for some of her past."

"She wasn't," May told her. "It took a lot of bargaining. Most of which involved having you two never come anywhere near her."

"Oh," Penelope said. "Whoops."

Phillip looked between them, his mouth hanging open, as the

Wolf King approached. "While I'm all for this pleasant reunion," he told them, "the Queen is opening a portal for us now."

And then the entire beach lit up in blue crackling lightning, and a tall, beautiful woman stepped out into the darkness. "Children," the Wicked Queen said with a smile. "So lovely to see you again."

CHAPTER 17

I t'd been twelve years since Jack's father had planted the Wicked Queen's beans on this land. At some point, the beanstalk had collapsed, the magic apparently just getting used up, but in that time, a lot of the remaining beanstalk had been reabsorbed by the forest or cut for fires by the local villagers. Well, at least the villagers who hadn't had their houses cave in from the toppling plant: Here or there, you could see the outline of where the beanstalk had hit, in that there was a specific lack of houses there now.

Then there was the enormous chasm shaped like two giant feet about a hundred feet past the base of where the beanstalk had been. There were even *fewer* houses there. A lake had sprung up in a few places from the footsteps where the giant chased

Jack's father into the distance, but the initial hit, where the giant had landed . . . that was far too deep. Nothing would grow there.

And here was Jack, growing another beanstalk. Add that to the list of things he'd owe people for later. If there was a later.

The ground rumbled a bit as the first sprout broke through the dirt and began to rise toward the sky. Though the day was cloudy (made sense, given there was an entire castle in the clouds above him), at least it wasn't as dark as the last time he'd done this. That night hadn't been Jack's favorite memory, the beanstalk rising toward Malevolent's castle, with Phillip and . . .

And, well, whoever else might have been there. Stop it. Stop thinking about things that aren't supposed to be *thought* about!

To distract himself, he pulled out his sword and the potion Jill had gotten for him, then poured it over the glass-like blade. The sword glowed oddly as the potion soaked in to the weapon, absorbing right into the blade. Huh, it worked. Hopefully.

The potion now empty, he put the bottle back in his pocket, replaced his sword on his back, then pulled out his grandfather's Story Book. He quickly flipped through it, reading the specific pages that held everything he needed to know. No one knew all of his plan, other than the Charmed One, who didn't approve but agreed that there was no other choice. He'd come up with it while traveling to the Wicked Queen's castle with Jill, trying to ignore his sister during the long trip by reading through the Story Book just like he was now. And a few pages seemed to keep jumping out at him.

And that's when he saw *it* and realized what it might be. Now that Gwentell had confirmed things from the Queen's raven—he smacked the fairy awake so she'd be ready, and she smacked him right back—he knew that this was the right plan. There was no turning back. The moment he arrived with the harp, that was it.

The first sprout now crept higher than the trees, and just like last time, Jack figured it was easier to rise with the magic than to climb. Did his father climb it? The man had planted the beans at night and woken the next morning to find it there, so Jack supposed he had. That couldn't have been fun, especially considering that the whole way he must have been thinking about his wife, Jack's mother.

Before the Wicked Queen killed her.

Stop it.

Jack stepped into a loop on the beanstalk, grabbed another shoot, and wrapped it around his wrist to make sure he didn't get knocked off if the stalk hit anything hard, like clouds. What were clouds made of, anyway? Would he hit one and bounce off? They looked pretty bouncy. Maybe that was something he should have talked to his father about. That, and why the man never came back for Jack yet let his daughter serve the woman who killed their mother and kept their father in prison, using her as what, bait? A secret weapon? Or was it more just that he couldn't stop Jill when she had the chance to strike back?

That thought led Jack to think about Phillip, safe somewhere on his throne, probably having servants feed him grapes carefully sliced into perfect likenesses of the prince's face. Would he be thinking about his part of the Queen's prophecy? Or what about Malevolent, who said that the prince would eventually cause her death?

Yeah, right. *If* that happened, it wouldn't be for, like, decades.

Jack was high enough now to see over the trees, and he swallowed hard. He was already higher than he'd been last time he'd been on the beanstalk and was quickly approaching the height he'd once reached on a witch's broomstick. Had that really only been half a year ago? So much had changed.

Like never seeing May again.

Stop it stop it stop it.

The beanstalk jumped suddenly, and Jack's feet lost their hold, the shoots around his wrist the only thing keeping him from falling right off. His stomach dropped past his toes, and he frantically grabbed for something, but the shoot he managed to reach just ripped off in his hand. Meanwhile, the shoots holding his other wrist sounded like they were ripping out by the roots.

And then, for no reason he could think of, his heart quieted down, and he stopped breathing in quite so quickly. Instead, he closed his eyes, then reopened them. He gently swung himself away from the main beanstalk, hanging out over a whole lot of nothing, then let his momentum carry him back toward the stalk, just close enough for him to reach it with his legs, just close enough for him to kick off . . . assuming the shoot would hold.

What other choice did he have?

Jack kicked off, and out he swung, out over the path the last beanstalk had fallen, the destruction it left behind clearly visible from this height. He began to turn back around, to swing back toward the main stalk, only to have the shoots holding his wrist groan, then rip. Off Jack fell—

Only to slam against the main stalk, just a few feet lower. His swing had barely worked, but barely was still good enough.

And yet he still wasn't breathing hard, and his heart still wasn't racing. On his back, he could almost feel his sword glowing, but he hadn't slowed time down or done any of the other tricks he'd been taught by Captain Thomas.

Well, unless you called staying calm a trick. Which, in a lot of ways, it was.

Jack worked both his hands and feet into shoots this time, securing himself much more safely as the tip of the beanstalk continued to push up against the lowest cloud. Apparently it had hit and caused the rumbling that still threatened to knock Jack off the stalk at any moment. And even more apparently, the clouds turned out to be floating rocks, or something just as hard, as the beanstalk was having as much trouble with this cloud as it had the base of Malevolent's castle.

Jack shook his head, not sure why he hadn't figured that out before. If a giant could live in a castle in the clouds, how could the clouds NOT be floating rocks? What else would hold a castle up? It was just logic, really, something he honestly should try relying on more often.

And then, something odd happened. A crack appeared in the rocks, right about where the beanstalk was pushing up through. The crack grew bigger, then suddenly exploded open, and a hand as big as a house reached down through the white rock to grab the beanstalk like a weed.

The hand yanked abruptly, and suddenly the entire beanstalk was rising up and through the hole, dangling before a man the size of a mountain.

"Well well," the giant said, his breath blasting against Jack like a unpleasantly stinky wind. "Look what we have here. Another little thief, trying the same trick as the first one. Never repeat, little thief. It will always get you caught." He pulled Jack off the beanstalk and raised him to eye level.

"Oh, right," Jack said. "Good advice. I guess."

"Well, down you go," the giant said, tossing the beanstalk away like a weed, then dangling Jack over the very empty hole, a lot of very empty air, and some very hard ground. But before he let go, the giant paused, then sniffed in, the vacuum of his nose pulling Jack closer with each inhale. The giant's eyes widened, and he stared at Jack.

"Your blood," he said. "It smells just like that last thief, the one that I never caught!"

Giants could smell blood? That might have been good to know.

CHAPTER 18

Weirdly, Penelope was the first to act. The princess stood up, her eyes back to their usual half-mast, and curtsied to the Wicked Queen.

Then, as she stood back up, she threw something small and sharp right at the Queen.

The whatever-it-was stopped right in midair, just inches in front of the Queen's forehead.

"You must be Penelope," the Queen said, and the object snapped in half. "I appreciate the effort, my dear, but we can't have you trying such things again." She glanced over Penelope's shoulder, and three goblins moved to grab the princess and drag her off, Penelope silent the entire time.

"If you hurt her—" Phillip started to say, but the Queen just held up a hand.

"Oh, Phillip, we really don't have time right now for your inane little threats. Do be a nice boy and keep that mouth shut, please."

And just like that, Phillip's mouth slammed shut. He clawed at his lips with his fingers but couldn't open it even a tiny bit.

"And you, my darling little month of May," the Queen said, turning to May finally, looking her over. "You've grown, haven't you?"

"People do that," May said, her hand on the glass ball in her pocket. And then the image of Penelope's splinter stopping in midair flew through her head, and she let go of it, then took her hand out of her pocket, deliberately keeping any thought of the Fairest out of her mind. She couldn't do anything, not now. Not yet.

The Queen smiled. "Oh, my darling, there was *never* anything you could have done.

"This isn't you," May said, not trusting herself to say much else. Too many other things kept bubbling up. Most of them would get her killed.

"It isn't?" The Queen pretended to be confused.

"It's not. This *isn't* . . . you aren't the woman . . . who raised me." She took a deep breath, desperately trying to keep herself calm.

Beside her, Phillip groaned, falling to his knees, pushed by an invisible force. Almost robotically, he bent over and kissed the Queen's foot, then stayed bowing low to her.

"You really should follow your friend's example here and address me with more respect, May," the Queen said softly. She looked past May, and more goblins came for Phillip. The prince caught May's eye, and he shook his head violently.

The message was clear and was the same one that she couldn't stop repeating in her head.

Unfortunately, May's heartbeat was so loud in her ears she almost couldn't hear anything else.

Who was this monster who would do that to another human being?!

"You seem . . . upset," the Queen said, stepping closer to touch May's cheek. May jerked her head away, and the Queen's eyes narrowed. "You would do well to not disobey me right now, May. We aren't talking about some simple grounding for a bad grade or you dyeing your hair. Not anymore. My punishments now are far, far worse."

"Don't . . . *please* don't hurt them," May said through clenched teeth. Her entire head seemed to be beating in time with her heart. "I'll come with you, I'll do what you want, but *please* don't hurt either of them."

The Queen paused, then moved in close, just inches from May's face. "One will betray you, May, and the other will die for you. You know that's going to happen, and I don't think I'm spoiling anything by saying that time will be here very, very soon. So I can't very well agree to anything of the sort, now can I?"

May didn't see the look this time, but goblins grabbed her arms and legs and carried her away as the Queen turned and walked calmly back toward the portal. May watched her go, her hands clenched into fists, until a goblin pulled some sort of hood over her head, and everything went dark.

Hours passed, or maybe just very long minutes. It was hard to tell what was going on while being carried. They didn't even bother tying her hands and feet together, just carried her by her limbs so that she had no leverage at all to escape. Not that she didn't try, but it wasn't anything like when the dwarfs had taken her. Now, she knew that if she did get away, she might be leaving Penelope and Phillip behind. And who knew what would happen to both of them without her there.

This was why they were supposed to stay *away* from her! She couldn't do this if other people might get hurt too!

The sizzle of the portal came and went, and May heard goblin feet slapping on stone. They carried her up and down stairs, everything silent besides the occasional muttering here or there by the goblins, mostly complaining about having to carry her so far.

Finally, they tossed her into the air, and she shouted in surprise, only to land on something fairly soft. One of the goblins yanked the hood off, and she quickly looked down, hoping it wasn't anything horrible, only to find an enormous bed sculpted from gold.

"Sleep tight, Princess," the goblin said with a creepy smile, then pushed the other monsters out the door and slammed it shut behind him. She heard one lock, then another, and a third. They weren't taking any chances.

Not only was she alone in the room, but so was the bed, apart from one lone chair. Bars covered a large window that looked out into darkness, and May couldn't be sure if it was still night, or if there just wasn't anything to see. For all she knew, she was in some other dimension without a sun. Or maybe it had an evil sun, one that sucked the light out of the world. And maybe the full moon turned wolves into people, instead of the other way around.

That's it, distract yourself. Don't think about what's waiting for you outside the door and what's coming . . . soon, if the Queen could be believed. And why would she lie?

Someone knocked on her door. All three locks turned, and May quickly went to hide behind the door, ready to surprise whoever entered.

She ended up almost punching Penelope, who stumbled into the room like she'd been pushed. The princess looked around, holding something folded and clothing-looking in her arms.

"Hello?" Penelope said as the door slammed shut behind her, the locks turning again.

May tapped her on the shoulder, and Penelope whirled around and punched her.

"OW!" May shouted. "It's me!"

"Oh, I'm so sorry!" Penelope said. "You, well, you surprised me!"

"I SEE THAT!" Her cheek throbbed where the girl had hit her, and her jaw felt sore. Not exactly what she needed right now. "Is that all you came in to do, hit me?"

Penelope shook her head. "I actually didn't intend to do that at all."

"Shocking."

"If you say so." She held out the fabric in her hands, which May could now see were two dresses that looked like they cost more than her friends' families back home made in a year. "They told me that we had to get dressed up to officially appear before the Queen."

May took one of the dresses, a shimmering blue that she knew was meant for her. It looked like every drawing of Cinderella's dress she'd ever seen. "What does that mean, appear before her?"

"Well," Penelope said, "from what the guard said, it sounds as if she intends us to declare our loyalty to her in front of her subjects, and if we don't, we'll be sentenced to death." As all the color drained out of May's face, Penelope leaned in conspiratorially. "You know, if this all comes down to the fact that I tried to stab her with a cursed spindle splinter, I am going to be pretty annoyed!"

CHAPTER 19

Jack hung upside down over a boiling pot, swaying in the breeze. Most castles didn't have much of a breeze going inside, but this one was probably big enough to have its own clouds. Which probably had their own castles.

Beside him, the giant hummed softly to himself as he sliced carrots, each one bigger than Jack's house, then tossed the slices into the pot.

"I've been meaning to try this recipe," the giant told him. "You wouldn't believe where I found it. You don't see many human stew recipes. Well, not anymore." He chuckled, and the force of it sent Jack swaying even harder.

"You don't need to eat me," Jack told him, just in case that was unclear.

"Now why would I waste such a bold opportunity by not doing just that?" the giant asked him, pausing in his slicing. "Have you ever eaten human?"

"Can't say that I have."

The giant shook his head, making *mmm*ing noises. "You might be small, but you're like a fine spice. Add just a bit to a stew like this, and the whole thing is just . . . like an explosion in your mouth."

Jack nodded upside down. "Okay, that's fair. We all go for different things. I like sweet stuff. You like explosions. But you know what would taste *better*—"

"Nope," the giant said. "None of that, now. I'm not some backward land giant, lad. Poor fellows down there. Too much air, I think. Goes straight to their heads." He tapped his forehead. "Up here, things are a bit thinner, and that's the way I like it. Last time I went down there . . . well, I don't remember all of it, but you wouldn't believe the headache I had the next day."

"You go down to the land a lot, then?"

"Last time was your . . . father?" the giant said, raising an eyebrow. "Brother? It's so hard to tell with you things, you all look alike to me. If you weren't so flavorful, and maybe didn't steal so many of my things, I'd just let you scurry on your merry way, smushing you underfoot as needed to keep you from infesting the place."

"We're not exactly ants."

"All depends on your height, I suppose." He looked up for a moment. "I feel as if I've seen pictures of ants, haven't I?" He shuddered. "So many legs. How you can ride those things I'll never know."

"I wouldn't look down, then, because there are like four of them right below you."

The giant jumped, and the entire building shook. He quickly realized that the floor was antless, then shook his finger at Jack, chuckling a bit. "Got me with that one! If you keep it up, you'll go in the pot straightaway, and I'll just deal with the slight chewiness you people get when you've been cooked too long."

Jack swung back and forth in silence a bit, then decided that he'd probably never have a better time to ask. "It was my father, by the way," he said. "I heard he stole a goose from you."

"That he did," the giant said, and his chopping became a bit louder, each knife stroke biting into the table just a bit deeper. "Never found that goose, either."

"Or my father, I take it."

"No, though as I said, it's a bit foggy." The giant dumped the remaining carrots into the stew, then began to slice up something enormous and green that confused Jack until he realized it was a tree. "I know I chased him and almost had him, but some other little man got in the way. Had this whole trap worked out, this other human did. Almost got me."

"This other man . . . what happened to him?"

"*Him* I got," the giant said, and smiled at Jack.

Phillip's father. Not the news Jack had been hoping for, but not exactly a surprise, either.

"You know, if you let me go, I could take you to the thief," Jack told the giant, picturing the monster attacking the Wicked Queen's castle, taking out half her army.

"Oh, I know where he is," the giant said, dropping sliced tree trunk into the stew, then stirring it around. "Or at least where he's *going* to be."

"You . . . what?"

"Won't be any of your concern, though, will it?" The giant patted his stomach. "Not unless you stick around for long enough to give me indigestion!"

"How do you know where he is? I thought you couldn't find him."

The giant smiled. "Now, that seems like the sort of question I don't have to answer, given that I'm the one cooking you and not the other way around. Can I get you anything to eat while you wait? This recipe calls for one of those tiny chickens to be baked, then swallowed by you. Adds flavor."

Jack shook his head. "Thanks, but I can't say that I'm very hungry."

The giant raised an eyebrow. "Didn't want to use that as an opportunity to escape?"

"Would it have worked?"

"Of course not. But I like that you've resigned yourself. No need to get all gamey from running around willy-nilly."

"I do what I can."

Something tugged at his hands, then stopped. He pointed up at his feet and soon felt something tug there, too. He quickly grabbed ahold of the rope with both hands and crossed his legs around the rope above where he was tied.

"I just feel like an inconsiderate host, you not eating and all," the giant said. "But I won't force it down your throat." He held up his enormous hands. "You're far too small for that. I'm sure I'd just end up smearing it all over your face."

"You're very considerate, but honestly, I'm fine."

"Suit yourself." The giant stuck a ladle into the soup, then blew on it and gently tasted it. "This seems about ready. You seem like a decent fellow for a human, even if you are descended from the most vile creature ever to walk the land."

"You'd be surprised how many times I've heard that."

The giant laughed. "One last question before you go. What exactly did you come up here for? Seems like it'd have been far safer to stay hidden away, what with smelling exactly like the thief and all."

Jack shrugged, which must have looked odd upside down. "Oh, I was here to steal a harp from you."

The giant paused, then reached up around his neck and pulled a chain out. "This?" he said, dangling something golden in front of Jack at the end of the chain.

Jack just sighed, shaking his head.

"Kept it safe by my heart, ever since your father tried to get it," the giant said with a grin, setting the harp down on the table next to him. "You know, for safety."

"Looks like you were smart to do it," Jack pointed out.

The giant laughed. "That I was. Well, enough talk. In you go!" And with that, he grabbed the rope holding Jack suspended above the stew and yanked. The rope snapped, and Jack went tumbling straight into the pot.

CHAPTER 20

May looked at herself in the window, the night pitch-black behind it. Her dress shimmered as she turned, almost like magic. It was probably the most beautiful thing she'd ever seen, and wearing it, she imagined that all the stars in the sky had looked down at her and thrown up all over her.

The whole thing made her sick. But she would play pretend, she would play at Cinderella again, dress up in this costume and play the good guy for the Wicked Queen's villain, if that's what it took. She would live out the story, no matter what the story was, as long as Phillip and Penelope were safe. The Queen didn't want them, just May.

So whatever it took. And then she'd be free to find some way out, to fight back somehow . . . assuming it wasn't too late.

She smoothed her dress, knowing that the Queen could see any potential wrinkle as an insult, then carefully brushed her hair, her stomach turning over and over for far too many reasons.

Penelope stepped out of an adjoining room wearing a pink dress that almost hurt May's eyes to look at, it was so impossibly beautiful. Penelope, though, didn't seem to even notice, and instead was carefully trying to find places for her few remaining spindle splinters.

"Why can't there be any pockets?" she said eventually, dropping her hands to her side in defeat.

"They really weren't very considerate of us taking weapons in, were they?" May said, smiling slightly. "I wouldn't bother. She'll know."

The glass ball at the small of her back behind the dress's sash said differently, but Penelope didn't need to know that. This had to be a surprise, or the Queen would stop it.

Penelope bit her lip. "Maybe. But I don't especially like the idea of going in without anything to help us out if things get rough."

"Things aren't going to get rough," May said. "I'm going to make sure they don't. You and Phillip are going to go home, no matter what. Trust me. And trust me in there. Do what I say, and follow my lead, okay? I can't have you both . . . I can't have any-thing happen. Especially not given what the Queen said about Phillip and Ja . . . Phillip and the other one."

"Jack?" Penelope asked, and May winced. "I wonder how he's doing. It'd be nice to see him and say hi, if he's here."

May just glared at the girl, but a knock at the door inter-rupted her before she could think of something suitably clever to say. A goblin opened the door and gestured politely for them to leave.

"You ready for this?" May asked Penelope.

"Every day I'm awake is a good day," Penelope told her with a smile.

Fair enough.

The goblin led them down a corridor made of black stone, while four other goblins fell in behind them, each one holding an axe as tall as they were. May tried to follow their path, just in case she needed to make a quick getaway at any point, but there were so many hallways and stairs and twisting paths that she couldn't remember which way left or right was half the time and eventually just gave up.

Which, of course, was when they reached the throne room.

Large columns of stone rose all the way to the ceiling, or

descended all the way to the floor . . . it was hard to be sure. Between the columns, red eyes appeared and disappeared, shadows flitting in and out of the darkness. Even the goblins behind May were nervous, though the one leading them seemed to be at least faking confidence. He probably didn't want to get in trouble with the Queen for disrespecting her either.

The Queen herself sat at the very far end of the throne room, on an elaborate bone chair twice her height, rising like a living thing over her, as if it were about to attack anyone standing before the throne. Maybe it was.

To her right was a coffin made of ice, just like the one May had seen in the Palace of the Snow Queen, right before everything stopped making sense.

Snow White.

The Queen stood up as the two girls approached. Behind them, Phillip entered with another group of guards and quickly caught up to them.

"Be prepared to run as soon as I attack," the prince whispered as he reached them. "And do not look back, no matter what you hear."

May looked at him, then cleared her throat. "Your Majesty?" she said, stopping in place.

The Queen tilted her head in response, and May continued. "The prince here is planning on attacking you to help us escape. If I might suggest to Your Majesty that she have his guards hold his arms and legs to keep anything . . . unpleasant from happening?"

Phillip looked at her with his mouth wide open, but Penelope shook her head. "She's got a plan," the princess whispered to him.

The Queen slowly smiled. "Since you ask so nicely, May, I cannot help but grant your request." She gestured, and the goblin guards grabbed both of Phillip's arms, and two others moved in close to catch him if he escaped the first two.

"Of course, you know why you are here?" the Queen continued.

"For sentencing, Your Majesty," May said. "And I am fully prepared to declare my loyalty to you if you wish, whatever you say . . . if you might find it within your heart to release my two friends here."

The Queen's smile grew. "That is an interesting thought. But what use do I have for you to give me your loyalty, when I might have it whenever I desire?" She gestured, and May fell to her knees, exactly as Phillip had.

"Because . . ." May said, gritting her teeth as she fought to raise her head. "Because, Your . . . Majesty, you will . . . never know . . . if I might escape. Or disobey. You cannot . . . watch me at . . . all times."

"Let her go!" Phillip shouted, and the Queen turned her attention to the prince. Abruptly, May could stand, and she leapt to her feet.

"NO!" she shouted. "Ignore him! I'll do whatever you want, just let those two go!"

The Queen slowly turned her gaze back to May, and she shook her head. "You were doing so well with the respect, May. But one can only keep up an act for so long, I suppose. You come before me with no power yet offer me the only thing you have left, your will, in order to save your friends?"

This was it: She had no more time. May stood back up, and put both her arms behind her back, keeping her mind as empty as possible. "So if I do, will you let them go, then?"

The Queen smiled. "Oh, May. Of course not."

May nodded, then tore the glass ball out of her sash and whipped it as hard as she could right at the Queen.

The Wolf King's hand closed around it before it had even gone two feet.

The wolf opened his hand and looked at the glass ball, his eyes widening.

"My dear," the Queen said, shaking her head. "You choose a poor time to rebel. What is it, my servant?"

The Wolf King looked May right in the eye, his eyes disbelieving, his hand closing around the Fairest. "It is . . . nothing," he said, his eyes locked on May's. "Some . . . pathetic attempt to hurt you, your Majesty. I will destroy it."

Did he know what it was? Not that May did exactly, but the wolf seemed to recognize the Fairest somehow. But why wouldn't he just tell the Queen what it was?

The Queen's eyes narrowed, but she nodded. "Your loyalty is an example to us all, my friend."

The wolf bowed, then exited quickly, throwing one last look at May before he left, taking their only hope with him.

"Now," the Queen said, "such an attempt deserves a punishment, doesn't it?"

The Queen beckoned, and two goblins carried in a silver tray, stopping before Phillip and Penelope. The Queen raised a hand, and the tray's lid lifted off and into the air, revealing two beautifully red apples.

"Sometimes it's nice to stay in theme, don't you agree, May?" the Queen said.

"Don't do this," May whispered.

"I won't do anything," the Queen responded. "They just look hungry, don't they?"

Phillip and Penelope both straightened, then reached with shaking hands to the apples. They each grabbed one, then slowly brought them to their lips, struggling against the Queen's magic.

"Don't do this!" May repeated, shouting this time. "Don't hurt them!"

"Lessons must be learned!" the Queen said. "Besides, if a poisoned apple is good enough for Snow White, why not these two? Now, my two delightful royals . . . please start eating. There's no need to wait for the rest of us."

Phillip glanced at May, then put the apple to his lips and opened his mouth.

CHAPTER 21

As Jack fell toward the boiling stew, he concentrated, closing his eyes, flipping around so he was looking back up at the giant and pulling his sword off his back. Fortunately, the giant hadn't bothered taking it, not really worrying about it any more than a human would have worried over a bee's stinger.

Let's hope the giant had a Jack allergy.

Time slowed as he gently fell, almost like a leaf in the wind. He pulled the end of the rope down to him, yanking Gwentell along with it. The fairy opened her mouth to shout in surprise but didn't get a word out before he grabbed her and tossed her into his hood, then tied the end of the rope to his sword's hilt.

Then he threw his sword at the passing giant's belt as hard as he could.

The sword sunk in, and Jack wrapped the rope around his arm as he continued to fall for a moment, everything still slow. Finally, he let time resume and jerked into a swing straight at the giant.

His momentum slammed him into the giant's pants hard, but he managed to hold on to a large handful of cloth. Climbing up the giant's pants, Jack reached the belt and yanked his sword out as the giant turned back to the table below, reaching for the ladle.

The giant sniffed in loudly. "You already smell so good, little thief-son!"

The fairy snorted in his hood, and he tapped her to be quiet. The giant dropped the ladle into the stew, stirred it for a moment, then brought the ladle to his lips, full of steaming-hot non-Jack stew.

A moment later, the monster spit stew everywhere.

It was a compliment, really. Humans must really have an impressively powerful taste!

The ladle slammed into the table hard enough to throw the dishes a foot in the air, steaming hot stew flying everywhere. "WHERE ARE YOU!" the giant screamed, his fist following the ladle, and again the dishes left the table.

"He looks mad," the fairy said, poking her head out of the hood as Jack inched around the belt towards the giant's front.

"I can smell you! If you run, I will hunt you down to the ends of the earth or the beginnings of the sky!"

"He looks *really* mad," Gwentell said. "I wouldn't want to be you, man-child."

"If he eats me, he's getting you, too," he whispered to her.

She stuck out her tongue at him.

The harp was so close, right there on the table. All he had to do was make his way across a raging giant, find some way up to the table, and take it. How hard could *that* be?

"I WILL CRUSH YOUR BONES ONE BY ONE!" the giant shouted, turning around and around as he searched for Jack, then began to move away from the table.

That wouldn't work. Every step took him hundreds of feet from where he needed to be. He had to slow the giant down somehow.

Jack pulled out his sword and stabbed the giant as hard as he could right in the creature's back.

"Uh?" the giant said, his foot stopping in midair a good twenty feet off the ground.

Oddly, the spot where Jack had stabbed the giant had already stopped bleeding. Or . . . not so oddly. Apparently Jill's potion had done the trick. But now was not the time to worry about it, as the giant's hand came flying in to slap the spot Jack had just attacked.

Jack leapt to the right, then grabbed the giant's pant leg and stabbed him again, using the sword to slow his momentum by cutting the monster's pants as he fell.

The giant slapped his leg, then yanked it up by his pants to drop the leg on a wooden chair, bending down to look for Jack.

Jack looked back up and waved. "Thanks for the ride!" he shouted. The giant shouted back, only using his hand instead of his voice, smacking his own leg as hard as he could, forcing Jack to jump for it.

He landed hard on the chair, rolling to get as far away as he could. A second slap hit just behind him, and the force sent a hurricane force wind straight into Jack, sending him up and off the chair.

He flung his arms out, reaching desperately for the chair's edge and barely catching it with his fingers, only to have the giant bend down to look at him hanging there off the chair, his breath sending Jack swaying backward and forward with each inhale and exhale.

"You. Are. Mine." The giant pushed a hand up from under Jack, and he fell into the giant's palm, rolling to the center of it. The giant slowly raised his hand toward his face.

Conveniently, it also carried Jack right past something very much harpish.

"Which bone should I break first?" the giant growled, raising his free thumb right above Jack's head. "Or shall I just go with all of them? You'll taste just as good as a paste, I'm sure."

"That's awfully nice of you to say," Jack said. "But I really can't stay for dinner." And with that, he stabbed the giant's palm and leapt off the hand to the table. He quickly stood up, only to get knocked off his feet by a fairy slapping him in the face.

"You almost got us eaten!" she shouted.

Jack shook his head to clear it as the giant screamed in rage far too close. Had the fairy always been so strong?! She really packed a punch!

The giant's screams shifted from anger to satisfaction, and both hands raised in fists above the table.

That wasn't good.

"The harp!" Jack yelled.

"Okay?" the fairy said with a shrug. "And what do you want me to do about it?"

Jack glared at her, then dove for the golden, glinting statue just out of reach, just as the giant's fists came down, collapsing the table out from under Jack, the harp, and the conveniently flying fairy.

Jack and the harp, at least, tumbled into nothingness, the floor coming up far too fast.

What was that song again?

He quickly strummed the harp's strings as he fell, but despite it sounding extremely pretty, he had no idea how to make individual notes.

"Oh, just let me do it," said the fairy from above him, diving down to meet them. As the floor drew closer and closer, and the giant's hand came rushing down at them from above, the tiny fairy climbed over Jack's hands and pulled one, then two, then three strings, only to lose her hold on his hand and fall off.

Abruptly, the moonlight wasn't the only thing making the harp glow, and Jack realized for the first time that the side of it was a statue of a woman. Mostly because the statue turned to look at him with a questioning look.

"Don't you dare leave me here!" the fairy yelled, but the giant's dusty room turned like a page, and Jack found himself falling into a throne room filled with columns and black stone, along with quite a few people.

Jack slammed into the floor far too hard, the harp hitting right beside him. The wind went rushing out of him, and it took him a moment to remember how to breathe before he managed to push himself to a standing position, his sword out and ready for whatever he might be facing.

As it turned out, he was facing the Wicked Queen, standing before her throne. And she didn't look surprised in the least.

"Your harp, Your Majesty," Jack told her, breathing heavily. "As promised."

"Jack?" whispered a voice behind him.

Jack turned around to find May, Phillip, and Penelope all staring at him, the two girls dressed in sparkling gowns, Phillip . . . not as much, all bound in iron chains and being held by goblins. Oddly, Phillip and Penelope both seemed about to take a bite out of an apple, but as soon as he appeared, their hands dropped to their sides as if something had just let go.

This was it, the same scene that the man in the final Eye challenge had shown him. The scene where he had fought Phillip, then—

"And here we all are," the Wicked Queen said with the hint of a smile. "And now, one shall betray my granddaughter, and the other shall die. Which shall be which, I wonder?"

CHAPTER 22

I am ready to face my death," Phillip said, stepping forward. "Let me lay down my life that these two princesses shall be free."

"Shut up, Phillip," Jack said quietly, pulling out his sword. This was it. Everything he planned for all came down to this, and one mistake would make it all pointless.

"I am done listening to you," Phillip practically spat at him as the prince pulled against his chains. "You joined the Wicked Queen, Jack. You betrayed us!"

Jack nodded. "Eventually, everyone gets tired of losing. You'll figure it out someday."

"I'll kill the prince if you'd like, my Queen," said a familiar voice, and Jill stepped out of the shadows from the Queen's side.

She grinned cruelly at Phillip. "I'd do it even if you didn't ask me to, honestly."

"We're not quite there yet, my dear," the Queen said, her eyes on Jack. "You have delivered me what I asked for, my newest Eye. And for that, I will grant a request. But what will you choose? Leaving all of this behind, leaving your friends in my care . . . or would you have me free them?"

"They're no friends of *mine*, Your Majesty," Jack said, gritting his teeth and deliberately ignoring the feeling of May staring right at him.

"*Don't* do this," she said quietly, so quietly that maybe no one else even heard her. But Jack heard her, and it made his chest ache.

"No?" the Queen asked. "You trained to be an Eye, true. You left them, and you say you want to leave this world behind as well. But I see into your heart, Jack. You would choose them, if I gave you the opportunity." She smiled. "So I shall ask you once again—"

"You have already given him the opportunity!" Phillip shouted, struggling to free himself while the goblins laughed. "And he chose evil! Face me, Jack, for our freedom! Give me a sword, and we shall see once and for all which of us is the better man!"

Before Phillip could say another word, Jack concentrated, disappearing only to reappear at Phillip's side. The prince didn't even have time to move before Jack punched the royal boy right in the face. The goblins howled with laughter, dropping their chains, but the prince just smiled.

"Finally," he said, and swung his chains straight at Jack's head.

Jack ducked beneath them while May shouted a name.

Phillip's.

Jack's face pumped bright red, and he pulled his sword off his back, the weapon glowing white with just a hint of black around the edges.

"Don't make me do this, Phillip," Jack almost spat. "You can't win."

"I cannot?" the prince said, and swung out with his chains again, forcing Jack back a step. "How many stories end with the villain victorious?"

"This is *not* a story!" Jack shouted, cutting right through the chains to keep them from hitting him. "And you're *not* the hero!"

"And you are?" Phillip asked him, circling around him, forcing Jack to circle as well. "You believe you fight for the good of all here? On the side of the WICKED QUEEN?"

One of the goblins moved to strike Phillip, but electricity spat out of the Queen's hand, sending the goblin crashing against the wall behind it. "I think we should let these two have their discussion," she said, and Jack could almost hear her smiling.

Phillip picked up the fallen goblin's sword, the cut chains hanging from his wrists. "The tragedy of this is that I once considered you my friend," the prince said, and swung out.

Jack easily slapped the sword away. "Really? That makes one of us."

"Don't do this," May said, her voice low and hoarse. "Jack, *please* . . . don't hurt him."

He threw a glance her way, saw her tearstained cheeks, and suddenly he had trouble breathing. Why were they here now? Why did they have to see this?

"*Kill* him, Jack," the Queen said. "Kill this prince, my Eye, and I grant you freedom from this world. I grant you a world without royalty, a world without magic, a world where a boy as clever as you would be admired far and wide."

Phillip struck again, then again, and Jack easily parried each time, his eyes locked on Phillip's. And then, reflected in the prince's eyes, Jack saw blue fire.

Jack turned his head, and there, just like he'd seen six months ago in the middle of the sky in Giant's Hand, when May had fallen right out of it, was a blue fire circle. And inside it . . . inside it were trees, a shining sun, and no sign of magic or princes.

"Kill him, my Eye," the Queen said softly. "And you will be free to leave this all behind."

Jack turned back to Phillip just as the prince launched a punishing series of blows. Over and over the prince struck with all his might, bashing Jack's sword with his own, taking chunks out of his own weapon, he hit so hard. And with each hit, Jack stepped backward, toward the Queen and away from May.

"You betrayed her!" Phillip shouted, fire exploding in his eyes. "She believed in you, and you betrayed her, me, your entire world! For your own selfish gains! And now you would run from your mistakes, from your betrayals? You would FLEE?"

Jack gritted his teeth, having trouble focusing on anything beyond the prince. Who was Phillip to judge him?!

Jack sidestepped the prince's blow and slammed the flat of his sword into Phillip's sword arm as hard as he could. "You have no *idea* who I am," he whispered, then kicked Phillip in the stomach, sending the prince sprawling across the floor, his sword sliding back to its unconscious goblin owner.

Jack advanced on the dazed prince, the glow of his sword

slowly being replaced by a black emptiness. "You're such a *hero*, Your Highness," he said. "You're so amazing, aren't you? Doing good just comes so easily to you. We should all just love you, shouldn't we?"

"Kill him," the Queen said quietly, and Jack gripped his sword so tightly his knuckles turned white.

Phillip watched him advance, showing no fear, ever the perfect royal. "Kill me," he said. "And with me, anything good or noble left in your life!"

"You're three months too late for that," Jack said, then looked at May—he couldn't help it, he looked at her, then quickly turned his head.

It would have to be fast. Don't think. Just do it as quickly as possible.

"NO!" May screamed.

"I *knew* this was who you are," Phillip said, staring up into Jack's eyes with absolute hatred.

"You're more right than you know," Jack said, raising his sword in the air. He looked one last time at May, his sword right above Phillip's head. "Good-bye," he whispered, then drove the sword down.

May's chains separated cleanly in half.

"NO!" May shouted again, then stopped, looking at her now-free hands. "Wait . . . what?"

Jack grabbed Phillip by his shirt and tossed him straight at May, then cut Penelope's chains as well. A goblin swung at him, but he ducked, time slowing as he did. Four swings later, and four goblins lay unconscious on the ground.

"GO!" he screamed at Phillip, pushing the prince into May. "Get them OUT of here!"

The Queen sighed, and the goblins' unaware bodies rose, picking up their swords, and attacked. "I truly had high hopes for you, Jack," the Queen said as Penelope grabbed a sword and joined Phillip against the goblins. "I knew you planned this, but I still hoped. Yet, the Mirror is never wrong, as much as I might have wished it."

"There's a first time for everything," Jack said, turning away from the others, not able to look at them, knowing what was coming. "Phillip, GO!"

"Jack, come with us!" May shouted as she defended herself from the unconscious goblin's sword. Jack turned, not sure what he could say, and caught her eye. "*Please*," she whispered.

And then a goblin smashed his sword into her head, and she fell to the ground. The goblin brought his sword up, just as Jack had done to Phillip minutes before, holding it above May's head.

Someone screamed, but Jack couldn't tell who it was. The goblin's sword paused, and Jack looked at the Queen.

She wouldn't do it. She'd been after May this long, there's no way she'd just let her die.

The Queen smiled at Jack, and the goblin drove his sword down.

And with that, Jack threw his sword right at the Queen's heart.

The Queen raised a hand, and the sword froze in midair, just inches from her chest.

"Now, now," she said. "You knew that wouldn't accomplish anything, didn't you?"

Behind him, the goblins' bodies dropped back to the ground, including the one attacking May. Phillip scooped May's unconscious body up and ran toward the door with Penelope. "Maybe not nothing," Jack whispered.

"One will betray her, and one will die for her," the Queen said, frowning at Jack. "If you won't betray her, then that only leaves us one option."

And with that, Jack's sword reversed in midair.

Jack turned to look at Phillip and at May, her hair almost covering her face. He'd known this would happen from the moment the Queen had told May the Mirror's words six months ago.

He couldn't have betrayed her, not in a million years.

And with that, the Queen drove Jack's sword right into his back.

He gasped both in pain and shock as the world turned to nothing, collapsing first to his knees, then to the floor.

"What a shame," the Queen said, her voice sounding miles away. "You could have been truly great, Jack."

Jack smiled weakly. She saw it coming, and she still had no idea.

And with that, Jack's heart stopped, and he died.

CHAPTER 23

NO!" Phillip shouted. Penelope grabbed his arm and tried to pull him out of the room, away from the Wicked Queen and her minions, but he struggled against her.

Penelope shouted his name, forcing him to look at her. "We need to go if we're going to escape." Phillip turned back to the room, back to Jack's body. Lian, the Eye, stood over it, almost in a daze. She kneeled down and turned Jack over, then placed his sword on his chest and gently touched the blade, closing her eyes and dropping her head out of respect. Apparently they had been closer than Phillip had known.

Even after Jack turned to the Wicked Queen, even after he betrayed them, Phillip never wished this. He had fought Jack in a fit of anger, but this, *this* is where that anger had led. And

Jack had done the one thing Phillip had not even considered he would: sacrifice himself for the others.

Lian picked up Jack's body along with his sword and bag. She gently, almost solemnly, carried him to the blue fire portal and laid him down within. "I hope you enjoy a world without any of this," she said quietly as the portal flickered then collapsed, disappearing in silence.

Then she turned toward the Wicked Queen and pulled out her sword.

"Oh, Jillian," the Queen said, not unkindly. "Are we finally here?"

Lian nodded, and lightning erupted from the Queen's hand. Lian slapped it away with her sword once, then again, advancing on the Queen. "I never knew him, because of you," she said, her voice deadly quiet. "First my mother. You took her from me. Then my father, you took him too. And now you take my *brother* from me?"

Brother?!

Lian held up her sword, glowing a bright white, then disappeared, only to reappear directly in front of the Wicked Queen. Moving faster than Phillip could see, Lian swung her sword at the Queen's face.

The Queen, however, caught it easily in her hand. Where

blood might have flowed in anyone else, the Queen's hand was remarkably untouched.

"Did you really think you could hurt me?" she asked the Eye softly. Lian rose into the air, struggling against the unseen force of the Wicked Queen's magic, then screamed as she hurtled across the room, slamming against the wall right next to Phillip.

Penelope was right. They had to go now, or they would *never* leave.

But after what Phillip had just seen, they could not leave without Lian.

"GO!" Phillip shouted, pushing May's unconscious body into Penelope's arms. He bent down and scooped Lian up and over his shoulder, then followed the other two right out of the throne room.

"Oh, little Prince," the Wicked Queen said from right behind him. "You can't run from me."

He whirled around, ready to attack, but no one was there. Of course the Queen would have her tricks, her magic. He could not stop for anything, trick or not.

Lian jerked, then kicked him hard in the back, knocking him to the floor. "What did you do that for?!" she shouted at him. "You do *not* rescue me. Not you. Not *ever*!"

A goblin attacked, but Lian took it and four others out without even looking at them.

"She would have killed you," Phillip said, picking himself up. "And she will kill us all if we do not find a way to escape."

"*You* caused this," she hissed. "You made him throw everything away like that!"

Phillip's anger bubbled back up. "I did nothing but confront him over his joining the Queen. Something you convinced him to do!"

Lian snarled, then shook her head. "You have no idea how much I didn't do this to him. This goes against *everything*. Everything!" She took a deep breath, then shook her head. "But now is not the time. You have one chance to get out of here, and it's by following me." She started off down the hallway to their left, one of five facing them, then turned back. "I do this because it hurts the Queen. I do *not* do this for you."

With that, Lian turned and ran off down the hall. Phillip reached out and took May from Penelope, who put a hand on his shoulder then ran with him to catch up.

The Queen's castle seemed almost empty in comparison to the garrisons of goblins they'd seen on their way in. Considering how many guards filled the city outside, he could not believe that there were none here. But they encountered no one, heard no one, sensed no one. The entire castle seemed dead inside, even if on the outside torches made it look lived in.

Unfortunately, even dead, the castle still moved. Shadows flitted here or there, and red eyes looked out hungrily from corridors that Lian wisely passed. Her glowing sword seemed to make them flinch and back away, but not for long, and as soon as they'd passed, the shadows followed them.

Down stairways they went, through hallways and random rooms, on and on until Phillip began to doubt that Lian knew where they were going.

"She doesn't, Phillip," said the Queen's voice in his ear, and Phillip whirled around, his goblin sword drawn, only to find no one there. "I will find you before you can escape. I'm on my way now. You can't run, Phillip. You can't hide."

"Don't listen to her," Lian shouted back. "She wouldn't be trying to scare you if she could reach us."

"You all hear her?" Phillip said without stopping.

Penelope nodded, while Lian just kept running, not looking back.

Finally, they came to a large wooden door, which Lian opened by sticking her sword through the door's lock. Three more doors followed, made of iron, steel, and brick, and each one unlocked as well.

"We are too far underground to escape," Phillip told Lian, but she just shook her head.

"I need to get something first," she said, and opened the last door, this one made of bone, revealing cages upon cages, one within another.

All were empty.

"No," Lian whispered. "NO! Where did you take him?!"

"Phillip," said the Wicked Queen from everywhere. "I suggest you listen to me. If you care about your mother and your kingdom, you should listen to my warning."

Phillip stiffened. "She is threatening my people."

"She *took* him," Lian said, ignoring him. "Why? What could she—" And then Lian froze, turning to Phillip, her mouth hanging open. "Oh *no*."

"She knows, Phillip," the Queen's voice said. "She knows what's happening. She knows about the giant."

"The giant?" Phillip asked, and Lian dropped her gaze, not able to look at him. "The giant?" he repeated.

"The one you've been looking for," she told him without

meeting his gaze. "The Queen, she must have taken my . . . taken the thief, the one who stole from him, and sent him to your kingdom. She'd hidden him away from the giant this entire time, but now that he's out in the world again, the giant will find the thief, and tear apart anyone in his way."

"He will destroy *everything*, Phillip, and you'll never return in time," the Queen told him. "Your mother, your kingdom . . . all gone. Because the giant isn't alone. He has six others just like him, and they're on their way. I'd say they have perhaps a week? No more, certainly. And here you are, powerless to save anyone and much too far away to reach them."

"*Monster*," Phillip whispered, gripping his sword. "I am glad you still live, that I might destroy you myself!"

"They don't have to die, Phillip," the Queen said.

"Don't listen, Phillip," Lian told him, but Penelope shook her head, strangely calm.

"We already know what he decides," the princess said, and gave Phillip a sympathetic look.

What did she mean?

"Tell me where you are, Phillip," the Queen said. "I will send you home. You can face the giants. You really are the only hope your people have, the only hope your mother has. And you know that. You've killed giants, more than you can count. Who else could save them?"

"You lie," Phillip whispered.

"NO!" Lian shouted. "Phillip, we need to escape!"

"That's not the choice he makes," Penelope said.

"I speak only the truth," the Queen said. "I've never lied to you. You know this. I told you one would betray my grand-daughter, and one would die. One has died, Phillip. And now it's your turn. Give up my granddaughter. Release her back to me, and you can save your people. A kingdom for one person. The choice is simple."

Phillip swallowed hard and looked down at May's face as he held her in his arms. He could not betray her. He could *not* . . . it was not even an option.

But neither could he leave his kingdom, his people to die at the hands of a giant.

Not when he could save them.

And that was it. One life versus those of an entire kingdom. And the Queen would not hurt May. She had been hunting her for too long. There must be a reason . . . there *must* be.

It did not matter. Betrayal was betrayal. But there was no choice here, not for him.

"*No*, Phillip," Lian said, her voice hoarse. "Whatever she's promising you, this is *worse*."

Phillip tried to speak, tried to explain, but there were no words. There was nothing he could say or do, other than despise himself and the Queen both.

"Only . . . only her," he said, barely able to get the words out. "Penelope and Lian come with me."

"You drive a hard bargain, but one that I find acceptable," the Queen told him. "Now. Open your mind to me."

Phillip opened his mind and, somewhere deep inside, felt a horrible presence flitter like a butterfly through his memories. He watched as if from outside as he followed Lian down the halls, through the castle, through the metal doors to the room with the cage.

And then a circle of blue lightning opened, and the Wicked Queen stepped out.

"A deal is a deal," she said, and just like that, Penelope and Lian both disappeared, just as May's eyes opened. Phillip carefully set her down, and she looked from the prince to the Queen.

"Just in time," the Queen told her. "Phillip just gave you up for his own freedom."

May turned to Phillip, her mouth opening without any words coming out.

And then, before Phillip could even say one word, he disappeared as well.

CHAPTER 24

Phillip had . . . betrayed her? Still groggy, May stumbled backward to slam into something that felt like metal bars. *Phillip* had? Where was Penelope?

Where was Jack?

No. NO. If Phillip had, then . . . then Jack . . .

The Queen just smiled at her.

"It can't . . ." May whispered, and just like that the room began to spin. She couldn't breathe. She coughed, just trying to get some air, trying to grasp at any thought that would come.

"It's very true, I'm afraid," the Queen said, still smiling. "And I'm afraid there's no one but you to blame, my little May."

May could barely hear her, like her voice was coming from

miles away. He . . . he couldn't be . . . she would know, some-how. She would *know!* "You . . . *liar*," May heard herself saying.

The smile disappeared. "You should remember what lack of respect gets you, my dear."

May felt an invisible hand latch itself around her body and slam her up against the bars, crushing her into the metal until she could barely breath.

She didn't care.

"YOU. *LIAR.* He's . . . alive!"

"I would shut your *mouth* if I were you," the Queen said, her eyes on fire with shadowy flames.

The hand squeezed, and May gasped.

"HE . . . IS . . . ALIV—"

The hand threw her across the room.

"Do I need to show you his body?!" the Queen shouted. "What will it take to show?!"

"There's . . . nothing," May said, every breath shooting pain through her chest. "You . . . couldn't . . . show me . . . anything. He's . . . *alive.*"

"I never thought you stupid," the Queen said, dragging May back into the air. "But this inability to see reality—"

"REALITY!?" May shouted, and kicked out. Her foot

slammed into the Queen's hand, and whether from pain or surprise, the magic disappeared. May collapsed back to the floor, but was on her feet instantly.

A sword. She needed a sword.

"You *struck* me!" the Queen said, her eyes wide.

May dove for a goblin sword on the ground, then aimed it at the Queen. "I'm about to do more than that."

Lightning played over the Queen's fingers. "You will have to suffer for that, of course."

May launched herself forward, swinging the sword straight at the Queen, only to have it slide off something that wasn't there. She struck again and again, never getting within a foot of the Queen.

And then a tiny bolt of lightning leapt from the Queen's fingers to May's chest, and May found herself on the floor, not sure how she'd gotten there.

"I could kill you right now," the Queen said from somewhere above her. "It would be easy. But I wonder if you might still serve some use?"

May just looked up at her, barely comprehending her words.

"Your friends are all gone," the Queen said, smiling slightly. "You have no one left but me."

"You're *happy*," May said, almost not understanding the word.

"Happy?" the Queen asked her, and she looked confused for a moment. "Of course not. Why would you suggest such a thing?"

"You took . . . *everything* from me." Her voice cracked left and right, but she just pushed through it, slowly sitting up. "Everything I had, you destroyed. My home. My family. My friends. You took everything from me and everything from them. It must have made you happy. . . ."

The Queen paused, then nodded. "I suppose I should be, shouldn't I? But like you, I wish it hadn't come to this. I knew it would, of course. I knew from the moment I first saw you in the Mirror, when I asked it to show me . . . well, there's time for that later. I knew when I stole you from your father and stepmother and brought you here as barely more than a baby. And I knew when Jack freed me from Rapunzel's jail. And I warned you."

"You *lied*," May said, her entire body screaming in pain as she pushed to her feet then picked up her sword again. "He's *not dead*."

"You can't kill me, child," the Queen told her. "Though you are welcome to wish me harm all you'd like. You can't hurt me, of course. Not physically." She frowned. "I'm beginning to forget what it feels like, caring for you. But I know that I did once, and strongly."

"You could never have cared and done ANY of this!" May shouted.

The Queen smiled. "We lived in that other world for so many years, and you still don't see how there's more to life than good and evil, May? Of course I cared for you. I loved you. Dearly. It was not always that way, of course. When I first found you, I knew that caring for you would lead us here, and I would be far safer just killing you as a child."

"You should have," May said, pointing her sword at the woman's heart again.

"Perhaps," the Queen said. "I *have* made mistakes. And the worst part is, I knew that I would. I saw them ahead of time yet was doomed to follow through on them if I wanted to ultimately triumph. After all, you can't take the good without the bad, can you? Everything I saw, all my mistakes, they will lead me to ruling over this entire world. You, here, now . . . it all leads to my victory."

"Trust me," May said, running the back of her hand over her wet face, "me being here right now doesn't lead you *anywhere* good."

The Queen's eyes flashed with anger. "I warned you, child! I *warned* you! I gave you the same knowledge I had about those two boys. If you had joined me, Jack would still live, and Phillip's kingdom would not be in danger. At least not until my armies descended upon it."

May shook her head in disbelief and advanced on the Queen, the sword shaking in her hand. "You . . . you can't be . . . this *thing*! The woman I thought was my . . . she wouldn't have hurt anyone!"

The Queen smiled. "I had hurt many, many people at that point, May. But that other world . . . it did strange things to me. Things I never would have expected. But I can see you don't care, do you?"

May shook her head, feeling a million miles away, looking down on herself and the woman she used to love, the woman she used to think she could save, could bring back from whatever she'd become. "You couldn't have just been a horrible monster? You had to destroy us all along with the rest of the world?! WHY! WHY did we have to suffer too! You said you cared about me, but all you've done since returning is try to hurt me! WHY!"

"Why?" the Queen said, then shrugged slightly. "Because I was curious to see if I *could*. After all, you speak the truth . . . if I did truly care, how could I hurt you? I had to be sure. And now I am." She reached out a hand, and lightning slammed into May, throwing her across the room, her sword landing far from her hand. "You see? I can hurt you with no qualms, May. That is what I needed to know. In the past, I've had . . . difficulty with certain people. I couldn't kill Snow, not completely. Part of me held back, and now she hovers between life and death forever. But returning to this world, I've purged myself of any weakness I previously had. And now I am worthy to truly rule."

May groaned, her entire head throbbing, while her heart seemed to be skipping beats from the electrical charge. She smelled something burning and suspected it might be her singed hair.

She pushed herself to her feet, only to fall back to the ground. A second time, and she fell again. The third time she managed to hold herself up, then stagger over to where her sword had fallen.

"You really won't give up until you've had your chance, will you?" the Queen asked her, watching May like a cat watches a mouse trying to run this way or that, away from the predator.

"You took me . . . for a reason," May said, just trying to make it to the sword. "You were . . . afraid. There's got to be . . . a reason. The Mirror must have . . . told you so." She reached the weapon but fell against the wall.

"Malevolent used the Mirror to find out how she would die," the Queen said, still watching her closely. "She was shortsighted, clearly. I had far more important questions for the Mirror than how I would leave this Earth." She tilted her head. "Though leaving *this* Earth did come up. And for a few years there, I wasn't quite sure if we would come back."

"You should have kept us moving," May told her, picking the weapon up, not believing how heavy it suddenly felt. "If the Huntsman hadn't found us, you wouldn't die right here."

"Oh, but it wasn't he who first found us, don't you remember?" the Queen said. "Someone stole something very special to me that morning. I believed it to be the Huntsman, but he was only after the crown, to fix the Mirror. He had no idea what else had been hidden in our house or that it had disappeared."

"That doesn't matter," May said, dragging the sword step by step toward the woman whom she finally, *finally* no longer saw as her grandmother. "Not to you. Not anymore."

"Very well," the Queen said. "If it will move things along, then by all means, kill me." With that, she opened her arms and waited.

May paused, wondering if this was a trick of some kind.

Then she decided she didn't care and stabbed the Wicked Queen in the heart.

The Queen looked down at the sword in her chest, then smiled. "Now, I hope that makes you feel at least a *little* better, dear." Then she pulled the sword out without even a mark. "This must be a bit surprising, I'm sure. But sometimes death isn't quite as final as we might think."

CHAPTER 25

Portal," he heard himself say. "Get me through the portal."

It was like a dream, slipping in and out.

"You had this all planned?" a girl's voice said. "From the start?"

Who was talking?

"One of us was going to die. The Queen saw it. I just took the choice out of her hands."

The other voice seemed to be angry. "You're trying to be a *hero* again?!"

"Nope. I learned my lesson. But she can't know what I'm doing. And if there's one thing I've learned, it's that you can get away with a lot more if no one knows what you're up to."

"I'll get you through the portal."

"Just make sure I have the Story Book. I'm going to need it."

And then the scene swirled away like it never existed.

"Are you sure you know what you're doing?" This time it was a male voice.

"Of course not. Have I ever been?"

"There's no turning back from this. You make one mistake, and you won't get a second chance. Not with her. If you even make it back."

"I'll make it back. I know exactly when my portal home is going to show up."

"If you even *want* to return."

And then just like the first one, that scene disappeared into a cloud, and there was nothing, just darkness, nothing more. No dreams, no voices, just nothing . . .

Jack gasped, and sprang up to a sitting position, frantically feeling all around his chest.

Instead of a wound, all he felt was a scar.

He let out a huge breath, then looked around. This wasn't the Wicked Queen's castle. In fact, it didn't look like anywhere he'd ever seen before. The woods around him weren't quite the same color green, like they were a bit duller than the ones he'd seen all his life. The sun overhead, while just as bright, shone in a sky that was a bit off the normal blue, and the clouds didn't look as stony as the ones he'd walked on earlier that same day.

Jill had done what he'd asked and gotten him through the portal. He panicked for a second, then felt his grandfather's Story Book at his side, along with his sword. Before he could forget, he opened the Story Book to the correct page and tore out an entire tale, adding the pages to the folded ones Gwentell had returned to him after confirming their accuracy with the Queen's raven.

The world around him seemed so quiet, which was good. He'd just died, after all, so quiet was a good thing. He pulled the empty potion bottle out of his pocket and smiled. It'd taken a few minutes, but the healing potion on the sword's blade had repaired the wound the sword itself had caused. Which was good, since he hadn't had a chance to test it, other than on the giant, or had much of a backup plan if the Wicked Queen decided to lightning him to death. Thankfully, she'd fallen for him throwing his sword at her exactly as he'd hoped, and things had gone as planned.

That was the benefit of people telling you what their magic mirrors had seen. Jack only wished she'd tell him more next time.

If there *was* a next time. Where was he? The Queen had opened this portal, so presumably she knew where it led, but where would she send Jack? She wouldn't have lied, not outright . . . he must be in Punk. But there were far too many ways to deceive someone without lying than he cared to think about.

One of those ways being to drop him right into a life-threatening situation. Or, as he usually called it, a Tuesday.

Other than the lack of a sun giant and the colors being a bit muted, this world looked enough like his home that he could have easily mistaken the two. Here, though, there'd be no magic. Or would there?

He picked up his sword and concentrated, trying to slow time. There was . . . something, like a bit of a jump, then another one, like trying to walk on ice. The magic was there, but he just couldn't . . . hold on to it, almost.

He slid the sword back into the scabbard on his back as a small tinkling, like a tiny bell, began to ring. Another one soon joined it, and another, each one a bit farther away. Was someone there?

"Hello?" he said, but the bells just continued, blissfully unaware of the confusion they were causing. He stepped toward the closest one, bending down to find a tiny bell attached to the tiptop of a bright red hat. The bell kept ringing even as he picked the hat up.

Why did this seem so familiar?

And then it hit him.

Malevolent's castle. The dungeon.

Picking up the imp by his hat and stealing it as leverage.

Uh-oh.

"I *totally* expected to see you here," said a voice absolutely dripping with sarcasm. "I was just saying how much I thought you'd show up out of nowhere, like the greatest present ever. It just seemed *so* likely."

Uh-oh uh-oh.

Jack pulled his sword out and turned around in a circle, far too aware that the sword was basically powerless, given that it'd instantly heal up anything he cut. "Who's there?"

"Did I make so little an impression?" said the voice, and something invisibly grabbed Jack and pulled him into the air. "I'm sure *this* doesn't bring back any memories."

A foot off the ground, then two in the air, and Jack struggled as hard as he could. Just like before, though, it accomplished nothing . . . whatever held him, he wasn't going to escape it.

So apparently magic *was* possible here. But how powerful was it? After all, he wasn't flying hundreds of feet into the air . . . he was barely a few feet off the ground, and even that seemed slow, like it'd been difficult to get him that far.

A tiny man dressed in a goldenrod tunic, his beard tucked into his bright blue pants, smiled widely, almost wider than seemed possible on his little face.

And as if that wasn't bad enough, another imp stepped out next to him. The new one wore a golden shirt and pants and was clean-shaven and hatless.

"What did you find here, cousin?" the new imp said.

"A present for me, just like the Queen promised," the first imp said. "The only human to humiliate me. Him and the girl with him." The imp checked around. "You're probably too *smart* to have brought her here too, huh?"

"Okay, just so you know, I'm catching the sarcasm," Jack said, glaring at the imp. "What are you even doing here? I didn't think magic could work on this world."

"Every spell is a struggle," the second, unfamiliar imp said with a sigh. "But when your name has power, and some horrible princess tells everyone in the world what that name is, sometimes you don't have much choice."

Something May said jumped into his head. ". . . Stiltskin?" Jack asked.

Mr. Stiltskin turned to the imp that had tortured Jack back in Malevolent's castle, and smacked his head. "You brought a human here who knows our NAME?!"

"*I* didn't bring him here!" the first imp said indignantly. "She did, as a payment on a debt, after I hid some big hairy guy's long lost love in the dream world. And I forgot that they knew! I was a *bit* more worried about revenge!"

"If you don't let me go, I'll scream your name as loud as I can!" Jack said.

"No one will hear you," the first imp said darkly.

"YOU, let me handle this," the second one said. He turned to Jack. "Your kind just won't leave me in peace, will you? I leave you horrible humans behind, only to find thousands of your kind here. And they don't even know what to call me, so keep calling me a leopard-con or something. What does that even mean?"

"Maybe we can make a bargain?" Jack said, and the golden-clothed imp's nose began to twitch.

"Bargain?" he said. "And what could you possibly have that I want?"

Jack didn't exactly have a lot on him, and the last thing he was going to do was offer up his sense of sarcasm. He couldn't give up his sword, either. He'd need it if he ever made it back home. And all that left him was—

"A Story Book!" he shouted. "A Story Book filled with tales of pirates in love with mermaids, wolves hunting down girls in red hoods, and man-eating horses!"

"A Story Book?" the imp said, raising an eyebrow. "How would *you* ever find one of those? They're pretty rare. . . ."

"I'm pretty amazing," Jack told him.

The imp with May's sarcasm snorted. "What good would that do us? What use would we have for a magic book that won't work here?"

"The stories won't disappear, even if the magic does," Jack told him. "And a storyteller is always in high demand, if I know, uh, the humans here."

"There *are* those two German brothers offering to pay gold for stories," the golden imp said. "And there's a human in France who is looking for the same thing. And one in Denmark."

"This thing *is* filled with stories," the red-hatted imp said, flipping through the Story Book. "We could make more gold than we'd know what to do with!"

"We'd have to hide it in pots, we'd have so much!" the golden imp said, his voice rising in excitement.

"Below rainbows!" the red-hatted imp said.

The golden imp paused at this, throwing his cousin a weird look. "Why would we do that?"

"So we'd always know where it was!"

"But wouldn't that mean anyone could find it?"

"Why would anyone ever think to look for gold at the end of a rainbow?"

"YOU did."

"I'm not stupid like humans are."

"You're CLOSE."

"Gentlemen!" Jack said. "We haven't discussed what *I* get!"

"YOU get?" the red-hatted imp said. "You get your life!"

"Oh, that book is worth at least three of my lives," Jack told him, hoping his math was correct. Both imps nodded reluctantly, so he plowed ahead. "But I'll only take the one life, and . . ." He pulled out the Story Book page he'd ripped out and showed the imps a picture. "I want you to send me *there*."

The imps squinted at the picture. "That would take most of the magic we have left!" the golden imp said.

"Why would you need it anymore if you have pots of gold?" Jack asked.

"I used to be able to spin straw into gold," the golden

imp muttered. "Never needed money before now. Life isn't very fair."

"You're telling me," the red-hatted imp said. "We're letting my mortal enemy go free!"

"Mortal enemy?" Jack asked. "Honestly, I barely remembered you."

"Even worse!" the imp shouted.

"So do we have a deal?"

The imps looked at each other and sighed, then nodded their heads. They put their hands together and concentrated, sweat breaking out on their foreheads, their eyes clinched close, and Jack felt something pulling at him, something that grew stronger and stronger.

"There it is," the golden imp said, gritting his teeth. "I found it. But it's in another time entirely!"

"Another *what* now?" Jack said.

"Hundreds of years in the future," the red-hatted imp said. "This really will drain us completely!"

"Well, if it's that far off, put me there a day or two ahead of time," he told them. "That'll give me a little time to make a plan."

The red-hatted imp sputtered at Jack's request, but the

golden imp just smiled. "A deal's a deal, cousin." He winked, and seemed to show the red-hatted imp something Jack couldn't see. "See, the deal is complete even if we drop him right . . . *here*."

"Wait, drop me *where*?" Jack said, but the imps disappeared as something dragged him away with enough force to double his entire body over.

Faster and faster he went, until finally whatever it was let go, and he popped back into the world, skidding to a stop on what felt like a road made of rock, which hurt in at least twenty different places. Had that been what the imp meant?

And then Jack looked up to find an enormous metal beast charging straight at him, screaming loudly in a strangely high-pitched squeal of anger as it descended on him, and he realized that THAT was what the imp meant.

"STILTSKIN!" Jack shouted at the top of his lungs as the metal monster descended on him. "STILT . . . SKIN!"

CHAPTER 26

Phillip reappeared back on the familiar battlements of his castle, Penelope and Lian both by his side. All around him, his soldiers and guards were shouting and pointing, and Phillip looked in the direction they were all staring.

There, on the horizon, were six giants, all as tall as mountains, all marching toward the kingdom, followed closely by a giant easily half again as tall, holding a club made of the tallest trees Phillip had ever seen, strapped together.

"Your Highness!" a man shouted, and Phillip turned to find the captain of his guard running toward him. "Thank goodness you've returned!"

"Goodness had nothing to do with it," Phillip said, finding it hard to swallow, his throat was so dry. *He* had betrayed May.

Him! Jack had protected her to the very end, something Phillip himself could not do!

"Where's my father?" Lian demanded, and the captain of the guard looked at her oddly.

"Answer her, my friend," Phillip told him. "Did you find anyone . . . out of place here? Someone who appeared much as we did?"

The guard nodded. "Yesterday, in the throne room. We almost killed him, but he instantly gave up. But how did you know?"

"He's a *genius*," Lian said, looking at Phillip like he were something unpleasant she stepped in on the road. "Where's this out-of-place man?"

"We locked him in the dungeons," the captain of the guard told her. "He refuses to answer any questions, just asks us for news every few minutes." He made a face. "It's quite irritating."

"Runs in the family," Lian said. "Bring him up here. He needs to see this."

The captain of the guard looked at Phillip, who nodded. Whether or not Jack's father needed to see anything, Phillip needed to see *him*. More than ever, after what had just happened.

Penelope touched his shoulder. "You made the only choice you could."

Phillip flinched from her touch and moved to the ramparts to get a better look at the giants. "How far would you say they are?" he asked the nearest guard.

"Maybe a week out, Your Highness. Possibly less."

He nodded, looking at the land in between the castle and the giants. Houses dotted the landscape in the distance, growing more plentiful as they neared the castle, until about a half mile out twenty-foot-high walls enclosed the city proper. "Evacuate everyone outside the walls into the city. I want it done by nightfall."

"Of course, Your Highness," the guard said, and ran off, passing the captain of the guard, who returned with a bearded man wearing horribly dirty rags.

"Your Highness," the captain said, and pushed the man to his knees in front of Phillip, two other guards holding swords on the bedraggled man. "As you requested, the man who appeared in your throne room yesterday."

"I know you won't necessarily believe this," the man in rags said, looking up at Phillip with a half smile. "But you made the smart choice."

Phillip froze. "Excuse me?" he said, his voice barely above a whisper.

The man shrugged. "Leaving the girl. You had to do it, or you might have lost your entire kingdom."

"Because of you," Phillip whispered. "I had to betray someone dear to me, leave her behind in the clutches of pure evil, solely for a tiny chance to save my people. All because of *you*."

"If that helps you."

Something inside Phillip snapped, and he leapt forward, dragging the man to his feet. Phillip grabbed a sword from one of the guards and shoved it into the man's hand, then stood back, taking another sword for himself. "Attack me!"

Jack's father just raised an eyebrow. "Why would I do that?"

"ATTACK. ME."

The man dropped the sword, so Phillip growled and picked it up again, then forced the man to take it. "I cannot strike you if you do not attack me first. I give you permission. Strike me, so that I might avenge my father's death!"

"That'd be pretty stupid of me, then, wouldn't it?" the man said. He pointed with his sword out toward the largest giant. "Besides, I think you want that guy."

"YOU stole from the giant!" Phillip roared, grabbing the man by his rags and holding his sword to the man's throat. "YOU caused my father's death as surely as that giant did! And now *you* made me leave her behind!"

"Phillip," Lian said behind him, "put your sword down, or I will take it from you."

Phillip heard guards surround her, but she didn't seem to care. "My father demands *justice*, Lian," the prince said, his mouth curled into a sneer. "May demands justice!"

"Is that what this is?" Penelope asked him. "'Cause it seems a lot more like guilt."

Phillip looked from the man, who smiled, to Penelope, who was glaring at him, and dropped his sword to the ground. "What . . . am I doing?" he said, sliding to the ground. "I do not know what to do."

Penelope squatted down next to him. "What would your father do right now?"

"He would ride out and defeat the giants."

"By himself?" Penelope snorted. "He wouldn't get far against seven of them."

A few of the guards gasped. "The king bested seven in one *blow*, Princess!"

Phillip looked between Penelope and the guard, then suddenly had the urge to laugh. He chuckled softly at first, then louder and longer, eventually shaking and having trouble breathing, he laughed so hard. "They were *flies!*" he said when he could breathe, between the laughter. "Not giants, flies! My father was a tailor and killed seven flies with one blow. He bragged about doing so, and someone believed that he meant giants somehow. He killed but one giant in his life, and that was almost by accident!"

Lian snorted, and Penelope gave Phillip an odd look. "What are you saying?"

"I am saying that he had no idea what he was doing!" Phillip shouted. "He died fighting the giant in the clouds because he only beat the one giant by luck!"

Penelope shrugged. "So?"

"SO?!"

"You've bested giants, quite a few more than seven," she said. "Who cares what your father did? What matters is what *you* can do. And you can save your kingdom, even if he couldn't."

"Is anyone else hearing this?" Lian said from behind him. "Am I really the only one who thinks we should just run for it?"

"Running won't help," the man in rags said quietly. "He has our scents. He'll hunt everyone in your kingdom down one by one until he finds us."

"How did you escape him the first time?" Phillip asked him.

"I tricked him back into the clouds," the man said. "Your father . . . we'd met before, on another adventure. He might not have killed seven giants, but there was no one more clever. He almost even outwitted me at one point."

Phillip almost laughed again. Jack's father . . . was complimenting his own on his cleverness?

"Together, we convinced the giant I'd escaped back up the beanstalk. He followed me up but took your father. I cut the beanstalk down and trapped him up there," Jack's father said. "He was never *that* big, though. He must have only been a teenager when I met him, because he's almost double the size now. He could climb down from the clouds and not hurt himself. There's only one option."

"We have to defeat him," Phillip said, standing up and wiping his face with his sleeve. For some reason, he felt better.

Lian stepped over to the wall. "So, how do we do this?"

"We?" Phillip asked her. "I never asked for your help."

"Oh, I'm going to help you now," she said, "and then you're going to help *me* take down the Queen once and for all." Lian paused, staring at her father. "She . . . stabbed Jack in the heart, Father. With his own sword."

The man raised an eyebrow, then threw a look at Phillip. "I see."

Lian and her father shared another look, but Phillip ignored them both, sizing up the houses between the giants and the castle again. Perhaps they might have a chance after all. "I may have a plan. But we will need help. And for that, I will need you two," he said, turning to Penelope and Lian. "What would you say to asking some friends for their assistance?"

Lian looked between Phillip and Penelope, then sighed. "I really don't like where this is going."

Phillip grinned. "No. You will not. Though I do hope you know where to find some mermaid tears."

His satisfied expression lasted for all of two seconds before a pirate monkey landed on his face, screeching in happiness to see him.

CHAPTER 27

The Wicked Queen pulled the sword out of her heart and handed it to May with just a trace of sadness. "You weren't the first to try that."

The sword dropped from May's hand as she struggled to speak. "But . . . you . . . no!"

"There's nothing there to hurt, May," the Queen said. "It hasn't always been such. At one point, I was much like you, of course. So much like you." She reached a hand out to touch May's cheek, but May shuddered and pulled away.

The Queen narrowed her eyes, and grabbed May's chin, pulling her toward her, electricity playing between her fingers. "I could kill you now," she said, her voice now quieter. "I could do it, don't you see? The part of me that held me back before, that part died in the other world. Magic is weak there, if it exists, and dies away quickly. So there. . . ." She moved, and her shadow moved a fraction of a second later, as if it weren't just an absence of light but a second figure. "There, these shadows that haunt me could not live forever. And neither could I."

"You didn't feel anything," May said, every word a struggle against the Queen's grasp on her jaw. "You *never* loved me!"

The Queen's eyes flashed like a lightning bolt, and she raised a hand to slap May, her face a grotesque mask of hatred. But she paused, then lowered her hand.

"Perhaps I should share . . . a story," she said, and gestured. The room morphed around them, and May found herself in a chamber that seemed to extend higher than the sky, all four walls completely covered with books. A table in front of her could barely be seen under stacks of books four or five high, with titles like *Thrilling Tales of Science* and *The Myths and Stories of the Norsemen*.

The Queen pointed, and May turned to find a book resting on a pedestal, its cover blackened and charred as if it'd been on fire yet somehow survived.

The Queen gestured at the book, then stepped away, her back to May. May rubbed her aching jaw, then, not knowing what else to do, she stepped over to the book and pulled open the enormous cover, wondering if it would fall apart in her fingers.

Instead, it felt as solid as a brand-new book. Inside was a beautiful painting, a watercolor picture of a girl with black hair and a joyful smile, holding an armful of apples.

Once upon a time, Princess Eudora lived happily with her king father and queen mother, the perfect family, content in every way. If the princess had a flaw, and many would argue that she did not, it would be that she was a trifle vain and believed herself to be the most beautiful girl to ever live.

Yet even with a dash of arrogance, Eudora was good and kind and loving, treating any and all equally and justly, even her uncle, who was jealous that the princess would take over the kingdom instead of he himself.

The next page showed a painting of the princess sitting by a well in a courtyard, singing with some birds, while a man dressed in black watched from above, his expression clearly not loving.

The man looked . . . familiar. Black hair and a gaunt face. Where had she seen that?

For a while, the princess lived happily, unaware of
her uncle's plot against her. But then her parents were
called away to visit another kingdom, and she was left
alone with the man. And her uncle wasted no time.

The painting here showed Eudora's uncle grabbing the princess from behind and stabbing her in the heart.

The court magician, desperate to save the girl,
tried everything he could. No medicine, no herb, no
magic he knew of could keep the girl alive. So, despite
his reservations, the man turned to the shadows to
save his princess.

This time, the girl lay on what looked like a funeral pyre while a river of shadows flew into the spot where her heart was.

Her heart was just a step away from death, so the
shadows healed it so that it might beat forever, then
removed it from her body and hid it away in a wooden
box, filling her chest with their evil. That evil kept her
alive, but turned her into a shadow of her former self.

The girl stood over the magician, who cowered in terror from her. One of her hands was raised, and blue lightning played through her fingers in a very familiar way.

Her uncle, upon learning she still lived, tried
again to murder her, but without a heart in her body,
Eudora could not be hurt. And the heart in the box
had its own protection: The shadows had placed a
cruel curse upon it.

Now the princess stood behind her uncle, who frantically attacked the girl, desperate to somehow kill the monster he'd unknowingly created.

Indeed, the princess's heart was now safe, but for
the very thing that had hurt her in the first place . . .

May turned the page, but the rest of the book had been ripped out. She put it back down on the floor, only to have it disappear in a sizzle of lightning.

"I apologize for the abrupt ending," the Queen said from behind her. "But the story revealed a bit too much. You'd be surprised how much power it took just to destroy those pages." She smiled mockingly. "The shadow's curse is less effective when no one knows it but me."

"So . . . they live in you now?" May asked, pushing herself away as subtly as possible.

"They do in this world," the Queen told her, her expression completely devoid of any love or joy. "As I said, in the other world they were weakened and dying. I would not have lived much longer, in fact. But . . . I was much like my old self, from before my treacherous uncle decided to murder me."

And despite herself, despite the stories, despite the cruelty and hatred and horribleness, May actually felt something other than fear of the woman. "Maybe there's a way to cure you," she said quietly.

The Queen smiled just a bit. "If there was, it has been lost to the ages. I myself don't have the power, and I am the most powerful magic-user still alive in this world. I know, for I killed any more powerful than myself early on."

"The fairy queens—"

"They would kill me as soon as cure me, but even they'd find that practically impossible. Not without the knowledge of the curse."

"The missing pages," May said.

The Queen smiled again. "There are those who knew, of course. Malevolent figured it out before she betrayed me. That was why I had to take the Mirror from her: She knew far too much. Of course, it turned into quite the benefit on its own, but I've found ways to make do without it."

Malevolent knew? If that was true, then the Queen's secrets had died with the fairy queen. But what, then, was the Fairest supposed to have done . . . ?

"And Snow White . . . she found out as well, as the Mirror warned me she would," the Queen said. "I sometimes wonder if she would have bothered if I hadn't ordered my stepdaughter's death in the first place. Again, that was my weakness. I could not do the deed myself, as too much of my former self still lived. Sometimes we fulfill our own prophecies, I suppose."

"Snow White knew?" May said.

"Not that she can tell," the Queen said with a smile. "She will never awaken from my poison. The one cure for that died long ago."

"The Charmed One," May said, and suddenly things began to fall into place.

The Queen gestured again, and the library disappeared,

replaced by a smaller room with maps all over the walls and tables. On the right side of the map (she would have said east, but who knew in this world what direction was what) were the occupied lands, with little statues of goblins, ogres, trolls, and other assorted monsters representing the Queen's armies, all staked out around the lands.

On the other side were the free kingdoms, and May recognized a few different places: Giant's Hand, the village she'd first appeared in; the Black Forest, where they'd found the Wolf King; Phillip's kingdom, which they'd visited shortly after releasing the Queen from the Palace of the Snow Queen; Bluebeard's kingdom on the shore; even Malevolent's castle. But there were far more kingdoms that she'd never seen and probably wouldn't ever at this point. And all those kingdoms had little figurines of men and women with swords, apparently representing the armies of those who remained.

"What do you see?" the Queen asked her.

May looked at the map, then at the Queen. "A bunch of toys. Why, did you want me to play too?"

The Queen smiled. "Be my guest."

May carefully chose a few human figures with swords, then smashed them into the castle marked Capitol, the Queen's kingdom. She swept away all the monster figurines with her arm, then knocked the entire table over.

A moment later, everything was just as it was and May slammed into the castle wall hard enough to knock the breath out of her.

"Let me show you what *I* intend," the Queen told her, lightning playing in her eyes. She gestured, and tiny portals opened over every goblin, ogre, troll, and monster figurine. Each one disappeared, then popped back into existence all over the map. No, not *all* over . . . in the free kingdoms.

Within the city and castle walls.

"It honestly isn't very complicated," the Queen told her. "The fairy queens are the only ones who could have stopped me from using magic to invade every single free kingdom at once. But my little Eye's last task for me ensured that the fairy queens won't be a concern, no matter how hard you worked to save them."

"What . . . do you mean?" May said, gasping for air. Whatever held her up on the wall also made it difficult to breathe.

"Fairy queens use music to perform their magic," the Queen told her. "Always seemed like a weakness to me. After all, it doesn't take much to throw a song off harmony."

"That . . . harp thing?" May said.

The Queen nodded. "Not the most powerful magic, I'll grant you. But sometimes a pebble is enough to start an avalanche. And as soon as the fairy queens try to stop me, I'll turn their music into something they never imagined."

The kingdoms on the left side of the map burst into flame, one by one. May thought she could even hear screams coming from the map, and cries of victory by the various monsters.

And the biggest monster of all just smiled. "You see what is to come. But I am not without consideration for what you once meant to me. Join me, May. Join me and rule this world as my heir, the future queen. You think you've known these people all your life through the stories you were told as a child. But those stories *lied*, May." She made a fist. "Snow White does *not* come back to life. The Wicked Queen does *not* die. And Cinderella . . . I offer her an entire world instead of a prince."

"And what . . . if I say . . . no?"

The Queen frowned. "Then you will be made into a lesson and put to death for all the world to see as I invade the remaining kingdoms in seven days' time."

"Why wait?" May gasped. "Why not just do it now?"

The Queen gave her a curious look. "I can't reveal *all* my

secrets, can I? Let us just say that Phillip isn't quite through helping me yet."

"They'll fight back," May said, the room starting to swim before her eyes. "The people . . . they'll fight. They'll . . . beat you. Evil always . . . loses to good!"

The Queen laughed. "Oh, my darling May. You've read *far* too many fairy tales."

CHAPTER 28

The metal beast roared to a stop, screeching its feet with a high-pitched squeal that rivaled its scream. And then, terrifyingly, a person poked their head *out the side of the monster* and shouted at Jack.

"What are you doing?" the apparently half-eaten person screamed. "Get out of the road!"

Something yanked Jack to his feet and out of the path of the metal beast. Horribly, the beast's translucent upper body revealed that it hadn't just eaten the one angry man, but a confused woman as well. Anger and confusion both seemed pretty legitimate feelings for having been eaten, so Jack forgave the yelling, wondering if he should try to help them escape, considering they hadn't been digested yet.

A woman pulled him from the stone road and onto another, less wide and differently colored stone road on the side, where a growing mob of people watched.

"Are you okay?" the woman asked him, holding his shoulders and staring into his face. "Did you get hit?"

Jack shook his head. "No, I'm okay." The metal beast that had attacked him had wandered away, and he noticed for the first time that the entire road was full of meandering metal beasts, all full of humans being digested.

Odd.

"You look so pale, though," the woman said, frowning in worry.

"Oh, I was dead a few hours ago," Jack told her. "Or pretty close. It's been a strange day."

"Call 911," the woman told a short, pudgy man in black clothes with thin white stripes. "I think he's delirious." She pointed at his armor. "Maybe he wandered away from a Renaissance Faire. Probably got hit in the head with a mace or something."

The man in the black clothes with thin white stripes pulled a small card out and began to push at it with a pudgy finger. The card made odd noises, and the man lifted it to his ear and began talking softly. Maybe the card was numbered 911 of a thousand? "I really am fine," Jack said, "but I could use some help. I'm looking for a girl named May. I'm not entirely sure where I am. Or where she is."

"What's her name?" the woman asked, turning Jack's head back toward her.

". . . May," he said for the second time.

"I mean her last name."

"Her last name? She's only had one as far as I know. Do you switch names a lot here?"

"No, her second name, her last . . . May *what?*"

"May, a girl I know," Jack said, getting irritated with this whole thing.

"I give up," she said, taking his hand and pulling him to some nearby grass. "Just have a seat. The cops will be here soon, and they'll figure things out."

Jack reluctantly sat down on the grass, not sure what cops were, but hoping they'd at the very least not make him repeat names over and over.

A black and white metal beast with crazy red eyes on its back came running down the street, screaming its high-pitched squeal, then screeched to a stop right in front of Jack. A man and woman dressed entirely in black *opened the beast up*—which practically turned Jack's stomach—then closed it again and walked over.

"What happened here?" the woman in black said.

"I think he's from a Renaissance Faire," the woman said. "He almost got hit by a car. Something's wrong with his head."

"Are you okay?" the man in black asked.

"I'm from another world," Jack told them. "My clothes look a little odd to you, I guess. But I'm just looking for a friend of mine. Her name's May. Can you help me find her?"

The man in black looked at the woman in black, and a moment later, Jack found himself being shoved into the metal beast's stomach. Surprisingly comfortable as it was, he waited for the two "cops" to walk away, then tried to open the beast back up and run, only he couldn't figure out how.

"We're going to take you to the hospital and call your parents," the woman in black told him as she opened a separate part of the monster. "What's your name?"

"Jack," he told her.

"Last name?"

"It's always been Jack."

She turned and looked at him. "LAST. NAME?"

Okay, seriously, was this some kind of horrible torture?

And then he remembered something May had said once, something that he hadn't even thought about at the time, but now—

"Winterborne," he said. "That's my, uh, last name." She'd called her grandmother Eudora Winterborne. Two names.

"What's your address?"

"I, um, can't remember, I'm too delirious."

The woman glared at him again, but pushed on something toward the front of the monster that had letters on it, like the monster had swallowed a book. "I've got a *Eudora* Winterborne—"

"That's HER!" Jack yelled. "That's my, uh, grandmother. She's taking care of me."

"Those Renaissance Faires can be nasty business," the woman in black told the man in black. "Kid probably got smacked in the head with a mace."

The monster ran on, as other metal creatures ran out in front and behind it, each one with at least one person inside it, slowly digesting. At least Jack knew that he could survive it as long as he got out quickly enough. He shifted back and forth, trying to keep anything from eating away at him while he waited for them to reach wherever it was that the cops were taking him.

As it turned out, it was to a large white building with giant white metal monsters waiting in front of it.

"Your grandmother isn't home," the woman said, dropping a small card like the pudgy man had talked into. "It isn't far, though . . . just over on Hough Street." Jack repeated the strange name to himself as she and the man opened the monster and stepped out, then opened the creature for Jack to get out too.

"What are you doing out of school, anyway?" the man in black asked him.

School. Would that be where May was now?

"I escaped," Jack told him. "You should take me back. It's only fair. I need to be punished, and I'm sure the school wants to do it."

The man looked at him oddly. "Maybe after we make sure you're healthy."

Two men in white came out and led Jack inside.

And that's when the torture began. Men and women in white asked him insane questions, stuck him with impossibly long and fat needles, and forced him through all sorts of demeaning and, frankly, pretty chilly tests.

Two hours later, Jack ran through the front doors, his armor in a bag on his back, wearing a T-shirt that said COOK COUNTY HOSPITAL; a pair of extremely baggy blue pants, tied at the waist;

and new shoes that had belonged to someone named "Dona-tion," apparently.

Odd names, here in Punk.

Behind him, the men and women in white screamed his name and ran after him, but he didn't stop. The man and woman in black had left, which was good . . . he couldn't take another nauseating ride in a metal monster.

Instead, he ran off in the general direction an unsuspecting nurse had pointed when he'd asked for the nearest school. May would be there, and if not . . . there was always Hough Street.

Either way, he had one last thing to steal.

CHAPTER 29

May closed her eyes, knowing this was the end. It'd been a good run, but her grandmother was going to kill her.

"It's not that bad," Jacqueline told her, taking the pop quiz out of her hand.

"You could totally just change that C to a . . . well, no, you're stuck," Moira said, grabbing the paper from Jacqueline, then shrugging. "What'd she say last time?"

"One more C, and I'm grounded until my grandchildren graduate college," May said. "The joke's on her, though. My grandkids are going to be geniuses and go to college at, like, age four."

"That'll teach her," Moira said, nodding. "Or you could just not show her."

May shivered. "She'll know. She *always* knows. Everything. Doesn't matter. I can't hide anything from that woman. It's like she can read my mind or something."

Some guy walked by them whom May hadn't seen before, and threw a look her way, then a second one. She frowned. New student? As Moira and Jacqueline kept offering suggestions, May watched as the new guy went up to a locker and started to fiddle with the lock, then looked at her again, then quickly looked away. He seemed to be wearing scrubs from a hospital, and he carried a very large, very clanky bag.

"Then, I'd take the ashes of the burnt test and burn *those*," Jacqueline was saying, but Moira stopped her.

"Why is that guy staring at you?" Moira whispered to May.

"I don't know," May whispered back. "Why are we whispering."

"Because he might be listening."

"From down the hall?"

"You understand how listening works? We make sounds with our mouths, and those sounds travel through air. Since there's air between here and there, it's possible that those sounds will actually reach his ears, even down the hall. It's complicated, so I get that you haven't figured it out yet."

May nodded absently. "Totally. What do you think he wants?"

Jacqueline frowned. "It looks like to get in his locker. Apparently, he doesn't want it bad enough, though. Maybe that's where he's keeping his actual pants."

She was right, the guy seemed to be twisting the knob over and over in one direction, like he had never seen a lock before.

Eh, why not? "Hey, they not have locks where you're from?" May said loud enough for the guy to hear her. "You need help or something?"

The boy looked up and blushed deeply. "I'm, uh, new here."

"I couldn't tell," May said, instantly feeling bad for him. "What's your combination?"

"My . . . what?"

"The numbers. They gave you in the office. Three numbers."

He blushed again. "I should go. I didn't, um, get numbers. I'll go ask them . . . where did you say?"

May pointed back toward the office, still staring at the boy. "You want me to take you there?"

He kept playing with the lock as if he might luck into the right numbers. "You don't need to be so nice. It's . . . odd."

May gave him a strange look. "What a normal thing to say. Well, good luck with making friends, what with your completely friendly outlook and all." With that, she turned around and walked back to Moira and Jacqueline. The next strange boy she met, she was going to insult straightaway. Apparently, that was what they expected.

"Weird," Jacqueline said. "He keeps looking over here."

May grabbed both of their arms and led them away, shaking her head. "Let's ignore the creepy boy and figure out a way for me to stay alive, how about that? You know what I need? A distraction."

Moira stopped, and gave May an evil look, grabbing a lock of her hair. "You know what would distract her from your test? Jacquie, you got any more of that blue hair dye?"

May's eyes widened, and she shook her head, stepping away from both girls. "NO."

Jacqueline and Moira both grinned evilly at her, and she took another step back. "NO!"

"YES!" they said, and grabbed her arms, dragging her toward the door.

As they led her out, chatting about where to put it and how blue to make it, May threw one last look over her shoulder. Maybe the strange, annoying boy would distract them, and she could make a run for it.

But the boy was gone, which was just as well. She didn't need help saving herself. If Jacqueline and Moira thought they could get away with this, they had another thing coming. And that other thing would be blue dye all over *their* hair too.

And with that, May grabbed the other girls and led *them* out the door.

CHAPTER 30

WHAT WAS HE DOING?! Jack had no idea how time worked, or how he could possibly be meeting May before he actually met May, or if that would change things when he DID meet May when she fell through the fire circle into his village.

He pushed his back against the wall, his heart racing. And to talk to her?! There was no reason to take the chance!

Not to mention the knob on the metal door with the numbers. Could he have looked stupider? Probably not, and that was saying something!

Another kid walked past him, giving him an odd look, and Jack realized he looked incredibly suspicious, especially with his bag full of extremely loud armor, so he coughed, shrugged, then pushed through doors made of glass into a room across from where he'd been standing, a room where other students in this enormous school seemed to be gathering.

The smell hit him first—slightly musty, slightly papery. And then he realized that this wasn't just a room. This was a room filled with books. FILLED with books. More books than he'd ever seen in his life, multiplied by about a thousand.

"Oh, *wow*," he said, stopping in place.

Then the doors of glass hit him in the behind as another student pushed in, and Jack decided that maybe the entrance to whatever this was might not be the best place to stand. Instead, he dove in, wandering between shelves absolutely filled with books.

"Can I help you find anything?" asked an older woman with a friendly face.

Jack opened his mouth, then realized he had no idea what to say. What kind of book could he ask about? He had no idea what any of them were!

"You know, just looking around," he told her, trying to act as if he had been in so many book rooms that they just couldn't impress him anymore. "Books. Stories. That kind of thing. You know."

She smiled. "Stories? What kind do you like? Maybe I can recommend something."

The panic hit for the second time, and he frantically searched his memory. May must have said *something* about their stories here! She'd heard of Jack's world, she'd heard of the Wicked Queen and Snow White . . . what had she called those stories?

"Well, I like fairy bottoms," he told the woman, giving her a knowing smile.

"I'm sorry?" she said, her smile fading. "*What* did you say?"

"Tails!" he shouted. "I like fairy tails!"

She gave him an odd look. "Fairy tales have actually been pretty popular lately, but I think we've got a few still in the library." She led him through the shelves, winding in and out, before bending down to the very bottom shelf and grabbing a few books. "What have you read?"

"The usual stuff. The one with Snow White."

"Ever read any Jack tales?" the woman asked without looking up.

Any *what* now?

"Can't say I have," Jack told her, his voice barely squeaking out.

She handed him a book called *English Fairy Tales*. TALES. Right. Whoops. "Those are fun. He's my favorite."

"English? Who is *he*?"

She stared at him. "Right. English as in British. From England. I mean Jack. I read all those as a child, I used to love them. 'Jack and the Beanstalk,' that kind of thing. You must know that one."

He nodded. "Pretty well at this point." Was this for real?

"Take a look, you might like some of the others. Here's a copy of *Grimm's Fairy Tales*, and Hans Christian Andersen. You might think you know the stories from movies and all, but the originals are very different."

Jack looked at the cover of the book *English Fairy Tales*, with a picture of a boy climbing a beanstalk, and nodded. "You have no idea how different."

She gave him another odd look, so he quickly thanked her and retreated to a table, like the other students did, and opened the beanstalk book first.

Once upon a time . . .

Jack read through the first story, then the next, and the next, his stomach dropping through his shoes. These were his *family's* stories! His father, his grandfather, even some hints of what he had done in the giant's castle in the clouds!

People could just read about his life without him knowing?! Were they watching him now, watching him read about himself, that they were then reading, and—

Probably not. But that woman had said she loved these stories and thought of Jack (or, well, all the Jacks) as a hero. But the Jacks in the stories did what Jacks had always done, which wasn't always heroic or anything . . . sometimes it was exactly the opposite, outwitting and outplaying people just to win.

But here . . . they liked that. Just like the Wicked Queen had said. Here, they admired people like him.

He set the *English Fairy Tales* book aside, feeling something odd that he hadn't felt in a long time, and turned to the next book, flipping through it only to stop abruptly at one story.

Snow White and the Seven Dwarfs.

This time, he couldn't even feel his stomach. He quickly flipped through to the end of the story, where Snow White looked like she died, so some dwarfs put her in a glass box and left her. Then along came a prince and woke her up, and the two got married. He shook his head. When had *that* happened? And the Wicked Queen went to the wedding and danced herself to death in red-hot iron shoes? . . . Uh?

Jack quickly read the entire story, then read it again. It had a magic mirror, so that part made sense, but when had the rest of this happened? Snow White had been in a coffin made of ice when he'd last seen her, before the Wolf King had stolen her away.

Wait.

Did that mean she could be woken up?

He quickly flipped through the next book, finding far too many familiar stories. "Rapunzel." "Tom Thumb," a boy who sounded a lot like a younger Captain Thomas, at least in size. "Little Red Riding Hood," just like the outfit Rose Red had worn.

All stories from his Story Book, the one he'd given to the imps in the past. Had the stories of his world really survived all those years? Apparently whoever the imps had sold them to had been pretty smart storytellers!

Of course, there were a bunch of stories that didn't sound familiar, like one called "Donkey Cabbages," and another called "Cinderella." Weird titles, but maybe those were made up at some point.

He'd have to read further; these could be useful. But he couldn't just stay here all night.

A girl stood up and carried a few books over to a desk, where a man stamped them, then handed them back. Only, the girl had also handed the man some sort of card, which he handed back to her with the books. She then walked out the doors of glass, books and all.

Had she bought them, paid for them somehow with the card?

Not that it mattered: Jack had nothing. But these books could be extremely useful. . . .

It wasn't like he hadn't done worse things already. So Jack picked up the three books, even the creepy stories about his family, grabbed his bag, and walked toward the man at the desk, who smiled at him.

Then, at the last second, Jack made a run for it.

Something screamed in his ears, but he didn't stop, plowing through the doors as the man shouted behind him that he needed to check something. With the grating screaming noise in his ears, Jack took off down the hallway and right out the door he'd seen May leave by, and didn't stop running until he reached some woods nearby.

All night, he read about his own family, about the heroes and villains of his world, and about the way all the heroes always lived happily ever after. But the heroes of the books weren't like Phillip, not for the most part. Usually they were just some kid, often not even a firstborn, who was smart enough to outwit whatever the story threw at him.

If people in this world really did look up to people who used their brains . . . why was he leaving?

The next morning, he crept up to the school, left all three

books in front of the door leading inside, then took off again. At least he didn't feel so bad about things now. And he had so many new ideas.

Now all he needed to do was find the Wicked Queen's house, which was somewhere on a Hough Street, whatever that was.

The iron shoes would be a good Plan B.

CHAPTER 31

Phillip concentrated, his entire soul dedicated to the task before him. This would be the difference between life and death, between the lives of his subjects and the ruin of his kingdom.

He held his work up to look at it critically, as every detail counted. "It is not very pretty," he said, tilting his head to get a better angle.

The guards around him stopped their sewing and gave the cord he had just sewn a look. Even the monkey looked up from his job to look at Phillip thoughtfully.

"I've seen worse, Your Highness," one said.

"You're doing a fine job, Your Highness," said another.

"'Tis unto a flower bloomin' in dawn's first breath, Your Highness," said a third.

Phillip shrugged. "I suppose it does not have to look good. How fare the rest of you?"

The others held their cords up for inspection, and Phillip nodded, then glanced out the window at the hundreds of yards of cord that led from the window to the courtyard below, gathering in huge piles below where other guards wrapped the cord onto wheels, and townsfolk and guards alike rolled those wheels out of the castle, through town, and out into the countryside.

"I'm back," Penelope said, and Phillip jumped. He never did hear the girl come in.

"How did your task go?" he asked her, noticing that she was covered in dirt and smelled like music.

The princess smiled, petting the monkey on the head. "I convinced some of them, and they'll work on the others. It might take a few days, but I think they'll be here."

That was a bit slapdash for him, given the stakes, but it was not as if he had any choice. "I would have preferred them here before the giants arrived, but I suppose we are on our own there. What about Lian? Has she returned?"

Penelope shrugged. "I'll have to see. I came straight here to see how the sewing's going. You've done a lot!"

"A prince does what one must," Phillip said, turning from

her back to sewing lengths of rope together to make an extremely thick, strong cord.

Penelope looked at him for a minute, then sat down next to him. "You know, I wasn't ever allowed to do this," she said, watching Phillip's needle threaded in and out. "Too many spindles involved. But the fairy queens used to find it very relaxing, they said. They'd often sit for hours, sewing, singing, telling stories . . ."

"We have no time for singing or stories, unfortunately," Phillip said.

"I have a story!" one of the guards said.

"No one wants to hear your invisible gnome story, especially not the prince!" said another.

"I *would* actually like to hear it at a later time," Phillip told the crestfallen guard. "For I myself had some trouble with an invisible gnome."

"Did he steal your pants too, Your Majesty?"

"Did he, Phillip?" Penelope asked, her eyes opening a bit wider than usual. "I'm guessing yes, considering you're blushing again."

Philip turned back to his sewing. "I do not see how that is relevant."

"The point is," Penelope continued, "they found sewing an

easy way to take their mind off their troubles." She nudged his shoulder. "Not that *you* have any troubles, right? But you just stay here and keep at it. I'll go find out if anyone's heard from Lian, or if the sharks ate her."

Phillip glanced up at her, at her gentle smile, and could not help but smile back. The repetitive task of sewing *had* taken his mind off things, things he would rather not remember.

Things like the look on May's face when he had left her in the Wicked Queen's clutches.

Penelope quietly left the room, or so Phillip supposed, as when he looked again, she was gone.

"Begging your pardon, Your Majesty," one of the guards said. "But why are the princess and that . . . other girl—"

"Lian," Phillip said absently.

"The, uh, Eye, yes," the guard said, his face clouding. "Not that it's my place to suggest that we throw her out the nearest window, as it's only a matter of time until she betrays us—"

"She would not be the first to do so this week," Phillip said quietly.

"But shouldn't those two be bringing our friends and allies here as soon as possible? Don't we need all the help we can get here to take care of those giants?"

The ground shook, just as it did every few seconds, as if in response. The giants weren't far off now . . . maybe a day, probably less.

"We will face more than the giants if we live through the attack," Phillip told the guard, and all the guards. "There will be evil greater than any of us have ever seen, and it will come calling for our very heads. And when it comes, we will need all the help we can find." He sighed. "Meanwhile, the giants cannot be faced with strength or numbers. Whatever we put up against them, they will overcome. It is their nature to overpower. But this . . ." He held up the cord. "This cord that we make . . . this has its own power. There is power in cleverness and wisdom, too. A lesson I would have done well to learn before now."

"So . . . say we survive . . ." the guard said.

"A mighty big 'if,' there," said another.

"Have faith, my friends," Phillip said. "Not because we are noble and good and worthy of victory, though I believe in this battle, we are. The noble, unfortunately, do not always win. No, victory goes to the side that outwits the other side. And I would be a poor prince if I did not try everything I could to save my people." He smiled. "Even a bit of trickery."

A hand touched Phillip's shoulder, and he looked up to see

Jack's father looking down on him with something resembling pride.

"I won't say what I'm thinking," the man said, "most likely because you don't want to hear it."

"You are correct," Phillip told him. "I would not want to hear it."

"Jack would be pleasantly surprised by you right now, Phillip."

Phillip shook his head, then stood up, dropping the cord from his hands. "This will have to be enough. Everyone, gather what cord you have and join me in the courtyard." He looked at Jack's father, then shook his head. "Even you. I will need your . . . expertise."

"With what, exactly?" the man said, raising one eyebrow and smiling. He knew, but he wished to make Phillip say the words. If words were all that stood between Phillip's kingdom and destruction, then words it would be.

"I officially request the aid of one Jack the Giant Killer in the slaying of up to and including seven giants that are currently on their way toward my kingdom."

The man nodded, still smiling. "All you needed to do was ask." He picked up a length of cord, then stopped once more. "Oh, and Phillip? This plan will work on six of them. Maybe. But not the big one. Not the one that killed your father. That one won't fall for this like the others will."

This time, Phillip smiled. "If you outwitted him, how hard can he be?"

And at that, Jack's father roared with laughter.

CHAPTER 32

May, now complete with blue streak in her hair, stumbled out of her front door looking bleary-eyed in the morning light. What felt like hours later, a beautiful woman with dark, slightly gray-streaked hair left as well, getting into one of the metal wagons waiting in front of their house.

And yes, they were wagons. Jack had realized that eventually. Embarrassingly eventually.

The wagon backed up into the road, then groaned much like May had as it rolled its way toward town.

Now was as good a time as any to steal the Queen's wooden heart box.

Dressed in his Eye armor once more, Jack sized up the house. It'd taken him long enough to find. Just knowing the name of the street hadn't helped as much as he'd have thought. How many streets did Punk need? Giant's Hand, where he'd grown up, had *one* . . . and not even that in some places.

Even when he'd found the right street, he'd come across a worse problem. So many houses! And all looked exactly the same!

Part of him wondered if he should just walk down the street, knocking on every door until he found the right one.

A smarter part of him decided to use what little magic remained in his sword to sniff out the Wicked Queen like a bloodhound.

And so here he was. He hadn't ever broken into a home before—just castles, really—but how hard could it be? There was bound to be an open door or window, after all. No one had the money to put locks on *every* way in or out, and who locked their doors anyway?

Apparently May and her grandmother, because both doors Jack found were locked tight. Not to mention the windows. All except one window left open on the second floor of the house (which in and of itself was insane . . . how much money did they have to be able to build an entire second story? Out of what looked like fake wood?! How could it even support itself?)

Second floors meant higher climbs, and climbing was the last thing Jack really felt like doing right now. Fortunately, a convenient tree rose near enough to the open window that one might climb it, shimmy out on a branch, then jump for one's life and maybe, if one was lucky, grasp the windowsill with the edge of one's fingers.

Jack, however, was not one to be lucky on any sort of regular basis.

"I just climbed a stupid beanstalk!" he said to no one in particular. "TWICE, really, if you count the last half a year!"

No one in particular responded, which didn't entirely surprise him. In fact, if someone *had* responded, Jack might have jumped in surprise, then suggested that maybe that person climb the tree, jump to the window, then come downstairs and let Jack in.

Life was never easy.

Jack stared up at the tree, ready to go. That lasted a minute or two, after which he actually got his hands onto the tree and began to climb. That lasted another minute or two before he realized that climbing trees in Punk somehow seemed more difficult. Trees back home always seemed to have convenient hand- and footholds, and one could scurry up them like a squirrel. Here, though, Jack scraped his way up, then slid back down (also scraping) no less than five times before realizing he might need to think this through a bit.

Behind him in the yard, there was some sort of metal sculpture, rusted metal rods with chains hanging down from them, the chains holding some sort of odd-looking seat. He looked from the chained seats to the tree and back, and realized one of these might be just what he needed. Out came the sword, its remaining magic giving it just enough sharpness to slice through the chains, which was fortunate. If he'd had to cut through them without any magic, the Huntsman would be there and gone for a few weeks before he'd finish.

Back the sword went into its scabbard, and back Jack went to the tree. He wrapped the seat around the tree and grasped an end of chain in each hand, then, holding the chains as tightly as he could, used them as support to anchor himself as he walked slowly up the tree.

This, in a way, was magic too.

Unfortunately, this kind of magic took forever, so he grabbed a branch that looked sturdy enough to support him as soon as he could, then used that branch to climb to the one leading to the open window. Inside he could see a familiar scene, and he pulled out the Story Book pages to compare.

Walls white as clouds. An enormous bed covered with soft lin-ens. A wooden desk with a now not-glowing square sitting on it.

Yup. This was May's bedroom.

He got a chill out of nowhere and almost fell from the tree then and there. She may not have known who the unconscious person was on the ground beneath her tree, but May still would have laughed at him, he was sure.

The jump didn't look quite so bad from closer up, so without thinking, Jack pushed off and went for it.

"Without thinking" was actually a very accurate description, for if he had thought, he might have realized that the branch, while sturdy enough to support him, would still flex a bit when he jumped.

As it was, his fingers passed through nothing, only to smack into the windowsill at the very last moment, catching him. His heart racing, he pulled himself up and into the house, deciding that this was the very last time he'd ever steal, no matter how many worlds needed saving.

May's bedroom may have looked exactly like the painting in the Story Book, but stepping into that painting was even odder than seeing it in front of him. He looked around, drinking it in, trying not to think about what had happened to May back in the

Wicked Queen's castle . . . and then realized that being in her room was kinda creepy, and he shouldn't just stand there not moving for any longer.

Besides, he had a house to search.

Flipping through his Story Book pages as he opened May's door, he came to the picture of the wooden box that May's grandmother had mentioned, or would mention later that night, when the Huntsman came. "Someone broke into the house, May," the Story Book had the Queen saying. "Someone stole my heart box."

The picture showed a mostly obscured box covered by books, clothes, and a bunch of unrecognizable things. Fortunately, he didn't have to know what they were, he just had to . . . well, recognize them. How hard could that be?

An hour later, he knew exactly how hard that could be. How many things could two people actually own?! The entire house seemed filled with objects, as far as Jack was concerned. They lived like royalty (no surprise), with almost as many books as the school had!

Just then, a *thump* right outside the house made Jack's heart stop, and he looked around frantically for somewhere to hide. The door he'd come in led to the front of the house, and from the sound of it, whoever had just returned was coming in that same direction. Behind him was nothing but wall, except for a small half door mostly covered in piles of books.

Well, he couldn't replace the piles, but at least he'd be out of sight.

He pushed the piles out of the way quickly, then yanked on the door. It didn't move, so he yanked harder and harder, and the door exploded open with a loud *creak* as he heard the footsteps outside stop.

Jack quickly pushed his way into a tiny alcove filled with more books, clothing, and a bunch of things he'd never seen, then pulled the door shut behind him. He pushed himself back, only to run up against something hard and . . . boxlike. . . .

Of course. He couldn't have found this five minutes ago?!

The footsteps were in the house now, slowly walking from room to room. Whoever it was must have heard him and started looking for him.

Maybe it was time. It had to be the Queen herself, and now was as good a time as any. He felt around behind him in the darkness, moving more by memory of the Story Book picture than anything, until his hand felt the wood of the heart box. He quickly pulled it to him and opened it, reaching a hand inside to feel something . . . pretty disgusting.

Then the disgusting thing *ba-bumped* in his hand.

It was her heart.

The Wicked Queen's heart.

HE HAD THE WICKED QUEEN'S HEART IN HIS HAND. AND IT WAS BEATING.

IN HIS *HAND*.

His mind couldn't take this kind of crazy, but what choice did he have? The footsteps stopped right outside of the half door that hid him, and he knew that he might not ever have another chance.

He took out his knife and took a deep breath.

Then he stabbed his knife right into the Wicked Queen's heart.

It didn't even make a dent.

"Hello?" said a voice. "You called about a leaking sink? I'm here to fix it. . . ."

And just then, the door swung wide open.

An old man wearing rumpled gray clothes and holding a box of tools stared at Jack; and Jack, one hand holding a beating heart and the other clutching his knife, stared back.

The old man paused, then slowly closed the door.

Then the old man ran, screaming.

Well. Uh-oh.

CHAPTER 33

May sat alone on her bed, knees pulled against her chest, staring at the dress made of gold that lay draped over a chair across from her. Goblin maids (still holding evil-looking axes and swords) had brought it earlier and taken her last one away. Apparently, becoming the Queen's heir was more formal than being judged a traitor.

She would appear before the Queen, wearing the Queen's dress, and pledge her eternal loyalty to her Majesty. And for that, she would get to live, and live well, as a Wicked Queen in training.

She stared at the dress, mentally running through the pledge the goblin maids had delivered on an elaborate scroll of linen. "I offer my loyalty and my love to Her Royal Majesty, for now and ever more," it began, then went on for a few more pages, or turns of the scroll, or whatever they called it.

Six months ago, a gold dress would have been for a school dance. A pledge would have been of allegiance. And goblins would have been . . . well, nowhere. In books. If there. She didn't read a lot of fantasy. Never found it believable.

And yet, there was another whole life that she had been meant to live, where a gold dress would have meant a royal ball, a glass slipper, and a fairy godmother.

Neither of those lives existed anymore, not really. She was never going to make it back to school, dance or no. She wasn't ever going to live with her stepmother again and leave her slipper at the ball.

Now, she was either going to join the Queen, or she was going to die.

May hugged her knees tighter and went through the pledge again. "I offer my loyalty and my love to Her Royal Majesty, for now and ever more." She had to do it. She couldn't just die. To give up, to say no to the Wicked Queen . . . she couldn't. She couldn't! She wasn't that person. She wasn't a character in a story who could do the crazy thing, the life-ending thing, and be satisfied that she'd made the right choice.

But joining the Queen . . . could she really live with herself? She'd seen how the Queen's subjects had lived, back in the safety of her stepmother's home. Even there, even protected by the fairy queens, she'd known that taking one step outside would have meant capture or worse. Just like what everyone else still living in her town had to deal with on a daily basis.

Could she really say yes to the Queen, knowing those people still lived in fear for *their* lives?

Yes. Yes, she could. Those people had, hadn't they? They weren't rising up or anything. They weren't protesting. They weren't rebelling.

No, they weren't, because they had more to worry about.

They had families and friends.

May had neither of those things. Not anymore.

This woman wasn't related to her. There was no blood there. She had believed the Queen to be her grandmother, but that was just more lies. It wasn't real. Or if it was, it wasn't anymore. Now there were magical curses and shadows living in the place of people's hearts.

All that mattered was that there wasn't a heart there now, and the woman felt nothing for May. Even if May still felt something for her.

The gold dress just lay there staring at her, another Cinderella costume for her to wear, another act to put on.

Someone knocked on her door and said in a goblin's guttural voice, "Ten minutes, Princess May."

Princess. That'd been fun at the beginning. Everything had been happier back then, back at the beginning, with princes and houses made of candy and rescuing Snow White. Giants, talking wolves, and invisibility hoods. Then, they'd found her grandmother, and—

Not her grandmother. The Wicked Queen.

May stood up and walked over to the dress, feeling it between her fingers. Gold wasn't soft. How could anyone be comfortable in something like that? And where had it come from? Golden thread led to Rumplestiltskin in her head, and she smiled at the thought of Jack hanging upside down outside Malevolent's castle.

What would Jack do here? He'd join the Queen . . . he already had. But he hadn't meant it. He'd had a plan. He'd tried to rescue them after all. And after everything, he wouldn't betray May. Phillip had, yes, but . . . there had to be a reason. But Jack hadn't even done *that*. Jack would make the pledge, she knew. Because living another day meant another day to figure something out, a way to escape.

And somewhere, she knew, she *knew* he had done just that.

But for her, there was nowhere to escape to, nowhere to go.

Phillip wouldn't give his oath without meaning it. He was such a fairy-tale prince . . . no lying, no trickery. He'd tell the Queen no, no matter the consequences.

"Five minutes, Princess," said the goblin at the door. "Do you need help?"

"Not me," May said, picking up the dress. "I've got this, all on my own."

The throne room practically burst with people, goblins, trolls, ogres, and assorted shadows floating overhead, each one looking like a trick of the light when you stared right at it. May waited outside with her goblin guards, both of which were sweating and shaking as much or more than she was.

Someone was announcing several apparently important people in the throne room, and each time, someone moved to stand in front of the Queen on her throne, bowing low. The Queen would acknowledge each one with a nod, though every few people, she would gesture, and goblins would take the unlucky lord or lady away, their screams echoing through the silent hall.

"The Princess May, to declare her loyalty to Her Royal Majesty!" called the voice, and May's guards started forward, almost stumbling over her feet. May followed a step behind, and gasps went through the crowd.

May smiled at the guests, the torches shining off the golden dress that May had ripped to ribbons, dropping the pieces like flowers as she walked through the throne room in her jeans and PUNK PRINCESS shirt.

"What is *this*?!" the Queen asked, her eyes narrowed to slits.

"Oh hey, Your Majesty," May said, throwing another piece of dress into the air. "I thought I'd add some festiveness to this whole thing. It felt like it was getting a little depressing."

The Queen looked to May's left and right, and goblins grabbed her by the arms and dragged her forward, forcing her down to her knees before the throne. "I take it that this is your way of refusing to become my heir," the Queen said quietly.

"I mean, I thought about it," May said, the goblins shoving her head almost down to the ground. "I didn't think I'd have the guts to do this, actually. But then I remembered something." She pushed back against the goblins and looked the Queen right in the eye. "I remembered that I've got more heart in my little finger than you do in your whole body. Though, to be fair, who doesn't?"

The crowd began to murmur, each of the assembled nobles looking at each other nervously. May couldn't blame them. The heart she'd just bragged about was about to burst, it was beating so hard.

"You choose *death*, then?" the Queen asked, her eyes striking May's like bolts of lightning.

"There's a boy I know," May told her, struggling against the goblins to stand up. The goblins, nervous about being killed in whatever magic destroyed May, released her almost thankfully, backing away slowly. "His name is Phillip, and he's a prince, but that doesn't really matter. Phillip taught me something a while ago, back on a pirate ship. He said that when you do something good and noble, you'll win."

The Queen stood up, lightning sizzling in the air.

"He was wrong," May told her with a shrug. "You won't always win. Sometimes you'll lose, and sometimes . . . well, bad things happen. But not trying? Not standing up to people like you?" She smiled. "Then we all lose. So no, I don't choose death, because that's giving up too. But I'll never join you, and I'll keep trying to take you down for as long as I can."

The room went absolutely silent for a moment.

Then someone, somewhere in the back, shouted, "Down with the Wicked Queen!"

And that's when things got ugly.

CHAPTER 34

The ground shook every few seconds now. The air smelled of rotten meat and mountains of sweat-covered clothing. And shadows fell across the entire land as the fireball that was the sun was blotted out entirely.

The giants had arrived.

Phillip stood with his back to a chimney on the roof of a farmhouse as the first six slowly walked toward him, spread out with hundreds of feet between each one. He was alone, of course. Penelope had tried to come with him, but he had made her promise to stay back.

If he failed, after all, someone needed to go find May and bring her home.

"HUNGRY!" shouted the closest giant.

"EAT!" shouted another.

"KILL!" shouted a third.

A mile or two behind them, the seventh giant, this one towering over the others as if they were children, laughed. "You'll get your fill, boys!" the seventh giant shouted, his voice traveling all the way to Phillip's ears clearly. "Just make sure you leave the thief to me!"

That one would be trouble. But the first six were the primary concern.

But he still needed to wait.

The ground shook again and again, and as the giants approached, Phillip had to hold tight to the chimney to avoid being shaken right off the roof. Another few seconds, and they'd be in place. All he had to do was wait and make sure he wasn't seen.

"Watch out that they're not hiding in the houses there," the seventh giant shouted.

Phillip sighed, then stepped out from behind the chimney.

Not two hundred feet away, a giant with a fire-red beard and hair stumbled backward in surprise. "HUMAN!" he yelled, and Phillip watched as the surprise turned to eagerness. It only took thirty seconds, which was quick for a giant. "EAT THE HUMAN!"

"Eat the human, yes," Phillip said quietly, holding his arms out, his sword still at his side. The seventh one was too far back to see what was happening, which was fortunate, as this never would have worked otherwise. If it even worked to begin with.

The red-haired giant grinned and slowly reached down for Phillip, licking his lips. Off to either side, Phillip heard the other giants shouting about their own human treats, and from the corner of his eye, he watched five other giants reaching down to various houses with various soldiers waiting as well.

"TASTY HUMAN," the red-haired giant said, and Phillip braced himself. The hand descended, growing to the size of a small cottage, and he could see entire feet of dirt beneath the creature's fingernails.

"Very tasty!" Phillip told it. "Better hurry or I'll get away!"

The message took a few seconds to reach the giant's brain, but when it did, the giant redoubled its efforts and bent over the house, his hand spread wide to grab the tasty human.

Just as the hand came within a few feet of Phillip, the roof opened up, and the prince fell right through.

The giant's hand followed, reaching right into the farmhouse after the disappearing prince.

"NOW!" Phillip shouted as he fell toward a large pile of hay on the floor of the farmhouse. The sewn cord noose hidden within the farmhouse's walls pulled tight, trapping the giant's hand just as Phillip slammed into the hay below.

"PULL!" he shouted, throwing himself out of the hay toward the barn door. Above him, the cord yanked hard, and the hand followed Phillip right out the barn doors.

Outside, teams of horses and riders galloped out of the haystacks they'd been hiding within, each one attached by a smaller cord to the large cord holding the giant's hand. And just as was happening in five other farmhouses, Phillip's horses all ran off toward the castle, yanking the giant forward.

The scream behind him was so loud, Phillip almost lost his footing as he ran, but he knew he did not have time to trip. The giant's falling body would take exactly fifteen seconds to hit the ground, and anything on that ground would be crushed to a pulp. Phillip planned on being nowhere close.

But while the other five volunteers all ran sideways, out of the way of their falling giants, Phillip ran forward, toward the legs of his redheaded, toppling giant.

The giant's collapse exploded a tidal wave of earth in every direction, and Phillip watched it coming as he sprinted toward the giant's feet, then jumped at the last possible moment to avoid whatever he could. The earth leapt up to meet his feet and pushed him higher, sending him flying into the air.

Fortunately, this was not his first toppled giant, and he flipped in midair, then landed carefully on the ever-shifting ground, still running as quickly as he could.

Wave after wave of earth came rushing at him as the other five giants hit, destroying the farms of far too many of his people but never even slowing him down.

There was no time, after all. The seventh giant had already seen what was happening, and though Phillip often lost sight of the monster in the trees, the giant's quick footsteps told him what was happening.

"I told you all to watch out!" the giant shouted. "The thief did this! He will pay, I will ensure it!"

"It was not the thief!" Phillip shouted, and climbed as quickly as he could up the nearest, tallest tree. He stood at the very top on two fairly sturdy branches and waved his arms at the approaching giant. "It was ME!"

The giant slowed its run and stared down at the insect-size human waving at him. "You smell of the thief, but you are not him . . . or of his blood, like the other one," the monster said. "I have no time for you!"

"I just killed six of your kind," Phillip told him. "One more, and I match my father's record. Face me, if you are no coward!"

The giant stared down at him, then laughed. "Perhaps the thick air down here has clouded my mind, little human, but I guess a quick snack won't turn my appetite."

The others didn't know the plan here. He had let Penelope and his mother both believe that they would capture all seven giants the same way. But they would not. Jack's father had known this, and together they had come up with a plan.

Unfortunately, the plan needed someone to act as bait.

Phillip watched as the giant reached down for him, and he remembered the past few months, wondering when he would sacrifice himself for May, protecting her from the Wicked Queen or some other imagined evil.

But instead he had chosen his people. And for his people, he would make the ultimate sacrifice.

This time Phillip didn't jump. This time he let the giant grab him, lift him hundreds of feet into the air, and swallow him whole.

CHAPTER 35

This was it. The Huntsman had come, and everything was happening exactly like the Story Book pages said. Jack watched and listened, glancing at the pages every few minutes even though he had them memorized now.

"Mmph!" the old man said from behind him, not really able to say much with the cloth tied around his mouth.

Jack sighed. "I really am sorry about this. I'll cut you free right before I go, okay? There's just a lot going on here, and I couldn't have you telling people I was here."

"Mmph," the old man said, making Jack feel even worse.

"You know, this house is about to be very abandoned," Jack told him. "Well, after it's searched by seven dwarfs. Whatever you want in it, you should take. You know, to say sorry. In fact, just take the whole house!"

The old man stared at him suspiciously.

"No, seriously!" Jack whispered as he heard the Wicked Queen hurry down the stairs. He quickly checked his pages and realized that right about now, May would be getting surprised by the seven dwarfs. Part of him had to fight the urge to run up and help her. A big part.

Then, something exploded, rocking the entire house, and he knew May would be down soon either way.

"That the best you've got, Your Majesty?" shouted a man's voice. "How long have you been saving that one up?" Jack glanced out the gap in the door leading to the living room and could see the Huntsman grinning at the Wicked Queen.

"You have no idea what you're doing, Sebastian," the Wicked Queen said. "This is beyond your understanding. You *must* leave me here!"

"Funny," the Huntsman said. "I remember you ordering me to bring you Snow White's heart, and I didn't do that, either. But my family is already *cursed*, my lady. What else could you possibly punish a betrayal with now?"

"I was not . . . the same person," the Queen said. "If you

take me back there, the shadows will return, and I can't be held responsible for what I do."

"Too bad you broke the Mirror, my lady," the Huntsman said. "Otherwise, the Wicked Queen would have seen me coming, wouldn't she?"

"I tell you truthfully, that person no longer exists," the Queen said quietly. "But there's enough of her left to deal with *you* if you don't leave *now!*" Tiny, pathetic little sparks of lightning passed between her fingers, intimidating no one.

Jack glanced at the old man, whose eyes were about as big as dinner plates. Jack just nodded with understanding. "You think that's all weird, I should tell you about a witch and her house of candy sometime," he whispered.

Upstairs, the dwarfs attacked May, and her shouts distracted the Queen long enough for the Huntsman to slap huge iron chains on her wrists. The sad sparks of lightning immediately disappeared, and the Huntsman smiled. "Looks like you're all out," he said, and fastened chains around her legs as well, then to her neck.

From upstairs, seven familiar-looking dwarfs carried down a struggling May, presenting her to the Huntsman like a gift.

"And who might you be, girlie?" the Huntsman said, a combination of confusion and amusement playing over his face.

May proceeded to share some names with the Huntsman, but none of them were hers, and none of them bore repeating.

The Huntsman gave her a look of admiration, then shouted at the dwarfs. "Get her back to the palace, or I'll have your axes! Then find that crown; we need it to use the Mirror!"

The Queen struggled, but the Huntsman just picked her up and threw her over his shoulder like she weighed nothing. He said something Jack couldn't hear that sounded suspiciously like magic, and a blue fire portal opened on the wall behind the Huntsman. Through the portal lay a tunnel, just like Jack had seen in the Story Book, at the end of which waited a woman.

Rapunzel. It was Rapunzel at the end of the tunnel.

Knowing that six months ago would have changed so much.

"Leave her behind, she's no one important!" the Queen shouted.

The Huntsman laughed. "If you care that much, the girl's definitely coming along." He started off into the portal, followed closely behind by the dwarfs carrying May.

The dwarfs would be coming back, so the portal would stay open. Jack waited in the house, knowing what was coming next.

One of the dwarfs tripped a bit in the fire tunnel, and May kicked out, throwing the lot of dwarfs right off balance. One tipped into the next, and May fell to the portal floor. She seemed confused, but the dwarfs leapt for her, so May backed away, then dove through the side of the fire tunnel, disappearing.

"You worthless axe-grinders!" the Huntsman yelled. "Can't you do anything right?!"

The dwarfs looked from one to the other, then shrugged. "Who cares?" one said, this one a bit grumpier than the others. "She was just a girl. The Mirror is all that matters. Without it, we'll never find a way to save Snow." The grumpy dwarf turned around and walked back toward Jack. "Come, brothers. We need the crown, not some human girl."

The Huntsman swore, then sprinted down the tunnel with the Queen, who watched everything without a word. Jack hid so the dwarfs could pass by, but he couldn't stay long . . . their search would eventually lead them to him and the old man, given that they weren't going to find the crown, currently hidden in May's pocket in a note from her grandmoth—from the Wicked Queen.

"I'm going to let you go," Jack told the old man. "Just run out the front door and don't come back for at least a day or two. By then, the dwarfs will be back at the Palace of the Snow Queen, where we'll find them later, and the Wolf King will fight them as we . . . well, that's not really important."

The man just stared at him.

"Right," Jack said, cutting through the old man's bonds but leaving the cloth over his mouth. "Now let's go!"

With that, the two ran out of the small closet they'd been hiding in, and Jack whipped the front door open and gave the old man a friendly shove out it, then went for the blue fire tunnel—

Only to immediately jump back into the closet as the Huntsman strode purposefully back toward the point in the tunnel May had escaped through. The enormous man stopped, examining the area carefully, then nodded and stepped through at the same point May had.

Jack gave the Huntsman as much time as he could, then, hearing at least one dwarf heading back his way, sprinted into the tunnel and dove through in the exact same spot May had fallen.

He hit the ground hard and, for a moment, wondered if he would have to kiss himself awake. The moment passed, and Jack picked himself up off a road he hadn't seen for half a year.

"Another one?" said a gruff voice behind him, then whoever it was gasped. "Jack?!"

Jack turned around to find his grandfather staring at him. "But . . . you just left!" the old man said. "And you look so . . . different!" And then his grandfather's mouth dropped. "NO. An

Eye? NO!" He shook his head, his beard tossing around wildly. "I kept you hidden from all that! You were never meant to follow your mother's path!"

"Just forget I was ever here, Grandpa," Jack told the man, struggling not to hug him. It had been so *long*!

"But . . . how?"

"I can't say," Jack told him. "But you said I just left? With the princess, right?"

Jack looked at the ground beside him to find Robert, the boy who'd bullied him his entire life, still lying unconscious, first from Jack's knee in his face, then from Jack's grandfather hitting the boy over the head with a food tray. The food still littered the ground, and Jack couldn't help but smile. "I really *did* just leave, didn't I."

A clicking noise made him turn back to his grandfather, who was holding what looked to be a dagger-size sword that slowly grew into a full-size weapon. "I promised myself you'd never join her, Jack," the old man said, aiming his weapon at Jack. "I *promised*. Your sister was a lost cause, but you . . . you were different." He sniffed loudly, and Jack realized the old man was crying. "I thought you could redeem our whole family, boy! I thought you were *better* than this!"

And with that, his grandfather swung his sword, and Jack had no choice but to block it with his own sword, which once more glowed eerily in the dying light. The glow lit the tears on his grandfather's cheeks, and Jack sighed, then put his sword back in its sheath.

"Sit down, Grandpa," he said. "We need to talk."

And with that, he showed the old man what was in the Queen's wooden box.

CHAPTER 36

"Q uite the inspiring speech," said a man in a large black cloak as the goblins led May back to her cell. The goblins froze in place as the Wolf King stepped in front of May, then ran off as he dismissed them.

"Oh yeah?" May said. "Inspiring enough for you to change sides?"

The Wolf King laughed his low growly laugh. "What did you hope to accomplish?"

May glared at him, then sighed. "I have no idea. But I couldn't just join her. I *couldn't*."

"Better than you have tried before," the wolf told her. "And it almost worked. But sometimes it's even worse when you get that close, only to fail."

Behind them, screams echoed in the throne room, and swords clashed against swords. The goblins had pulled her out as everything had descended into chaos, but it wouldn't last long, she knew. Not long—

And then the Queen's voice rose above all others, and everything went absolutely silent. "Perhaps I should get you to your cell," the Wolf King said, and gestured for May to follow him.

"Give me back my weapon," May pleaded with him. "The one you took, back at Malevolent's castle. She was convinced it would help take the Queen down!"

The wolf just looked at her. "You have no idea what you had there."

"I had the Fairest, whatever that meant."

"Do not *speak* of her!" the Wolf King growled. "You know nothing of what you speak!"

". . . Her?"

The Wolf King pushed her against one of the hallway's stone walls, flashing his teeth at her, despite still being in human form. "That was no *weapon*—that was a dream and nothing more!"

May glared right back. "Are we talking about metaphors

here? Because you're really going to have to be specific. I can't tell what's literal and what's not with you people."

The wolf growled again and pushed her back into the hall- way. "Never speak of her again."

"You keep saying 'her,'" May said, stopping in place. "The Fairest . . . she's a person? The fairest one of all . . . oh wow, that's not the name, that's a title. The most beautiful person in the world . . . we're talking about Beauty, like in 'Beauty and the Beast,' aren't we?"

"Do not speak of this further!"

May's eyes widened. "You're the Beast!"

The wolf bared his teeth again. "What *I* am is none of your concern!"

He pushed her through a door and into a more brightly lit room, surprising two goblin guards who'd been sleeping in their chairs. The Wolf King growled at both, then pulled one of the five cell doors open and pushed May inside.

"I rescued your Beauty, didn't I?" May shouted at him.

"She was never real!" the Wolf King roared. "She was only a dream! The *only* way someone could love me was in a dream!"

"A dream you loved too?" May asked, her voice dropping to a whisper.

"And what do you think the Queen would do if she knew?" the wolf sneered. "My dream love was taken from me once. What lengths do you think the Queen would go to in order to hold Beauty over me once more?"

"Whatever it took," May said softly.

The wolf just glared at her.

"It'd still be worth it, though," May said. "You know, if you really did love her. Dream or not."

The Wolf King roared, banging a fist against the cell, then turned and walked toward the door.

"You're welcome for saving her!" May yelled after him. "See you at my execution!"

"QUIET!" one of the goblin guards yelled at her, suddenly a lot braver now that the wolf was gone.

"Oh yeah?" May said, spreading her arms. "Come over *here* and say that!"

The other goblin stood up and smacked his sword against the bars. "He said quiet!"

May grabbed his arm and yanked it hard, bashing the goblin's head into the bars. She grabbed his shoulders and pulled him back against the door while the monster squealed and the other guard just laughed. A minute later, the second goblin's sword poked through the bars right at May's head, and she released the first one, who straightened up and stumbled out of reach.

"I wouldn't try that again," the second goblin said, grinning still.

"I think she was trying for the keys!" the first goblin said. "I felt her reach for them!"

"Well?" the second goblin said, pointing at the keys on the first one's belt. "Looks like she didn't get them, doesn't it? Maybe next time you'll be even stupider and just hand them over to her."

"Maybe if you'd been doing *your* job and watching my back, I wouldn't have been attacked!"

The goblins continued arguing while May slowly moved the knife she'd just stolen off the goblin up into her sleeve, then settled back into the corner of the cell, waiting for her execution.

CHAPTER 37

Jill watched from the castle walls as the biggest giant she'd ever seen picked up a tiny Prince Phillip and swallowed him. She frowned. "That seems like an odd plan."

"You're back just in time," her father told her as he came up behind her. "After all the hard work is done."

"I'm pretty terrible at sewing," she told him, still concentrating on the last remaining giant, who now resumed his onward march toward the castle, all because he could smell her father, and probably her, honestly. Stupid blood. "What exactly was Phillip's plan there? To give the giant indigestion?"

"I'm not spoiling anything," her father told her, putting a hand over his eyes to cover the now-visible sun giant once again. "Though I reserve the right to say it wasn't my idea if it doesn't work."

"LIAN!" shouted a voice, and Jill turned to find Penelope sprinting up the stairs to the wall. "What just happened to Phillip? The guards said he was eaten?!" The girl's eyes were wider than Jill had ever seen, and she seemed about as awake as a normal person for once.

Several responses swam through Jill's head, ranging from the blunt ("Yup, swallowed all up!") to the kind ("I'm sure his death will be quick, and he won't feel the stomach acid for very long") to her default response (a shrug).

She shrugged, going with the classic. "Apparently he's got a plan."

"Plans don't do much from inside a stomach," Penelope said, pushing as far as she could over the wall to see better.

"He's not even slowing down," Jill's father said. "This might end badly."

"We could always run away from the castle, and he'd probably follow," Jill pointed out.

"That'd be admitting defeat, wouldn't it?" her father asked.

"I'm pretty sure the giant eating us both will also be admitting defeat."

"Maybe he'll eat you first and give me a chance to escape."

"Spoken like a loving father."

"Be quiet, both of you!" Penelope shouted. "How can you be so . . . callous? Phillip might be dead!"

"Probably," Jill said. "But we have to look at the big picture. And they don't get much bigger than that giant out there. What do we do now?"

"We wait until the last moment," her father said. "Phillip might still come through."

The giant sniffed loudly in the distance. "I can smell you, little thief! I'm coming for you!"

"Maybe not the *last* moment," her father admitted.

The giant was less than a mile away now, and even if he did fall, he'd still almost reach the city. This was getting far too close, especially at the rate he was going. Yes, running would mean abandoning the city, but what had the city ever done for Jill? Also, the giant *would* probably follow them. Probably. She wasn't sure which side of that she came down on. Neither side was particularly encouraging.

And then, the giant paused right in midstep. His foot swayed in the air, then fell back to the earth with a huge shudder. The giant's face contorted into a very uncomfortable expression, and he grabbed his stomach as he seemed to be dealing with a loose morsel of food in his teeth, picking at it with his tongue.

"What . . ." the giant said, then stopped as his eyes rolled back into his head and he fell forward.

"He's too close!" Jill yelled as guards all around them began to panic and run from the walls.

"No, he's not," her father said, grabbing her arm. "Just wait."

The giant collapsed toward them, his mountain-high head getting closer and closer as he fell. His knees hit first, the jolt almost knocking them off the wall as the monster's chest and head hurtled straight at them.

Well, they were going to be crushed, that was it. Jill's last thought was that she really, really wished she'd been able to take the Wicked Queen with her.

Her father's last thought, though, seemed to involve throwing a rope over the city wall in the direction of the descending giant's head.

And then the head slammed into the ground maybe twenty feet away, and the resulting tidal wave of earth threw all three of them into the air. The walls began to collapse under them, and Jill grabbed Penelope as she slowed time down, avoiding any falling stones and making it to a safe spot in the wall, which just happened to be the spot her father already stood in. Of course he did.

Finally, silence took over, and Jill turned to her father, who just smiled and pointed down at the rope.

Someone was pulling on it.

Jill rolled her eyes. No. Way. There was no way. He was no Eye. He had no special training. He was just some kid. There was no way!

And then a hand appeared on the remnants of the wall, and her father reached down and helped pull Phillip up and over.

"Phillip!" Penelope shouted, and helped him as well, while Jill just shook her head. The perfect prince. "But . . . how did you survive?"

"I had it on good authority that one could grab on to the bit of skin hanging down over the throat of a giant," Phillip told her as Jill held her nose. Being eaten did *not* smell good. "And then it was just a matter of jumping at the right moment."

"I may have helped him with that," Jill's father whispered to her, and she rolled her eyes again.

"But how did you kill the giant?" Penelope asked.

Phillip reached into a pouch on a shoulder strap and pulled out a shiny-looking apple, with a guilty-looking smile. "I figured these should come to some use," he said.

"That's one of the Wicked Queen's apples," Jill said, her eyes going wide in surprise. "How many did you feed him?!"

"Just one," Phillip said with a shrug. "I only had the two, but apparently they are stronger than you would think!"

Penelope laughed, and Jill even smiled. It was hard to hate someone who smelled so horrible.

And then, tiny hands pulled themselves up the rope, and a golden fairy appeared over the side of the wall. "Finally!" she said.

"Gwentell!" Jill shouted, and retrieved the dirty, shaken fairy. "Where did *you* come from?"

"Your horrible, stupid brother left me in the giant's castle!" she shouted. "I had to ride along with him the entire way back here!"

"What's she saying?" Jill's father asked her.

"Same sorts of things," Jill told him. She bent down to whisper in the fairy's ear. "Jack . . . he died, Gwentell. The Queen killed him."

The fairy looked at her in shock, then snorted. "No, he didn't."

Jill gave her an odd look. Did she know? "What do you mean, no he didn't? I saw it happen."

"Eh," Gwentell said. "He's fine. Trust me, I've seen that man-child make it out of things that should have killed him a hundred times over." She brushed herself off, then gently flew up to Jill's shoulder. "Now, what's next?"

Jill smiled, then turned back to Phillip. "By the way," Jill said, "I did what you asked. The Sea King is on his way. He's marching his sharks and squids and everything over land and will meet us there."

"The fairy queens have decided to help us too," Penelope said, smiling at Gwentell. "They're on their way as well."

"Captain!" Phillip shouted, and a moment later the captain of the guard picked his way up the collapsed section of wall where Jill and Penelope had been standing moments earlier.

"Yes, Your Highness?"

"Gather anyone you can find," Phillip told him. "We'll need an army, if we can find one."

"Of course, Your Highness," the captain said. "But . . . for what?"

"We are going to attack the Wicked Queen's castle," Phillip told him. "We'll start marching at dawn!"

"Might as well get wiped out all at once instead of dragging it out," Jill murmured, and the fairy snorted.

CHAPTER 38

S o wait," Jack's grandfather said as he absently pounded away on the contents of the Queen's wooden heart box with a large hammer, frowning at the lack of progress. "How did the Wicked Queen come back? You skipped over that part. No one's heard anything from her in over a decade."

"We may never know the full truth of that," Jack said, turning around so his grandfather couldn't see him blush. "But that's not really the point. I need to figure out a way to stop that heart, Grandpa, and nothing I've tried has worked."

"If you know what's going to happen, why don't you just go stop it before it can?" his grandfather said.

Jack shook his head. "I got a bunch of headaches trying to figure that out already. If I changed things so the Wicked Queen wasn't freed, then I'd never need to go to Punk to arrive here when I do, which means I wouldn't be there to stop it, which means I'd go again, and on and on." He grimaced. "I need to make sure this sticks. And that means I need to wait until the point I left."

"So I probably shouldn't be doing this," his grandfather said, still hammering the heart.

Jack shrugged. "I'd be a lot more worried if I thought there was a chance of it working."

"Well, I'd suggest something from my bag of magical curiosities, but I just gave those to you—the younger you," the old man said, then gave Jack a suspicious look. "You still have them, right?"

Jack coughed. "Oh, I'm sure I gave them back to you or something in the future, unlessIlosttheminacollapsingcastle. Anyway, they're not here now. Any other suggestions?"

"I missed a big part of that sentence, but fine," his grandfather said. "I still can't believe you went over to the evil side."

"It's not the evil side!" Jack said. "I mean, it is, but I had to get close to the Queen if she was going to send me to Punk so I could steal her heart."

His grandfather glared at him. "You're just like your uncle. And look where that got *him*."

"Where exactly did it get him?" Jack asked. "I actually have no idea who my uncle is. My father wouldn't talk about him—"

"For good reason," his grandfather said. "Even your fool father had more sense than that idiot. But enough about your mother's less-than-intelligent family. *She* was a sweet girl, even for an Eye. Speaking of, can't you just use that fool sword of yours?"

Jack opened his mouth to say something, then closed it quickly. Whoops. He hadn't exactly tried that. And it *had* cut through frozen dragon's breath six months ago, when he'd rescued . . . uh, accidentally freed the Wicked Queen. "I was going to do that next," he said, then pulled his sword out and gave it a try.

The heart went right on beating, but the sword's glow reminded him of someone he needed to talk to.

He gently placed two fingers on the sword, closed his eyes, and concentrated on the Charmed One.

A second later, his body collapsed to the floor, and he found himself sitting beneath an oak tree in the middle of a grassy field.

There, with an exact copy of Jack's sword, was the Charmed One. Only, the sword was aimed right at Jack.

"She got to you before I could," the knight said, circling around Jack. "I failed you, Jack, and for that, I apologize. But I cannot allow you to leave here under her control."

"Apology accepted," Jack said, then paused. "Wait . . . what?"

And then he realized that though the sword had come with him through time, the Charmed One apparently had not. So . . . the knight wasn't in his head after all. Instead, the sword must pull him in from some . . . *other* place? Jack frowned, the whole thing giving him a headache again.

Then the Charmed One sliced through the spot where Jack's head should have been, Jack barely dodging it, and he realized that he'd have a *bigger* headache if he didn't pay attention.

"Well avoided," the knight said half-approvingly. "I see she has trained you well."

"Who, the Queen?" Jack said. "She didn't train me, you did! You gave me this sword. You just haven't done it yet. You will. In a giant's mouth."

The knight's eyes narrowed, and he attacked again. Jack blocked with his sword and leapt away, trying to force the man to talk to him. "You really did!" Jack shouted. "You trained me! To . . . not become this, actually. So it didn't go so well, but—"

The knight struck again, and again Jack defended himself, then moved away quickly. "I should have found you sooner," the Charmed One said. "I never dreamed she'd find you this early. I thought you were hidden away safely, where no one would find you!"

"Hidden me?" Jack said, and then barely dodged as the knight's sword flew straight at his chest.

"I cannot allow this, Jack," the Charmed One said. "If you've joined her, I will see your mind dead, and your body will soon follow!"

"WAIT!" Jack shouted, but nothing happened even close to that. The knight attacked again, and this time, Jack fought back. The knight swept his sword low, and Jack leapt over it, swinging out one-handed with his sword at the knight's shoulder.

The sword passed through the knight as if he were made of air, and yet the man flinched from what looked like pain. "First blood to you," he said.

"You're not bleeding," Jack told him.

The knight growled and attacked again, moving so fast that the Jack of six months ago would never have even seen a movement. But Jack of six months ago was presently galloping away on a man-eating horse. *This* Jack knew a thing or two more.

Jack concentrated, and the knight's sword hit nothing, as Jack completely disappeared, only to reappear right behind the man. Jack grabbed the Charmed One's cloak and yanked, pulling the man down, then drove his sword down at the man's unprotected neck, stopping just short of touching it.

"Despite how this looks, I really don't want to hurt you," he told the knight. "Seriously."

"And what exactly is it that you *want* to do, *Eye?*" the Charmed One said.

And with that, Jack let him up and concentrated, making a dreamlike wooden box appear in his hand. "I want to destroy *this.*"

The Charmed One slowly pushed himself to his feet, his face full of shock. "That's . . . the Queen's lost heart. But where did you—"

"I found it lying around in some other world," Jack told him. "The one the Queen fled to after . . . well, you know that story better than I do."

The knight nodded. "So . . . you tell the truth, or some version of it. You couldn't be her creature; she would never risk her heart being found. And now you want to destroy it but don't know how?"

"Not so far. That's why I came to you."

The Charmed One nodded. "While I rejoice that you still fight for the good, I also despair for your quest. Only one other ever learned the secret of the Queen's cursed heart, and she told no one."

"So?" Jack said. "Who is it? I'll go find this woman and get some answers."

The knight sighed. "You may have a bit of trouble with that. You see, the one I refer to was poisoned by the Queen before she could share her discovery." He smiled sadly. "And given that the only one who can wake this woman, me, is currently dead, I'd say we might have some problems with this."

CHAPTER 39

S now White?" Jack said.

"Her body is poisoned," the Charmed One said, his voice cracking. "The poison keeps her mind from returning. Some mixture of the Queen's, deliberately keeping Snow alive yet unable to live. Beyond cruel."

"So we just need the counterspell or whatever."

The knight opened his mouth, but no words emerged. Finally, he whispered, "There is none."

"There's *always* a counterspell," Jack argued, his hope fading. "That's how these things work. Magic can always be undone."

"In her cruelty, the Queen did create an antidote," the knight said. "Me. She created the poison to only be cured by a kiss from Snow's true love. And then she killed me with my own sword."

Though the knight had hinted at that, Jack still went cold at the idea that the sword he held had killed the man in front of him. "But . . . how is it that you're here, then? You know, I meant to ask you that, but there always seemed to be more important things going on—"

"You . . . meant to ask me?" The Charmed One looked confused. "But we have not met before now."

Jack shook his head. "You shouldn't be here arguing pointless points if you're dead. Let's get back to the important questions, like how can you exist here in this place if you're dead?"

The knight pointed at his sword. "You really know so little about the sword and its power? I'm surprised an Eye would be so ill-educated."

"I'm a surprising guy sometimes."

"Did the Queen tell you nothing of her bargain?" the Charmed One said. "Did she not share how she came into possession of these swords?"

"Let's assume I haven't heard the story in a while. But how about the short version? My grandfather's probably not happy with how long I've been out."

The Charmed One seemed confused again, then shrugged. "The Queen had often explored other realities. Worlds with magic similar but different . . . even worlds without magic. One in particular she thought might make a safe retreat if ever she needed to flee."

"I've seen it; it's nice," Jack said, not really wanting to think about that.

"But while exploring, someone met her between realities, another explorer like herself, someone else looking for knowledge. Though while the Queen wanted knowledge to use as power, this man sought knowledge for its own sake." The knight seemed to be staring off into the space, as if he were imagining the man. "The Queen spoke of him as having two pet ravens, one on each shoulder. That was what gave her the idea for her familiar, in fact. This explorer carried a spear and rode a horse with sixteen legs—"

"Seems a little excessive—"

"And when this traveler heard of the Queen's Mirror . . . he wanted nothing more than to speak to it. And the Queen agreed but traded the Mirror's knowledge for something equally as important to this traveler: one of his eyes."

"AGH!" Jack said, trying to sum up his feelings in as simple a sentence as possible.

"The Queen claims that the traveler had but three questions

for the Mirror, then left with a patch covering his missing eye." The Charmed One gave Jack a look. "And before you ask, I don't know the questions."

"I *didn't* ask."

"The Queen took this man's eye and fashioned it into the swords we—"

"NO."

"Wield, and each sword—"

"NO!"

"Much like the traveler, thirsts for knowledge. The magic each sword contains—"

"I AM NOT HOLDING SOME GUY'S EYEBALL!"

"Was given to it by the Queen, imparted to each sword individually. But each sword also contained everything that this man had seen. This is how each sword knows how to bend light past its user and move us through time faster than we might normally move on our own. This traveler had learned such things, and his eye had seen them—"

"I'M SERIOUS HERE. I'm not touching some guy's EYE—"

"But each sword also learns from its user." The Charmed One put a hand on his own sword. "And mine has learned well. I even managed to replace the Queen's powers within the sword so that she could not listen through it, nor use my sight as her own. But putting so much of myself in the sword has resulted in this." He waved his hand around bitterly. "I have moved on, the important parts of me, but the remnants . . . the part of me the sword knew . . . the sword can still access that part of me from the beyond."

Jack put his hands up. "WHOA. So not only do I have some guy's eyeball on my back, but it also has the essence of a dead guy in it? Do you understand why I'm having some issues with this? Also, how big was this guy that this thing could be part of his eye?!"

"He was quite large, I'm told," the Charmed One said, and Jack thought he saw the hint of a smile.

"You better not be enjoying this," Jack warned him.

The Charmed One sighed. "I am afraid that I cannot help you with your task of ending the Queen's reign."

"NO," Jack said. "If I have to carry this thing around with me, it's going to be of some use. If you can be in here and you're dead, then Snow White can stop on by too. And if I get the two of you together in here, then you can do the whole kissing thing and wake her up, right?"

The Charmed One paused. "I . . . do not know. Such a thing would require months of training—"

"I have months. I'm already six months in the past—"

"And could very well leave you as weak as a babe, unable to defend yourself."

"That's pretty much my usual day too."

The Charmed One looked more hopeful than Jack had ever seen him. "I would of course be willing to try. If you were to attempt such a thing, to allow me to see Snow once more—"

"Let's not give me more credit than I deserve," Jack said. "I'm just trying to un-Wicked a Queen. But yes, that'd be a nice side benefit. So where do we start?"

"You'll need a place where you can be alone for the training," the Charmed One said. "No distractions, no other thoughts. I have an idea of somewhere you could go—"

The Charmed One gestured and showed Jack an image. Jack shrugged. "Seems a bit run-down but as good a place as any."

"I would truly owe you, my friend," the knight said.

"Just . . . try to talk some sense into me next time we meet," Jack said. "I'm going to be pretty annoying and not want to listen. But sometimes, you just have to jump for it."

"I . . . don't know what that means."

"You'll see," Jack said, then woke himself up, leaving as quickly as possible after his victory.

He was finally able to out-vague the Charmed One!

CHAPTER 40

Jack woke up to his grandfather standing over him with a bucket of water.

"I'm up!" Jack shouted.

His grandfather dumped the bucket of water on him anyway.

"It's best to be sure," the old man said, and Jack just glared at him. "When a person falls asleep after touching a magic sword, it's best to not let them sleep too long. After all, you're no beauty, boy."

"Thanks for that," Jack said, standing up and grabbing his grandfather's favorite cloak, then using it to dry himself off.

"HEY!" his grandfather yelled, so Jack tossed him the soaking cloak.

"I have to go," Jack told him, looking around for supplies. He grabbed a sack and filled it with as much food as he could find, pulling a nonmagical horse bridle off the wall as well. "When the younger me comes back, don't tell him I was ever here, okay?"

"You're leaving?!" his grandfather said, dropping the wet cloak to the floor. "But why?"

"I figured out what I have to do," Jack told him. "And I'm going to have to do it somewhere else. Considering that 'somewhere else' isn't close, apparently, I'm going to need a ride. Fortunately, I know where one just went."

"Samson?!" his grandfather said. "You just got through being terrified of that horse!"

"Sounds like me," Jack said, throwing the sack over his shoulder. He stopped in front of the old man, paused, then hugged him. "I love you, Grandpa."

"That just shows you're a smart kid," the old man said, wiping his eye.

Jack laughed and moved for the door. His grandfather coughed, and Jack turned back for a moment.

"You've grown, my boy," his grandfather said. "I . . . I'm not sure I understand everything that's happened, but I'm . . . I'm proud of you."

Jack suddenly had trouble swallowing, and he nodded quickly and turned so his grandfather wouldn't see the lump in his throat. "Just . . . make sure I go with May when we get back, Grandpa. I wasn't sure at the time, but I . . . I . . ."

With that, Jack shook his head and left.

Outside, Robert and a few of the other boys were gathering in front of Jack's house.

"Well, look who's back!" Robert said, puffing out his chest. "Where's the princess, Jack?" He grinned widely.

Jack punched him in the face without stopping, knocking the older boy out.

The other boys gasped, and Jack threw a look over his shoulder to see if they were going to argue the point, but they all seemed to find something much more interesting in every other direction, so Jack shrugged and broke into a jog.

If he remembered right, the Huntsman caught up to them not too far out of town. Still, that was a while ago, and who knew what the Huntsman had done to Samson—

An evil whinny caught Jack's attention a second before two sharpened hooves drove through the air just inches from Jack's chest. Jack leapt backward and dropped the food as the boys behind him screamed, running in every direction at once.

"MAD HORSE!" one screamed, and Jack realized he couldn't remember the names of the boys he'd grown up with.

"It'll eat your face off!" another screamed.

"Take him, let me live!" shouted a third.

Jack pulled the bridle out of the sack and slowly stood back up. "Don't make this harder than it needs to be," he told the horse.

Samson, though, seemed to want to make it as hard as he could. He whinnied again, the sound echoing in the depths of Jack's soul, and again kicked out with hooves sharp enough and hard enough to break rock.

Jack shrugged and moved quicker than the horse could see. As Samson's hooves hit the ground, Jack was on his back, had the bridle between his teeth, and was gently patting the horse's neck.

Samson turned around to look at Jack in surprise, and Jack just smiled. "I know, it's confusing," he said. "You just saw me, but I was different. Also, you're probably not happy about those magic flower reins, huh?"

The horse's dead eyes promised raging evil and foul-smelling hate, so Jack sighed. "Sorry about this," he said, and yanked on the reins.

Samson yanked back, then bucked wildly, and the other boys scattered to escape the rampaging horse. Why didn't they just go, and stop coming back to see what was happening? Jack held tightly to the horse, moving with every buck.

Samson might have kept at it all night if he hadn't just carried Jack and May off into the woods, then fought the Huntsman. Unfortunately for the horse, there just wasn't a lot of energy left, and soon he calmed down enough to accept that Jack was going to be riding him around for a bit.

"That's okay," Jack told him, patting his neck again. "You can kill me in my sleep or something. We've got a long trip."

The horse whinnied in agreement and slowly walked toward the path out of town.

The journey took a little under a week, and then only because Jack managed to sleep in the saddle, fearing what the horse might do if he ever slept on the ground. Samson eventually grew used to him, even giving up on biting him whenever they stopped to take a break. Well, he still tried, but his heart didn't seem to be in it.

Five days in, they passed over the border of the Wicked Queen's occupied lands, avoiding the patrols of goblins who periodically walked the border. Officially, the Queen hadn't returned yet, so things weren't quite so bad. The Charmed One kept Jack up-to-date on his past self's progress as they went, and oddly enough, Jack reached his destination on the same day his younger self freed the Queen.

Jack dismounted, and Samson didn't even try to bite him. Maybe the horse was impressed by their destination. Maybe he hadn't ever seen a building so big.

Or maybe the Charmed One's abandoned castle spooked the horse just as much as it did Jack.

CHAPTER 41

Time seemed . . . inconsistent. At one point, Jack was sure two months had passed. He asked the Charmed One, who claimed it had been exactly one day since he'd arrived at the castle.

Then, Jack could have sworn that just a day later, the knight was worrying that three months hadn't gotten them anywhere.

"You're too concerned with yourself!" the Charmed One would shout, smacking Jack with a duplicate of his own sword. "The sword's magic has no interest in *you*. It already knows you! It wants to know others, to know all! You have to move past yourself and embrace the rest of the world to truly awaken its powers!"

"So give the world a hug?" Jack asked, and got smacked again.

Training, in other words, was slow.

Every night, Jack would dream himself back to the oak tree and train until the sun came up. Some nights, he'd sit quietly as the wind gusted past him, the Charmed One saying that magic was nothing more than the path a leaf of grass took as it blew wherever the wind carried it. Jack always struggled to keep the obvious response to himself: If leaves of grass caught in the wind had paths to follow, then really someone should just draw a map and save everyone a lot of trouble.

Other nights, he would explore the city at the edge of the Charmed One's field, watching memories he'd had locked away of Jill and him playing or of a blurry woman whose smile filled him with joy . . . his mother, he supposed. He must have been too young to remember her clearly.

This, too, was training, according to the Charmed One. Jack needed to know his own mind before venturing into someone else's, apparently.

That made about as much sense as the grass's path, unfortunately.

Each day, Jack would wake up and find himself in an old, dusty, dark castle that lay smack in the middle of the Wicked Queen's occupied lands. Bands of goblins roamed through the nearby town, harassing the villagers as they saw fit. Jack often argued with the Charmed One about going out there, maybe in some sort of disguise, to fight the goblins off, but the Charmed One always pointed out that if he got caught, the Wicked Queen would know, and that would be that.

Most days ended with him staring at the Wicked Queen's heart box, trying not to think about a girl with a blue streak in her hair.

What was May doing? Was she okay?

"Stop thinking about her!" the Charmed One would yell. "She's distracting you and keeping you from your potential!"

Where was she now? Had they rescued the fairy queens yet?

"You won't defeat the Wicked Queen this way . . . you need to *concentrate*."

Had she found her prince?

And that's usually about the point the Charmed One would smack him, in or out of his dreams. True, if he wasn't asleep, the knight couldn't touch him, but he did seem to get strange headaches out of nowhere at times.

Despite the Eye's warnings, Jack did progress. Soon, he could go in and out of his own mind with ease, watching memories of things he never should have remembered. Classes on princess rescues in Giant's Hand. The way Gwentell's wings sparkled as she fell to Penelope's curse. A certain princess's laugh. All were locked in his mind with a clarity he never expected.

Having mastered his own thoughts, Jack soon began training his body as well. The knight worked him through the typical Eye training that Jack had taken—actually, was taking right now, somewhere else—but the Charmed One wasn't satisfied with just that. Soon, he had Jack running over the tops of the castle's ramparts in the dark (and blindfolded to boot) and carrying a torch with his feet through the castle while walking on his hands.

Jack couldn't even imagine what such things must look like from outside the castle. People in town probably thought it was haunted.

But above all, Jack practiced with the sword, and the sword practiced with him. Together, they learned each other's balance, and worked to move in complementary forms. Jack would feel the sword wanting to strike, and he would move in such a way as to most easily let it, while the sword could feel his goal (usually to smack the Charmed One back) and work to accomplish it.

And still, he couldn't stop wondering if May was okay.

"Snow White's mind will be buried deep, far deeper than you've ever had to go," the Charmed One lectured him over and over. "It will be like diving into the ocean, only without a mermaid tear to help you breathe. You won't run out of breath in her mind, but you might forget who you are or why you're there. Above all, you'll need to hold tightly to yourself as well as let yourself go, both at the same time if you'll have any chance of finding her."

"You realize that contradicting yourself makes you really easy to understand, right?" Jack would ask.

"Magic is contradictions," the Charmed One would tell him. "The fairy queens change nature by contradicting nature's song. The Wicked Queen takes the spark of life and contradicts it into a deadly lightning. And you, with your sword, will contradict the very reality of this world with your own imagination."

"I am pretty contradictory," Jack would admit, and sometimes—not often, but sometimes—get a laugh.

The training grew more and more intense, and Jack found himself sleeping through both nights and days as his time ran out. There were times he'd awaken with a start, sure someone was watching him, only to find no one there.

Creepy castles were definitely creepy.

Finally, the day came, six months after he'd begun training with the Charmed One.

"You just died," the knight told him. "There's not much time left."

Jack knew this was true. And he knew that he'd soon be as ready as he could ever hope to be to dive into Snow White's poisoned mind and bring the Charmed One to her.

This was the only way to end the Wicked Queen's reign once and for all. It'd be dangerous, and there was no guarantee that it'd work even if he got it exactly right, but it was their only shot. Snow White knew how to stop the Queen's heart, and Jack needed that information.

He needed to do this, but not for himself. He'd made a mistake, a year ago at this point, when he'd first heard how a princess's grandmother was kidnapped, and there was only one way to make it up to her.

And so, as the Charmed One reported that armies of fairy queens and legged sharks approached the Wicked Queen's castle, sure to fail in their attack, Jack left the Charmed One's castle armed only with his sword and the wooden heart box, a year late but finally ready to rescue Snow White.

CHAPTER 42

May's execution day turned out to be chilly and rainy, which was the perfect kind of weather to have on your execution day, she figured. Her goblin guards delivered a black cloak to her and waited with swords drawn until she put it on. At that point, they opened her cell and led her back through the castle in silence.

There was enough noise outside anyway.

At some point early that morning, May had heard a familiar calling, familiar but completely creepy. It'd taken her a good hour of listening to it before she realized what the noise was.

Sharks were growling. Loudly.

Somehow, Phillip had managed to get the Sea King to bring his armies to the Wicked Queen's door. From the tiny silver fairy that appeared in her window, then disappeared as the goblins shouted at it, she figured the mermen weren't the only ones out there either.

So all in all, rain or no rain, May was feeling much more optimistic than she had in days, black cloak with the hood up and all.

In what had been an empty courtyard a few days ago now stood a raised platform of darkened wood. The Queen waited for her there, the hint of a smile on her face. Behind her was a smaller crowd of nobles than had been in the throne room.

"You look happy for someone who's about to be invaded," May told her from beneath the black hood that one of the goblins had pushed up.

The Queen just smiled wider. "We shall see."

Next to the queen waited the Wolf King as well as row upon row of goblin, troll, and ogre soldiers.

The Queen nodded at the wolf, who nodded back. She smiled and turned to May.

"Before you die, I know you'll be interested to see this," she said.

"You getting your behind handed to you?" May asked.

"My invasion of the free kingdoms," the Queen said, then opened a circle made of blue lightning. The circle flickered, then solidified, and on the other side, May could see a very surprised-looking woman in a crown, and panicking soldiers.

"Phillip's kingdom," the Queen said, and gestured for the Wolf King to step through.

Before the wolf could move, voices raised from beyond the palace walls, and a song drifted through the courtyard. The blue lightning circle fizzled and disappeared, and the Wolf King turned to look expectantly at the Queen.

"Oh wow, look who else Phillip found," May said. "Sounds like he's got a few fairy queens out there. Maybe all eleven of them?"

The Queen smiled again and gestured for a pair of goblins to carry something up to the platform, covered like May was in a black cloak. The goblins pulled the black cloth off, revealing a golden harp with a statue of a woman on it.

The harp that Jack had brought back. The day he'd died.

"Let's try that again," the Queen said, and again, the blue lightning circle opened.

The voices outside raised once more, but this time, the Queen laid a hand on the harp, and the statue of the woman opened her mouth and began singing as well. Only . . . it wasn't just one voice. Or several. It sounded like thousands, all incredibly off-key, all overpowering the voices beyond the palace.

If the goblins hadn't been holding May's arms, she would have covered her ears. The goblins didn't look too happy either.

The Queen stroked the harp's head, and the thousands of voices quieted. The blue lightning circle, meanwhile, was still going strong.

"Melodies are such a fragile thing," the Queen said, her hand still resting on the harp. "They can be disrupted so very easily."

"He's still got an army out there," May said, feeling much less confident than she had a second ago.

A sudden wind behind her almost knocked May off her feet, and she turned to find something large, green, and toothy beating its wings slowly as it landed behind her on the platform. An enormous green dragon stared down at her as if it wanted to bite her in half, while its rider, wearing black armor with a white circle on it, saluted the Queen.

The dragon had landed, but the wind hadn't stopped. May looked up, then more up, and up some more, the dragons extending farther than she could see, at least with the goblins holding her down. A few spat fire into the sky ahead of themselves, either too excited or too ready to fight to hold themselves back.

Phillip's armies, fairy queens, and mermen wouldn't have a chance.

The Queen turned to the assembled human lords and ladies, a smaller group than she'd seen only a few days before. "*Behold!*" she shouted, and her voice echoed far beyond the palace walls. "*Look upon the reward for any who would defy me! The pitiful armies of the free kingdoms have gathered, yet they are helpless before my dragons! And while they flee for their lives, I shall send my armies into each of their kingdoms to take over while their protectors are gone. Any living free-kingdom soldier will return to find their kingdom under my rule!*"

"Princess," said a voice from May's side, and she turned to see the Wolf King now holding her arm where a goblin had been.

"I'm already going to be executed," May whispered. "Isn't that enough for one day? Now I have to put up with you, too?"

The wolf narrowed his eyes. "I have given some . . . thought. To what you did for me."

"*Now I ask you, my former subjects and present revolutionaries . . . do you still question me? Do you still wish to follow this girl down her path toward death?*"

"Better tell me quick," May whispered. "Sounds like I'm not going to be around for long stories."

"I owe you," the Wolf King growled low. "You did indeed

save my Beauty and return her to me, whether you knew it or not. I cannot stay here, not anymore. I cannot let the Queen know that Beauty is free once more, so I'm leaving. And without my nose, she'll be unable to track me down."

"That's amazing for you," May said. "Tons of warm and fuzzy feelings while I'm waiting to die, so thanks for that."

"I have something for you," the wolf said. "It is as much a risk as I am willing to take. And I do this for the sake of my Beauty, and for her sake alone."

May felt something soft and delicate in her hand, and she felt the Wolf King let go of her arm, then the goblin on her other side let go as well. She looked down at the object in her hand, and then up at the Wolf King, who once more stood in front of the open lightning portal.

Was he serious?!

"And what of this girl? What of this child who you would follow down the path toward destruction? If you would follow her, who will offer to take her place here now?!"

The crowd below was silent, but May hadn't expected much.

The Queen gestured for the goblins to bring May forward, still looking out toward the crowd.

Instead, now goblinless, May ran full-tilt straight into the

Wicked Queen, knocking her off the platform and into the crowd. And from there, everything began to move very, very quickly.

The crowd panicked, shouting and screaming and running all at once.

The goblins shouted, struggling to reach their Queen, only to find the Wolf King's hand on their heads, knocking them back down against the wooden platform. The wolf glanced at her once more, then disappeared into the crowd below.

And May found herself with her arms still tied together, facing an unhappy dragon and a smiling Eye riding on his back.

"That was it?" said the Eye, whom May had never seen before. "*That* was your entire escape plan?!"

May snapped her ropes with the knife she'd stolen from the goblin guard, then leapt forward and sliced through the dragon's saddle straps. The saddle slid straight off the dragon's back, slamming the strapped-in Eye right into the wooden platform.

"It's a start," May told the unconscious man.

Behind her, the Wicked Queen slowly floated into the air over the platform, her eyes wild, and magic crackling all around her. "*Dragons! Attack the armies! Kill them all!*" She pointed at the enormous green dragon behind May. "And you . . . *kill the girl.*" She looked down at May, her eyes filled with rage. "You had your chance, May. But now I will burn your friends' kingdoms to the *ground!*"

And with that, the Wicked Queen gestured, and both she and the harp disappeared.

The dragon shrieked at May, then launched its open jaws right at her head.

And just like she'd seen Jack do six months ago, she took the flower bridle that the Wolf King had taken from Malevolent almost as long ago and given to her now, dodged to the right, and held the magical bridle out right where she'd been standing.

The dragon bit down and began to shudder. May grabbed the end, then leapt up on the dragon's leg to its back, pulling herself up by the bridle.

Above her, forty or fifty dragons were beginning their attack dive on Phillip's helpless armies below.

In front of her lay a blue lightning portal to safety. All she needed to do was jump through it, and she could be away from all of this.

It didn't take even a thought.

"What say you and me go for a quick flight?" May said to the dragon, then yanked back on the bridle.

With a horrible shriek of rage, the green dragon beat its wings and shot into the air like a rocket—a rocket aimed right at the attacking dragons.

CHAPTER 43

Merriweather was the first to fall, but not the last. One by one, the fairy queens collapsed to the ground as Phillip watched in horror.

And that is when he realized that this was all going exactly as the Wicked Queen had planned. After all, the fairy queens might have fought her if they had been spread around the free kingdoms. But here on the front lines, her magic had removed them all from the battle at once.

Lian looked at her father, then nodded and disappeared completely from sight as the shrieking dragons overhead began to advance, breathing fire in their excitement.

"You people do seem ta have a knack fer findin' some

dangerous-type situations," Bluebeard said from Phillip's side. "What's the plan?"

"Can your magic help us with the dragons, Your Majesty?" Phillip asked the Sea King.

The merman shook his head, his shark growling up at the great flying monsters. "Not this far inland. If they were over the water, I could do something. Here on land, I might take down one, maybe two."

The goblins atop the castle gates shouted insults and mockery, dodging arrows in between them. "They're not coming out," Penelope said from Phillip's right. "That doesn't seem like a good thing, them leaving us alone out here."

"She means for the dragons to burn us alive," Jack's father said. "Unless you can put some wings on those sharks, Your Majesty, I'd say it's time to unleash our secret weapon."

"Drop them," Phillip said quietly, and his general raised a flag in the air.

All among the armies, soldiers with belts and straps dropped something into carefully dug holes, then stepped back. As the dragons descended toward them, the ground began to rumble, and the human soldiers readied themselves.

"This is gonna be close," Bluebeard said, squinting up against the rain.

"It always is," Phillip told him as the first beanstalk broke the ground.

A moment later, a second, then a third beanstalk broke through, and soldiers began to strap themselves to the stalks, rising into the air as more and more beanstalks grew. Bluebeard was right . . . it would be extremely close, as the dragons would reach them before the stalks had fully grown.

Fortunately, they'd come prepared.

"FIRE!" Phillip shouted, and the soldiers riding the beanstalks took their bows off their backs and began launching arrows at the advancing dragons.

"Shark-tooth arrowheads," Bluebeard said with a grin. "That oughta knock a few scales off those things!"

And then Phillip watched something explode up from the palace itself, flying straight at the advancing dragons. "HOLD YOUR FIRE!" he shouted, and the order went out.

"What are you doing, Phillip?!" Jack's father yelled. "You don't change the plan in midplan! That is not how things go, not when *I* plan them!"

Phillip just smiled as an enormous green dragon flew straight into the dragon in the lead, knocking it into the second one. "It appears that we have more friends around than we thought."

Bluebeard roared with laughter. "That'll teach the Queen ta mess with our little princess, won't it?"

"Send the order up, General," Phillip said. "Hit any dragon EXCEPT the green one. DO NOT hit the green one, even if it means not taking the shot. Am I clear?"

"Clear, sir," his general said, and ran off to speak with his subordinates. Within moments, the archers were firing again, this time nowhere in the vicinity of the green dragon, who now had its claws locked on to the back of a red dragon.

Behind him, someone shouted, and Phillip looked up to find a burning beanstalk slowly crumpling to the ground. "Out of its way!" Phillip shouted, and everyone—sharks, mermen, human soldiers—scrambled out of the dying plant's collapse. A dragon crashed into a second stalk, that stalk slammed against a third, and both toppled to the ground.

"The dragons have the advantage, even with May up there," Jack's father said. "We need the fairy queens back up if we're going to have a chance here."

"Any suggestions along those lines?" Phillip asked him.

"I've got my only daughter on it," he said with a smile. "But we still need to buy ourselves some time. And other than running for our lives, I'm all out of ideas."

Just then, the castle's front gates opened, and goblins too numerous to count poured out of them, screaming for blood.

"I take that back, I say we attack," Jack's father said, and Phillip nodded, while the golden fairy in Penelope's hair shouted some sort of battle cry, holding up a tiny sword and waving it frantically at the goblins.

"Your Majesty?" he said to the Sea King. "Shall we?"

The Sea King smiled. "I'm actually sorry I tried to drown you with a tidal wave, human."

"You apologized to *him*?!" Bluebeard shouted as they both rode away on their sharks toward the goblins. "You've NEVER apologized to me, and you apologize to him? He didn't even DO anything! That princess of his and the little Eye did all the work!"

"You saved me, Phillip," Penelope said, and nodded at the goblins. "I think that was pretty amazing, personally. Now, are you ready?"

"Very," Phillip said, and together they spurred their horses toward the goblins, Phillip with his sword, Penelope with her splinters of wood.

Lian slowly moved through the castle, the glow of her sword visible only to her. The harp had to be dealt with, or Phillip's armies would be massacred outside. From the sounds of the dragons overhead, maybe now was a good time to hurry.

The corridors were fairly empty, which was good, because she didn't have time to run into a distraction. Goblins would be one thing, and easily handled. Another Eye would be a bit of an issue. And even worse would be—

"Jillian," said a voice from about her knee level. "I have to say I'm a bit disappointed in you."

Yup. That would be worse. Jill sighed and dropped the invisibility, as Captain Thomas could see right through it anyway.

"I will accept your surrender, then," Captain Thomas said, gracefully saluting her with his sword. "And then I shall take you to Her Majesty for your punishment."

"I'm going to pass on that one, sir," Jill told him, and launched out with her sword.

Unfortunately, Captain Thomas easily countered it and smacked it out of her hand. "You must have known that wouldn't work. There's been only one Eye who was ever my match with our swords, and you're not even close to as good as the Charmed One."

The tiny man leapt up, grabbed Jill's hood, and slammed her to the ground, then placed his sword to her throat. "Now, shall I accept your surrender?"

Jill started to say no, never, or something suitably impressive along those lines, but before she could get a word out, Captain Thomas flew from her side and slammed into first one wall, then the other, then the first again, before dropping unconscious to the floor.

"There's your first problem," Jack told Jill, giving her a hand to help her to her feet. "You know you're supposed to hold *on* to your sword, right?"

CHAPTER 44

Didn't you die or something?" Jill said, grinning despite herself.

Jack shrugged. "What am I, some kind of hero?" With that, he walked right past her, and Jill, a bit startled, ran to catch up.

"Where are you going?! What are you even *doing* here?"

"It's been a little longer than you think since I've seen you last."

"Longer than a week?"

Jack smiled. "A bit. I've got a plan on how to take out the Wicked Queen, but if it doesn't work—"

"*When* it doesn't work," Jill corrected.

Jack paused and looked at her for a moment. "I wish I could say I missed that."

"I wish I could say you're making more sense than usual."

"I've got the Queen's heart," Jack told her, pulling out the wooden heart box and opening it. Jill gasped, then stabbed it with her sword.

"Really?" Jack said when the heart kept on beating. "You really think I wouldn't have tried that?"

"Who knows with you?"

"ANYWAY, I've got a plan. Snow White found out how to stop the heart, which is why the Queen poisoned her. So I'm going to go see what she has to say."

Jill froze again, and Jack grabbed her arm and yanked her to keep her moving. "But," she said, "Snow White's—"

"Not so much awake," Jack said with a nod. "I know. I did say I had a plan, didn't I?"

"The Charmed One," Jill said, the pieces falling into place in her mind. "So you think you can somehow get both you and him into Snow White's head and wake her up somehow? That's a pretty stupid plan, Jack."

"Why break tradition with a smart one? Speaking of bad plans, how's our father doing?"

"Oh, he's off fighting some war outside. I'm sure he's fine. He's got a good head on his shoulders."

"Let's hope it stays there," Jack told her. "I thought I heard dragons coming in. And the Charmed One thinks that the Queen's using the harp I got—"

"Yeah, I'm already caught up on things," Jill said with a sigh. "So, Snow White's in the throne room. You know who else will probably be there?"

"Just offhand, I'd guess the Queen. Probably the Wolf King."

"Maybe a few guards, too."

"Maybe."

They reached the door to the throne room, and Jack glanced through the crack.

"How many do you mean when you say a few?" he asked.

"Three?" Jill said.

"There's more than a few," he told her, stopping his count at around fifty.

"And the Queen?"

"I don't see her. Maybe she's busy."

"There *was* an execution going on," Jill said, and Jack looked back at her questioningly. She realized what she'd said and quickly shut her mouth, but Jack just stared at her.

"Who?" he whispered as loudly as he dared.

"Okay, you're going to probably not take this well—"

"WHO?!"

"It's probably too late anyway, and honestly, it was supposed to be a big public thing, and—"

Jack growled and began walking away, out toward the courtyard.

"Where are you going?" Jill demanded.

"That might be the stupidest question I've ever heard you ask," he said without turning around.

She grabbed his arm, but he yanked it away from her. "You *can't* go out there," she hissed at him. "You've got a chance to kill the Wicked Queen once and for all, and you're going to waste it by rescuing a princess?!"

"Yup," Jack said.

Jill grabbed his cloak and slammed him against the wall. "THINK about this, Jack! Either she's already gone, in which case there's nothing you can do, or the best chance you have of saving her is getting Snow White back. That's all you can do now—"

"You don't even *care* about her!" Jack shouted far too loudly.

"NO!" Jill shouted. "I don't! I care that the Queen killed my mother! That's *all* I care about! That's all I've cared about since I can remember!"

Jack started to yell back, then sighed. "She was my mother too."

Jill nodded. "I know. She liked me best, though."

He glared at her, and she glared right back.

"Help me with the goblins," he told her, "then I'll take care of Snow White, and *you* go rescue May. That's the only way I'm doing this. Deal?"

She gritted her teeth, and he repeated himself. "DEAL?!"

"FINE! As soon as the goblins are out, I'll go find your little princess. Happy?!"

"Not for almost a year now," Jack told her, and the two of them ran back to the throne room.

Inside, over one hundred goblins watched as the throne room door slowly opened, only to reveal an empty hallway.

"Hello?" one said, then flew backward into the guards behind him.

"Who's there!" another shouted, and this one fell forward, bashing his head into the floor.

"It's one of the traitor Eyes!" one of them yelled. "Strike out with your weapons, you're bound to hit them!"

And with that, the goblins began attacking anything and everything.

Thirty seconds later, the number of conscious goblins had been cut in half, and within a minute, there were only two standing.

Jack knocked their heads together and almost laughed. "Okay, maybe I didn't need any help," he said to Jill, who reappeared next to him.

"I've wanted to try that for so long," she said, a huge grin on her face. "A little knowledge is a dangerous thing. And a little knowledge might have been all they had."

"Go," Jack told her, looking past the throne at the coffin of ice propped up next to it, the silhouette of a woman just barely visible through the frost.

"If you mess this up without me, I'm coming back for *you*," Jill told him.

"Fair enough."

Jill shook her head, then ran off back down the hall. As soon as she was out of his sight, though, she reversed course.

The harp came first.

The sky filled with fire and dragons. May plummeted between beanstalks, claws, and teeth to slam into a blue dragon spewing fire on the merfolk below, then yanked up to fly her green dragon into the underside of a giant red dragon above her. Her dragon attacked with all four feet, and the red dragon screamed, then crashed into a beanstalk, sending both dragon and beanstalk toppling to the ground.

Flames exploded just to her left, and May threw a look back to find two smaller green dragons chasing her down, both ridden by Eyes. She dodged right, then left, fire swirling around her on all sides, then yanked up on her reins to send her dragon almost vertical. She gritted her teeth and held on as tightly as she could with her knees as the dragon flipped upside down, then straightened back to horizontal, having looped behind both of the other dragons. May yanked on the reins again, and her dragon spat fire to the side of the green dragon on the right, crashing it into its partner, and both toppled to the ground.

The Eyes might be faster than she was, but *they* hadn't seen a lifetime of movies with plane stunts, either.

But the dragons weren't the only threat. She heard a shout and glanced down to see Phillip and Penelope surrounded by goblins on all sides, while Bluebeard fought crazily to try to reach them from one side, and the Sea King and his mermen did the same from the other.

Without a thought, she dropped her dragon toward the

ground, a blast of fire exploding behind her through the spot she'd just been.

Phillip looked at Penelope, who smiled at him sadly. "At least you're going out next to your true love," she told him.

He could not help but smile. "You seem so sure of that."

She shrugged as the goblins advanced. "It's okay. I've warmed up to you, too." She held out her hand, and Phillip took it and squeezed.

A horrible roar filled the air, and something enormous and green slammed to the ground just in front of them, fire exploding from its mouth.

The goblins shrieked and ran in all directions, and Phillip looked up to see a blond girl in a black hood smiling down at him.

"Your Highness," May said, and saluted him.

There were a thousand things he wanted to say at that moment. Apologize. Explain. Beg her forgiveness.

A thousand things, but all could wait.

"The Queen," Phillip told her, pointing at the castle. "She is the key. If we have any hope of winning this, she must be our priority."

May looked at him for a moment, then nodded. "Agreed."

She started to spur her dragon back into the air, but Phillip raised a hand. "May, I—"

She shook her head and stopped him. "Later, Phillip. Stay alive, and you can grovel then. Deal?"

He smiled. "Deal."

And with that, May's dragon leapt into the air, and Penelope grabbed Phillip's hand to pull him back into the battle.

Jack slowly pulled the lid off Snow White's coffin, not sure what to expect. Part of him thought the Wicked Queen might be waiting for him within. Or some sort of monster. Or just anyone but Snow White.

But no. There she was, as beautiful as everyone said . . . hair black as night, eyes closed, her hands crossed over her chest. She looked older than the paintings of her, but it *had* been almost fifteen years since anyone had seen her. And just because she'd been poisoned didn't mean she'd stopped aging.

He bent down, took out his sword, and rested it against her hands.

This had better work, he thought as he used the Charmed One's training to dive down into Snow White's imprisoned mind.

As Jack fell forward, his body limp, his mind diving into the murky depths of nothingness at the top of Snow White's consciousness, a blue circle of lightning appeared, and the Wicked Queen stepped out of it.

"That was clever of you, Jack. Almost up to one of your father's little tricks." She played electricity between her fingers. "This time, though, I'll make sure I don't leave the task half-finished."

As she raised a hand, crackling with lightning, the entire throne room rumbled. The ceiling crashed in, goblin-size rocks tumbling to the floor, and an enormous green dragon landed on the rubble, breathing fire just over the Wicked Queen's head.

"Hey, Grandma," May said from the dragon's back. "He followed me home. Can I keep him?"

CHAPTER 45

I knew you'd make a magnificent heir," the Wicked Queen told May, then put both her hands on the sides of Jack's head, lightning crackling from them in the dark. "But this changes nothing."

"Jack?" May said, her voice just above a whisper.

"He's alive," the Queen told her. "But not for much longer. Presently, he's most likely lost within Snow White's mind." She smiled. "Unfortunately, he won't survive long enough to find his way back."

May shuddered from a combination of relief and fear. She'd known, she'd *known* he was still alive! And there was no *way* she was going to let that change now. "Get. Away. From. Him."

The Queen paused, then shook her head. "I don't think

so. Snow has a secret I can't have getting out." The Queen laughed. "To think, he spent this much time to try to outwit me, only to lose at the end. Everything he's done, it's all been for nothing!"

He swam through layer and layer of memories, some familiar, most not. At one point, he remembered a very vague thought of trying to save . . . someone. But who?

And who was *he?*

His feet touched ground in what had to be the scariest-looking woods he'd ever seen, with trees that looked like they wanted to eat him. He shuddered—the sap dripping from the trees' mouths looked far too much like drool.

A girl screamed, and he used his sword to chop his way through the evil trees. He found a man dressed all in green standing over a younger but still familiar-looking girl.

Was this why he was here? To save a girl from a man in green?

His sword glowed, and he touched it absently, only to have everything flood back in an instant: who he was, why he was here, everything he'd had to leave behind to make it this far—all stored in his sword, just like the Charmed One had left a part of himself in it years before.

But that could wait. He was here for Snow White. Only . . . why did she look so much younger?

The Huntsman held a knife over her, while Snow White held a tree branch between them, using it like a sword to hold him back.

"Don't do this!" she shouted.

"The Queen has given her order!" the Huntsman said. "She wants your heart, and if I return without it, she will have me killed!"

Jack struck out at the Huntsman, only for the sword to stop in midair, a one-eyed man made of glass holding it in his glass hand as sand fell through his body.

"You don't belong here," the man of sand told him.

"Neither does she," Jack told him, and yanked back on his sword.

It didn't move.

"I lost one of my charges," the man of sand told him. "I will not lose another. Continue on, and you shall be trapped here forever as well."

Jack dropped his sword and kicked out, catching the man in his glass stomach and crashing him backward into the Huntsman. Both fell to the ground, and the Sandman dropped Jack's sword, which Jack grabbed as he ran past Snow White, dragging her to her feet to follow.

"Who are you?!" she shouted.

"I'm Jack," he said. "Apparently, I rescue princesses."

Something snarled behind him, and he threw a look over his shoulder to see the man of sand rising to his feet. Jack waved, then turned around just in time to plow right into the man.

"Trapped it is," the man said, and sand trickled down between his hands. "I've held her here in her own nightmares for years and will do the same for you. Let's see what *your* nightmares are, Jack."

"I've been living my nightmares?" Snow White said, still holding the stick in her hand.

"Looks like that might continue for a while," Jack told her.

Jack woke up alone, back in the Queen's throne room. The Queen stood with her back to him, whispering something quietly while holding something in the air.

"What . . . ?" Jack jumped to his feet, only to have the Queen spin around, holding May by the neck off the floor.

Jack screamed out in rage and struggled to move, but the Queen just held him in place, slowly choking May as the princess held out a hand to Jack. He screamed again, calling for May over and over, not able to move—

And then the Wicked Queen crumpled to the ground, Snow White standing over her with her stick. As Jack watched in horror, the Queen dissolved into sand, filling the man of glass, who lay on his side on the ground.

"Maybe we should get out of here," Snow said, slowly aging to look more like she had in the coffin. "I for one am tired of living made-up stories. I can't believe he made me think I was young and scared again!" She growled in frustration.

"You . . . cannot leave," the man of glass said, only to scream as seven dwarfs each grabbed a leg or an arm and carried him off, much like they'd carried May into the blue fire portal. "It doesn't matter!" the man shouted as he was dragged away. "You cannot leave with her; she cannot awaken!"

"That brings up a good point," Jack said. "I'm going to need your help for a second. Can you keep him busy while I bring in a friend?"

Snow White smiled. "How hard can it be?"

The man of glass wrenched free from the dwarfs and shrieked with rage.

And as Jack watched, the man split into a thousand pieces, each of those pieces turning into one of his nightmares. Giants the size of mountains. Sharks with legs. Witches with no faces. Huntsmen, imps with golden hats, Wolf Kings, Sea Kings, mermen, evil fairy queens, Wicked Queens, as well as far too many other things he didn't even recognize. Cats wearing pants. Trolls beneath bridges. Shadows of shadows. All horrible. All nightmarish.

"You . . . got this?" Jack said, backing away from it all.

Snow grinned. "It'll be fun. Besides, what can they do? Dreams aren't real."

A dream-Malevolent breathed fire at them, and Jack felt the heat. "Maybe you've been wishing on too many stars, cause those feel real."

Snow White laughed wildly. "I've been stuck in my head for far too long. It's time I got to have a little fun too. Who's first?!"

And with that, she grabbed the Wolf King and kneed him in the stomach, then threw him into the Huntsman and leapt at the nearest witch.

Jack nodded. "You got this." He touched his sword, and reached up and out of Snow White's mind, looking for the one person who might put an end to all this.

May noticed the wooden heart box at Jack's side, and suddenly something clicked into place. "*He* stole it," she said quietly. "From our house. He . . . he planned this all out?"

"I underestimated him," the Queen said. "I underestimated the whole family at one time or another. His father. Certainly his uncle, the Charmed One. Even Jillian."

"Uncle?" May said.

"Let's go back to that 'even Jillian' part," said a voice from May's side, and May glanced up to find Lian holding the golden harp, now with a gag in the harp's mouth to stop her from singing. "By the way," Lian said, "I think there are going to be some angry fairy queens showing up soon."

The Queen sneered. "You cannot hurt me, Jillian. None of you can, don't you realize that? Jack stole my heart for nothing! It is unbreakable. The curse protects it, even as it turned me into this!"

"Let's see about that," May said, then shouted "ATTACK!" The dragon leapt forward, its wings sweeping into the sides of the room and knocking stones to the ground as it snapped its jaws at the Queen.

She just smiled, and the dragon froze in place, his mouth wide open.

Then the Queen's smile disappeared as she flew across the room and slammed into the floor. Lian appeared over her, her sword pointed at the Queen's throat.

"May, get away from her, let me handle this!" Lian shouted,

only to catch a bolt of electricity full in her chest, crashing into the wall behind her, and slumping to the floor.

"I took in the betrayer's family," the Queen said, glowing with rage and magic, "knowing that this day would come, but using them anyway. And now they think they can hurt me? Even without the curse, they have no power to rival mine!"

Fire exploded all around the Queen but swept around her to each side like a river splitting at a fork. "Again!" May yelled at the now-free dragon.

Again, fire exploded from the dragon's mouth, and again, the dragon froze in place.

And Lian attacked once more.

"She can't take us both on!" May yelled, knowing that wasn't true but also knowing the longer they distracted the Queen, the longer Jack had.

A shadow fell over May's eyes, and everything went dark and chilled, like the dead of winter. She shivered, feeling colder than she ever had in her life, like there was no warmth anywhere in the world. "Can't I?" said a voice from what felt like miles away.

It felt like Jack was gone for hours, swimming back up from the depths of Snow White's nightmares, through the horrible forest, through a tiny little house sized just right for seven dwarfs, through the Wicked Queen's laughing face, even, to emerge cold and horrified to a warm oak tree. He quickly glanced behind him at the trail he'd left, a glow shining its way back down that matched the glow in his sword.

"C'mon!" Jack yelled, and grabbed the Charmed One's arm, pulling him right back down.

Now that he'd found Snow White, the path was easier, and the nightmares passed by so quickly Jack almost didn't have time for them to terrify him. Finally, he reached the bottom, where everything was far too quiet.

"Snow White?" he said.

He heard heavy breathing, and turned around behind him to find a woman holding two swords in her hand, barely able to stand, on top of what seemed to be a pile of the worst things in the world. "You . . . certainly took . . . your time," she said.

"Snow?" the Charmed One said, his voice cracking.

"Aleister?" Snow managed to say, right as she collapsed to the ground. The Charmed One was by her side in an instant, even as all the nightmares disappeared, leaving only a man filled with glass.

"You . . . can't leave," the glass man said.

Jack punched him in the face, and the glass man went silent.

"It's been so long," Snow White told her prince, and Jack got the feeling she'd forgotten anyone else was even there.

"Far too many years," the Charmed One said, tears running down his face. "We need to get you out of here."

"I knew you'd come for me," she told him. "No matter how long it took, I knew you'd come."

The Charmed One leaned down and brushed her cheek, then hugged her tight. "I did. Nothing could have stopped me." He frowned, looking up at Jack. "Darling, I need to know . . . you found the Queen's weakness, didn't you? What did you learn?"

Snow White smiled. "It was so obvious, I should have known. After all, her uncle was the one who committed the crime. The magician who saved her used dark magic, and dark magic always has an ironic curse. The only one who could stop her heart now is someone who shares her blood, just like her uncle."

The Charmed One glanced up at Jack, whose mouth dropped. All this time . . . the Queen had kept the one person who could harm her right under her thumb.

"Ironically, there's a tiny part of the real Eudora still left that keeps her from killing any of her family members," Snow White continued. "She could only poison me and has needed others to do her dirty work for her, for any who share her blood. No matter how much she might want to, that pure part of herself keeps her from going through with it. Or, at least it had . . . maybe she's killed that part of herself."

"I'm going to free you from here now," the Charmed One told Snow White, brushing her hair out of her face. "I'm so, so sorry it took so long."

"It doesn't matter, not anymore," she said. "We have all the time in the world now."

The Charmed One slowly nodded, then leaned down and kissed her lips lightly.

Snow White disappeared right out of his arms, and the knight let out a choked sob, then stood back up. "Tell her . . . I'll always love her," he told Jack.

Jack nodded. "I will."

The Charmed One stood up, let out a deep breath, then saluted Jack with his sword.

Then the Charmed One disappeared as well.

The dragon breathed fire into the shadow, but the shadow ate the flame like a living thing, leaving nothing behind.

"Lian?!" May shouted, but no one answered her.

"You're all alone now, my little month of May," said the Queen. "Just as I said you would be."

"No!" May shouted, and the dragon breathed fire again. "I'm not alone. There will always be people who stand up to you!"

The Queen appeared before her, the shadows disappearing. "Will there?" she said with a grin.

"There will," said a new voice from behind the Queen, and May gasped as a beautiful woman with skin as white as snow held a beating heart in her hands, a knife to it. "It's been a long time, Eudora."

The Queen's eyes went wide, but she sneered. "Snow. So it comes to this. You have my heart, you ridiculous girl. What are you waiting for?"

"Nothing," Snow said, and stabbed the heart.

The heart didn't stop beating.

The Queen laughed, and Snow grabbed her chest, dropping the heart. "It seems only fair," the Queen said, walking slowly over to the shaking Snow White. "I take your heart, you threaten mine. It seems as if it's my turn again."

May slowly slid off the frozen dragon and crept toward the heart on the ground. She picked up what looked to be a goblin blade, then everything went bright white as a bolt of electricity hit her.

"*You*," the Queen said, picking up her heart and holding it over May, as May struggled just to stop shaking from the jolt. "You shall not *touch* that!"

"Only . . . a blood relative," Snow White said, then shrieked in pain as the Queen focused on her once more.

A blood relative? Images flooded through May's mind, images of the Queen's Story Book, the picture of the man who had tried to murder the Queen . . . a familiar-looking man.

Suddenly, she remembered where she'd seen him before.

"The portrait back in my father's home," May breathed.

The Queen turned to her. "You are *not* my granddaughter. You can do *nothing*!"

May smiled, only to struggle to breathe as another bolt of lightning hit her. "I'm . . . not," she said, gritting her teeth. "But . . . your uncle . . . was my . . . great-grandfather!"

The Queen shook her head. "I knew I shouldn't have let my uncle escape. Took me far too long to track him down, and by that point, he'd hidden his son away. Leave it to Snow to find his grandson first, along with his grandson's only daughter."

"I tried to . . . take you away," Snow said to May.

"But I got to you first," the Queen said with a smile, "and even claimed you were my granddaughter, yet no one would believe me! The last thing they expected was for me to hide you, my one vulnerability, in plain sight!" She laughed. "Or am I lying now? Is this all part of my ruse?"

"Let's find out," said a voice behind May, and Jack leapt past her to push the Queen's heart right into the woman's chest.

The Queen gasped, dropping May to the ground. Jack threw his sword to May, who caught it.

"Good-bye, Grandma," May said, then drove Jack's sword right into the Wicked Queen's heart.

And with that, the shadows began screaming, exploding out of the Wicked Queen with the force of a volcano. The castle began to shake, windows exploded, and even dragons began screaming outside.

In all the chaos, May almost missed that the Wicked Queen's heart beat once more, then finally, mercifully, stopped for good.

CHAPTER 46

May dropped the sword and caught her grandmoth–great-aunt as she gasped for breath, shadows pouring out of her chest. Jack helped May, and together the two gently laid the woman on the floor.

"Oh, May," Eudora said, and May could barely hear her voice. "I can feel them . . . they're leaving. The shadows. They were so weak . . . in the other world. They let me–"

May didn't say anything, just stared at her, a thousand feelings going through her head.

"I didn't . . . I didn't want to come back," Eudora said. "I didn't want to leave. I was happy there . . . with just us."

"The things you did . . ." May said, then stopped, unable to speak.

Her grand-aunt nodded and closed her eyes. "You . . . you are my only family, May. You are all that's left."

"Grandma," May said, her voice cracking, and her face felt wet for some reason.

"My beautiful month of May," Eudora said.

And then May's grand-aunt died.

May silently stared at her for a moment, then looked up at the boy sitting next to her. He looked . . . older somehow. More serious than she'd ever seen him, and worried, too. Worried for her.

He put his arm around her and hugged her tightly, and she hugged back just as hard, not wanting to let go.

He dropped his arms and nodded at Snow White. "We should make sure she's okay. Her and Jill."

May paused, then nodded and went to check on Snow White as Jack ran over to Lian.

The woman was stirring as May approached, and opened her eyes as May touched her arm. "Are you alright?" May asked.

"I have no idea," Snow White said, and tried to sit up only to wince. "The Queen—"

"She's gone," May told her, nodding behind her.

Snow White looked over her shoulder, then let out an

enormous breath. "I can't tell you how many years I've waited to see that. But where's my husband?"

"Um, let me cover this," Jack said, and spoke quietly to Snow White, who shook her head over and over, tears falling as Jack went on.

Lian limped over to May and nodded. May nodded back, then said, "I still don't like you."

"Oh, me either. Like you, I mean. I like me just fine. Just . . . just don't hurt my brother again."

"Oh, I won't," May said, then paused. "Who's your brother?"

Lian laughed, looked at her, then laughed again. "Eh, you'll figure it out."

"*Again*, I still don't like you."

Jack, meanwhile, held out his sword to Snow White, handing her the hilt. She took it and looked at him curiously. "The Charmed One that you saw was a memory in the sword," he told her. "And in here." He tapped his head.

She looked at the sword. "So . . . that *was* him, though."

"A memory of him, yes. He's gone now, but that's his sword, if you would like it."

She smiled, then shook her head. "I'd rather *see* him when my time here is done." She handed Jack back the sword and nodded at Lian. "You two have really grown up, by the way."

"You . . . know who we are?" Lian said, smiling nervously.

"You're his niece and nephew," she said. "Of course I know who you are. You were barely walking when I last saw you . . . and *you* had just been born," she said, pointing at Jack. "I guess it's been a few years."

"I'm . . . sorry?" Jack said, giving her a confused look.

"Jack's your brother?!" May shouted at Lian.

"The Charmed One is my uncle?!" Jack shouted at Snow White.

She laughed. "He always did like his secrets. . . ."

"Did you know that?" Jack said to Lian.

She shook her head, faking innocence, then sighed. "Okay, fine, yes. But I couldn't tell you. Father kept telling me not to say anything. He figured you wouldn't do what you had to if you thought you were royalty."

"What?" May said.

"The Charmed One was the prince of Charm," Lian said. "And my mother was the princess. Though I guess when our grandparents died, he became king, but she had . . . passed on at that point. So that makes us—"

"A prince," May said, staring at Jack.

". . . and a princess," Lian finished, glaring at her. "Not that the kingdom really exists anymore. The Queen took it over years and years ago."

"The castle's still there," May said quietly.

Jack glanced up at her questioningly, then quickly looked away. "None of that matters," he said.

"You are the heirs to Charm," Snow White said, putting a hand on Jack's shoulder. "In honor of your uncle and your mother both, I would say it matters quite a bit. There's much you could do to restore your kingdom."

"*Snow White* knows who we are!" Lian whispered to Jack, glancing sideways at the woman.

Snow White just shook her head. "Maybe that can wait."

May helped her up, Jack took her other arm, and together the two helped her walk out of the throne room, while behind them, Lian pointed to Snow White and whispered, "She knows who I am!"

Before they could exit, though, a growl from behind them reminded May of something. The four turned to find the green dragon, now freed of the Queen's spell, looking extremely angry.

"Uh, can someone reach those reins?" May asked. "Anyone? Lian, you're closest."

"Let me repeat that *I* never liked *you*," Lian said, and disappeared, only for the dragon to whip its head out and knock the girl aside.

The dragon roared and reared back to set fire to the entire room, when the throne room doors burst open, and something flew straight into the dragon's open mouth. The dragon snapped its jaws shut, looked confused, then toppled over, shaking the entire building as it landed.

"Nice shot," Jack's father said to Penelope, who stood in the doorway, holding a few splinters of spindle.

Penelope smiled back politely. "I've had lots of practice."

Phillip cleared his throat, looking at May, then his eyes went wide when he saw who stood next to her.

"Your Princeness," Jack said with a short bow.

Phillip stepped forward, then hugged Jack roughly.

"This is really not necessary," Jack said, frantically trying to free himself.

"You live!" Phillip said, wiping at his eyes. "I could not be happier at such news!"

"That makes one of us," Lian said.

"Don't fight, kids," Jack's father said. "Let's get Snow White out of here, and we'll deal with everything else. The mermen and fairy queens are on their way to all the kingdoms the Queen attacked to bring the goblins back here. But someone will need to be in charge of what happens to them all."

May started to say something, then just nodded. "I'm on it."

"You?" Jack's father said.

"It's a long story, but it looks like Her Wickedness here is the Queen's heir," Lian said.

"There's also the matter of the Charmed One being my uncle," Jack said.

His father started to say something, then glanced at Snow White and nodded. "I couldn't tell you. None of us could. If you'd known, you might have grown up like—"

"A spoiled royal," Phillip said.

"And who would want that?" Penelope said with a smile, taking Phillip's hand in hers. May saw Phillip blush, then match her smile, not letting go of her hand. "Now, can we go home?" Penelope continued. "I could really use a good night's sleep."

May laughed, half because of Penelope's comment, half from relief. Phillip started to say something to her, probably to apologize again, but she just shook her head. She was too tired to deal with that now; it'd have to wait. Besides, she had someone far more important to talk to.

As the others began to file out of the throne room, May held back, waiting to say something, anything to Jack about him leaving, about . . . a lot of things.

But when she looked, he was nowhere to be found, almost like he'd disappeared into thin air.

CHAPTER 47

The courtyard exploded in cheers as May, Phillip, and the rest filed out of the castle. Mermen, human soldiers, and even a fairy queen or two surged forward to greet them, the noise reaching all the way up to the ramparts, where Jack watched, unnoticed by the crowds below.

"The Wicked Queen is dead, by Princess May's hand!" someone shouted, and everyone went crazy.

"She's going to get all the credit for this," said a voice from behind him. Jack didn't bother looking up as Jill stepped up to the rampart next to him. "Figures."

"She deserves it," Jack said.

"So do you," said Jack's father from his other side. "So does Jill. Of course, I deserve more praise than *any* of you, since I planned this entire thing, but I'm too modest to ever suggest that."

"YOU planned this?" Jill said with a snort. "Nice try. Jack surprised us both. Don't bother pretending."

"Speak for yourself, young lady," his father said. "I had Jack set up from the start. Why do you think the Charmed One blocked his memories? At my order, so that the Queen couldn't find him."

"Did you set me up to free her too?" Jack asked quietly, still staring down into the courtyard.

"Well, no," his father admitted. "I'd planned on you freeing *me*, not her. But sometimes kids can be disappointing."

Jack smiled in spite of himself as Phillip was lifted up on his soldiers' shoulders, followed by May. May kept shaking her head, but that just encouraged the soldiers, and the cheering got louder.

"It's just not fair," Jill said, sighing as she turned away from the celebration.

"Aren't you the one who always says that we're not heroes?" Jack asked her. "We're the ones who get things done, no matter what?"

"Yeah, but it'd be nice to be *thanked*."

Jack's father reached out and hugged her. "Thank you, Jill," he said, his voice sounding strangely not-mocking. "Your mother would be proud."

Jill paused, then hugged him back, sniffing loudly. "Well, okay, I'll take that."

His father turned to Jack, still hugging Jill. "So what, Jack? You still hate me, or do you want a hug from your father too?"

Jack turned, starting to say something, then sighed, shut his mouth, and hugged them both.

"Your mother loved you both so much," his father said quietly. "More than you can imagine."

Jill sniffed again, and Jack bit his lip to keep himself from following her lead.

"So, what now?" his father asked. "I take it we're not going to join the party downstairs."

Jack shook his head. "I think they're better off without us." He moved back to the castle's ramparts and looked down at May, who was smiling and laughing. "They've got their own stories to follow, and we've got ours."

"You don't even want to say good-bye?" Jill asked. "I mean, *I* don't, but they all annoy me."

Jack gave May one last look, then shook his head, turning his back on the courtyard and everyone in it. "Nope," he said, forcing a smile he didn't feel. "I think everything got said back in the Fairy Homelands."

Jill slapped him too hard on the shoulder. "That's the spirit! Though let me know if you ever want to take the Queen's harp and mess with Merriweather a bit. I'd totally be on board for that."

"No one's messing with any fairy queens," his father said, leading them away from the ramparts. "Well, not today. There's too much to do."

"Do?" Jack said.

"Oh, you'll see," his father said with a grin.

CHAPTER 48

Dust filled the room, and Jack paused to try to wave some out the window. The Charmed One's castle—his *family's* castle—had gotten pretty dirty. Granted, it had been dirty during his training, too, but he'd been a bit distracted then. Now that he wasn't so busy, it felt right to clean it up a bit.

His father watched him from where he sat sideways on the castle's throne. "I told you there was a lot to do," the man said. "Though you look like you could use some help."

"I sure could," Jack told him, handing him the broom.

"Doesn't a father have the right to make his children do chores for him? Where *is* your sister?"

"Exploring," Jack said, going back to sweeping. "She said something about finding some world-ending magical something or other in the basement, and wanted to experiment with it. I think she's just bored and wants to cause trouble before we go to Phillip's coronation next week."

"Sounds fun," his father said. "Maybe I should go help her with that."

Jack sighed. "Please don't do anything stupid. It's only been a month since everything kind of settled down, and I'm not really ready for another adventure just yet."

His father smiled. "But you *will* be?"

Jack narrowed his eyes. "I'm committing to *nothing*."

"That's what I thought," his father said, hurrying out of the room to find whatever trouble Lian had found and most likely make it worse.

Somehow, having his father out of the room made cleaning go that much faster, and Jack fairly sped along until a blue flame exploded in the room, almost making him jump out of his shoes.

And out of that blue flame stepped someone he'd never expected to see again.

"Hey," said a blond girl wearing a crown and a light blue tunic over the same pants she'd always worn. Her hair was much shorter now, and the blue streak was gone.

"Uh," Jack said, stopping his sweeping and leaning on his broom. "Hey."

"It's been awhile. I haven't seen you since . . . she died. You never visited."

"I've been a little busy."

May nodded. "Me too. I've had the goblins out looking for the proper rulers of all the kingdoms the Queen took over. If any are left, I want them back in charge. And if not, we're going to hold elections. Gonna do that in my kingdom, either way."

"Elections?" Jack asked, going back to sweeping.

"Everyone votes on who they think is the best person to lead," May said, looking out the window. "That's not me. I'm no princess."

Jack smiled a bit at that. "I don't think any of us are who we thought we were."

May turned to him and nodded toward the window. "That's my stepmother's house, you know. Just down the road."

"Here?" Jack frowned, feeling like he should have known that for some reason. But that wasn't it . . . wasn't there something else having to do with her stepmother or the house?

May nodded and watched him clean. "You know, you left the

Fairy Homelands before we could talk about what Merriweather told you."

Jack stopped with a sigh. "I'm sorry I left like that."

"You should be."

"I just *said*—"

"You left something behind, remember?" she said, then pulled out a piece of paper from her pocket. "Dear May," she read. "I spoke to Merriweather, and she told me about your family. You have a stepmother and some stepsisters, it sounds like, waiting for you. You were meant to live with them, only the Wicked Queen stole you away. Your stepmother is evil, by the way."

May stopped reading for a second. "She is, you were totally right about that." Then she went back to the letter. "Merriweather would have saved you from all of that, though, if the Queen hadn't taken you. She would have introduced you to a prince, your true love. He was supposed to give you this slipper—" She held up a crystal slipper. "The slipper is magic and feels hard as glass unless your true love gives it to you. Then it will feel like it's made of air."

She tossed him the slipper, and he grabbed it, his eyes widening. May went back to reading the letter. "I don't know that I'd trust it or anything, a translucent shoe telling you how to feel. But that's me. And speaking of me, I have to go, May. I have to fix things. You were meant to be with that prince, and the Wicked Queen stopped that. And then I made a mistake and set her free again. This is my fault, and I need to make up for it. Please don't follow me or look for me in any way. Hopefully, this will make up for things. Jack."

"This shoe is pretty soft," Jack whispered.

"I know," May told him. "That's how it felt when you left it for me too."

"Um . . . " Jack said intelligently.

She stepped closer. "You shouldn't have left, Jack. That was pretty stupid."

"I . . . I had to fix things."

She slowly shook her head. "No. We had to fix things. And we did. But neither of us could have done that on our own."

"That's a fair point, but—"

"Shh." She took his hand and smiled. He couldn't help it, he smiled back. "So. Prince Charming, huh?" she said.

"Prince *of* Charm, really," Jack pointed out. "The town's name is Charm, so—"

"You really don't know when to be quiet, do you?"

"I really don't."

She shook her head, then stared up at him. Jack took a deep breath, closed his eyes, and leaned forward—

"If you two are through," someone said from the doorway, and both of them blushed and looked up to find Jill covering her eyes. The golden fairy Gwentell sat in her hair but seemed far more interested in what was going on than Jill did. "You may want to come outside. I might, *might* have just traded our father to a witch by accident."

Jack had never hated his sister more than at that moment. "You can't handle this yourself?"

"I could," Jill said. "But he seemed a little taken by the witch. You really want to roll the dice that we'll end up with an evil stepmother? I hear that never ends well. Can we go rescue him now, please?"

"You know," May said, still bright red. "Some would say I'm an expert in the area of evil stepmothers. I could come along, make sure you guys don't mess it up."

Jack grinned. "I'm pretty busy and all, but I guess you can come if you want."

"Don't worry," May told him. "I'll have you back by midnight." And with that, she grabbed his hand with a laugh and pulled him right out the door.